W9-BUY-092

HALFHYDE ORDERED SOUTH

HALFHYDE ORDERED SOUTH

Philip McCutchan

ST. MARTIN'S PRESS INC.
NEW YORK

Library of Congress Catalog Card Number : 79 – 66344
ISBN : 0 – 312 – 35689 – 7

ONE

It was a filthy passage. The westerlies howled smack into the fo'c'sle and superstructure of the old battleship to send solid water hurtling over the compass platform. Ton upon ton of water fell upon the anchors secured with compressors and rope stoppers, with lashings and strops on stocks and shanks – water that rushed aft as the deck lifted to submerge the great 16-inch guns in the swivel turrets and continued in its headlong rush past hatch coamings and davits to thunder down and meet the Southern Ocean once again as the greybeards lifted to the Captain's stern-walk. Everything, everywhere was under a blanket of spindrift. Wet pervaded body and soul, messdeck and galley, wardroom and cuddy. Men of the watch on deck huddled where they could, with luck, find shelter of a sort and yet maintain a lookout and be ready to answer any emergency call from the Officer of the Watch, as wet and storm-tossed as themselves. The word had been passed below by voicepipe that the watch would not be relieved until the weather moderated; and that might not be for days yet. Lieutenant St Vincent Halfhyde, Officer of the Morning Watch, glowered from the compass platform, seeking a sight of Cape Horn through the spindrift and the huge, rearing crests of grey water, seeking other shipping at large in the dreary wastes at the world's foot. One of the great seaways of world trade, Cape Horn was seldom without a number of windjammers beating round into the Pacific from east to west or running the other way before the great west winds that blew almost continually right round the world in the high south latitudes until, below the Cape

5

of Good Hope, they merged into the Roaring Forties to sweep the ships on for the Leeuwin and the Great Australian Bight. The route was not so often used by Her Majesty's ships of war – and just as well, Halfhyde thought mutinously, as he felt the tremendous shudder of the great ironclad beneath his feet. Almost 12,000 tons of obsolete battleship was Her Majesty's Ship *Meridian*, 12,000 tons that stood in urgent need of a dockyard refit which the Lords of the Admiralty would not sanction; instead, the old *Meridian* was being delivered to the Chilean Navy by gracious consent of Her Majesty Queen Victoria and by virtue of the jingling of a little gold into the coffers of the Treasury in London. The Disposal List . . . yet Halfhyde's vigilance was not only for the ship and for any windjammers that might be encountered trying to round Cape Stiff under lower topsails, but also, since this was no ordinary ship-delivery run, for the fighting-tops and gun-turrets and streaming ensigns of Vice-Admiral Paulus von Merkatz commanding the Special Service Squadron of the German Emperor.

*   *   *

Only a month earlier when serving with the fleet in the Mediterranean, Halfhyde's life had been very different. The Fourth Torpedo-Boat Destroyer Flotilla under the command of Captain Watkiss, Royal Navy, had been lying peacefully alongside the quay in the harbour of Mers-el-Kebir below the shadow of the French Foreign Legion fort and the base and arsenal of Oran. St Vincent Halfhyde, Lieutenant-in-Command of HMS *Vendetta*, had just shifted into plain clothes with the intention of taking his galley into Oran, there to sample the pleasures of French women and Algerian wine, when Prebble, his First Lieutenant, had come to his cabin with a message delivered by hand, from Captain Watkiss in the leader.

His face cold, Halfhyde had opened the missive and read: '*Vendetta* from *Venomous*: You are to report aboard immediately.'

'The literary style of the good Captain Watkiss changes but little from one year to the next, Prebble.'

6

'Yes, sir.'

Halfhyde tapped the message. 'Have you any idea what he wants, Prebble?'

'No, sir. Not precisely, that is. But a carriage went alongside *Venomous* half an hour ago, and a French officer boarded, and left again within five minutes.'

'A despatch?'

'Likely, sir.'

Halfhyde nodded. 'Very well, Prebble, thank you. I shall obey the order and trust that temper will not coerce me into planting a foot in Captain Watkiss' backside. I had other plans for this afternoon.' Ahead of his First Lieutenant, Halfhyde climbed to the upper deck and was saluted over the side by the Officer of the Day and the gangway staff, the former frock-coated and wearing a sword belt. It was a warm day, with no more than a gentle breeze stirring the dust along the wharf. Halfhyde glanced up at the tricolor of France floating from the flagstaff over Fort Mers-el-Kebir, at a bearded sentry of the Foreign Legion standing with his rifle by the main gate. An outpost of France, and *les belles dames* waiting a few miles away across the harbour in Oran . . . much sea-time of late had kept the men of the Fourth TBD Flotilla away from the fleshpots of the shore, and Halfhyde would not be the only one suffering the effects of abstinence and frustration. Shore leave had been piped for that afternoon, although the liberty men had not yet fallen in for inspection; when they did so, the duty watch would wait enviously for their turn next day. Halfhyde ground his teeth angrily: for him it was worse, for the cherry had been seized from between his teeth. Desire stirred uselessly in him as he caught a glimpse of a long dress, a parasol and an elegant figure on the fort's battlements. An officer's wife, flaunting beauty before suffering beasts . . . the land forces of any country had a better time of it than the Navy, and the Frogs in particular never neglected the demands of nature! Halfhyde, tall and angular, stalked on towards *Venomous'* gangway. At its head he was met by Beauchamp, Watkiss' First Lieutenant, an officer wearing the thin stripe of a senior lieutenant between his two thick gold stripes. Salutes were punctiliously exchanged and Halfhyde enquired what was afoot; Beauchamp, a nervous man at the best of times, seemed jumpy and spoke in a low voice as though attack might come at any moment.

'Captain Watkiss is – ' He stopped. Halfhyde, from the corner of his eye, saw why: from the starboard after door below the shelter-deck a rotund figure had emerged bearing a telescope. This was Captain Watkiss in person; and he gave tongue.

'Captain Watkiss is what, Mr Beauchamp, pray?'

'I – I beg your pardon, sir.' Beauchamp sweated, but was saved by a purely fortuitous circumstance: Captain Watkiss had seen, across his deck and the yellow-brown dust of the wharf, the young woman upon the battlements of Fort Mers-el-Kebir. He dropped his monocle from his eye to dangle at stomach level from its black silk toggle, and brought up his telescope with its gleaming pipeclayed turks-heads, a tattoo-ed snake emerging upon his forearm as his cuff lifted.

'I'll be damned! A woman! It's all the Frogs think about, is it not? Damn foreigners! Feller that brought the despatch smelt like a chemist's shop – I felt obliged to keep my backside against the bulkhead – you never know. Ah, Mr Halfhyde.'

'I was ordered aboard, sir –'

'Yes. No need to tell me my own orders, Mr Halfhyde. I dislike that.' Captain Watkiss snapped his telescope shut. 'Come below. And you, Mr Beauchamp.'

'Aye, aye, sir.'

'You may use my ladder.'

Beauchamp almost bowed; Halfhyde kept a straight face. Captain Watkiss' tone had indicated a great concession, democratically made: the starboard ladder, like all starboard ladders throughout the ship, was marked by a painted notice reading CAPTAIN ONLY, notices that were always removed before an admiral came aboard and were replaced immediately he had gone. Descending past this disgraceful example of Godhead, Halfhyde reached the Captain's cabin and, with Beauchamp, was bidden to a hard-seated chair. Captain Watkiss removed his gold oak-leaved cap and installed himself at his roll-top desk, which he opened with a rattle and brought out an envelope the seal

8

of which he had already broken. 'We are under orders for England, Mr Halfhyde. Not the flotilla. You and I only.'

'I see, sir. And may I ask, for what purpose?'

'You may not,' Captain Watkiss answered promptly. 'The purpose will be promulgated at a later date.' He thrust out his jaw and placed his monocle in his eye. 'You may rest assured it will prove a matter of much importance, however – of much importance for our country and the Empire. That's fact, I said it. Mr Beauchamp?'

'Sir?'

'The flotilla will cast off and sail for Gibraltar the moment all my ships have steam. See to that.'

'Aye, aye, sir.' Beauchamp paused. 'Leave – '

'Has been piped, yes, I know that, but it will not now be given, Mr Beauchamp, as you should know without being damn well told.'

'Sir, the liberty parties will already be going ashore.'

Captain Watkiss lifted his telescope and shook it at his First Lieutenant. His face deepened in colour. 'Then *stop* them, Mr Beauchamp, stop them instantly – and tell all my commanding officers to get back any men who have been landed, personally if they can find no other way, or I shall have them all in arrest and you too, Mr Beauchamp. And they are to report the moment they're ready to proceed to sea.'

'Aye, aye, sir.' Beauchamp left the cabin in a hurry and Captain Watkiss, clicking his tongue in annoyance, apprised Halfhyde of a little more of their shared orders which had come, it seemed, from the Admiralty by telegraph to the signal station at Gibraltar. From Gibraltar, the Captain-in-Charge had passed them to the French authorities in Oran; thus far, at any rate, there was no secrecy. But Captain Watkiss insisted pompously that secrecy would come.

'I would not be required upon some minor matter, Mr Halfhyde.'

'Indeed not, sir.' Sarcasm tinged Halfhyde's voice. 'And I?'

'Oh, as to you, I can't say,' Watkiss answered off-handedly.

'However, we are both to leave my flotilla at Gibraltar and embark aboard the homeward-bound P & O from Bombay. When in the Channel and off the Isle of Wight, we shall be taken off by a steam picquet-boat out of Portsmouth Dockyard and we shall report to the Commander-in-Chief for his disposal.'

'And the flotilla, sir?'

Watkiss looked disagreeable. 'My flotilla, God help it, will pass under the care of Mr Beauchamp until a post captain can be appointed to take my place. As regards *Vendetta,* Mr Half-hyde, you will hand over to your First Lieutenant immediately upon arrival in Gibraltar.'

'I shall do so with confidence, sir. Prebble's a first-rate officer, well fitted for command.' Halfhyde was indeed as pleased by this news as Prebble himself would be. Prebble had come up from the lower deck, making the long hard climb via the hawse-pipe to the intermediate rank of Mate, and was a little old for his present subordinate position: he could well do with the experience of command that would lead to advancement in the service, and that he would acquit himself adequately was a foregone conclusion in Halfhyde's mind. The relevant informa-tion imparted, Halfhyde was dismissed to return aboard his own ship and prepare for sea. Fires had not been drawn and within the next two hours, with all their ships' companies aboard, the five vessels of the Fourth TBD Flotilla had cast off from the wharf and were nosing in Line Ahead towards the Mediterranean, Captain Watkiss standing squat and square upon his navigating bridge as the routine farewell signals were politely made to Fort Mers-el-Kebir and its loose-living officers, and to the port authority in Oran. Gradually the town faded away on the port quarter, its two component parts, the seaport with the old Spanish town to the west of the ravine of Oued Rekhi, and the new French quarter to the east, seeming to come together be-neath the great mountain that backed them. The sea was calm and flat; as night fell the bow waves of the flotilla creamed back along the sides in brilliant phosphorescence. Halfhyde, with little else to do but breathe deeply of the good fresh air as he walked his small quarterdeck, pondered on the future. The orders were very non-committal but Halfhyde accepted the point that Watkiss had made : a post captain would not be hurriedly withdrawn from his flotilla and hastened into home waters without excellent reason. The ways of the Lords of the Admiralty were largely unpredictable and wrapped in mystery, but were not capricious to that extent. And where did he, Halfhyde, fit? He knew that he had done his duty, that his command had been well conducted; though still unable upon occasion to curb his tongue and his forthrightness, he would not be going home to face reprimand and censure followed by half-pay as had once been his lot. He grinned to himself as he paced, bracing his tall bony body automatically to the slight roll of the deck. He had always had that reputation for a degree of insubordination, for occasional acid rudeness to senior officers when he had seen through blind stupidity and pomposity – and God knew Watkiss was very often both and there had been many sharp exchanges over the past months. But Watkiss, who was largely an impossible man to serve under and was accustomed to making mincemeat of those of his officers who quailed before him, tended to respect an officer who stood firm and would not be bullied; and he had one great virtue : he dealt with his problems himself and did not pass his strictures on to a higher level. His reports, if biased towards giving maximum glory to himself, were largely fair upon his subordinates, and a mere lieutenant could not ask for more than that. Halfhyde's bursts of frustration would not have been the subject of adverse report. So the mystery remained : why were he and Captain Watkiss to be apparently bound together for disposal by the Commander-in-Chief at Portsmouth? Halfhyde grinned again. ' For disposal ' always had a dustbin ring, yet when used in regard to personnel it was no more than a routine service expression giving the disposer power to make his own appointments of the officers or men concerned. And again, in this case, why?

By next morning's first light Watkiss' flotilla had rounded Europa Point into Gibraltar Bay and had entered the inner harbour to go alongside the wharf, passing the homeward bound P & O at anchor in the bay, a great ship with a black hull and buff upperworks like one of Her Majesty's ships, wearing the

Blue Ensign in indication that her master and a proportion of her officers and men were enrolled in the Royal Naval Reserve and committed to fight as Queen's men in time of war. Immediately the leader had berthed, Captain Watkiss was seen to embark in his galley and proceed across the inner harbour below the great brown eminence of the Rock, to report to the Captain-in-Charge in the dockyard. As Halfhyde mustered his ship's company to bid them farewell, the bugles started blowing reveille over the regiments and corps in garrison, and a little later, from the direction of Red Sands, came the stirring sound of the pipes and drums as a Highland battalion paraded. The garrison began to come alive to a new day, with redcoats visible along the defences, and the shouts of NCOs coming from Hesse's Demi-Bastion, Cornwall's Parade, Chatham Counterguard, Forbes' Battery, Casemates and the Land Port. Soon, back across the water came Captain Watkiss. As he neared the flotilla he clambered to his feet and stood dangerously, foolishly really, in the sternsheets. He removed his gilded cap and waved it energetically as his coxswain reached out a steadying hand. As he passed, each vessel cheered ship, a storm of sound echoing out across the blue water as the sennit hats, hastily donned by the seamen for the occasion of bidding their Senior Officer goodbye, were waved in the air. Watkiss finally replaced his cap and saluted. He must, Halfhyde thought, be feeling happily nostalgic. Cheers were always heartening, but it was at least debatable whether on this occasion they were expressions of relief. Captain Watkiss reached *Venomous*, climbed to his quarterdeck and vanished below, and within two minutes the signals had started as expected : *Venus* had been slow to secure alongside; *Vortex* had a length of codline hanging judas over her stern plating; and Mr Halfhyde would be taken off by Captain Watkiss' galley for the liner as soon as *Vendetta*'s new commanding officer had placed in the report a stoker who had been observed peering from a hatchway wearing a dirty singlet as his Senior Officer passed by.

*   *   *

'Mr Halfhyde, I have certain information from the Captain-in-Charge. You will report to my cabin in ten minutes. They call it a stateroom. Number Five, on the starboard side of the upper deck.'

' "A" deck, sir – '

'Oh, don't argue, Mr Halfhyde, I dislike it intensely, and you are still upon Her Majesty's service whether or no you are aboard a civilian vessel.' Captain Watkiss bounced away along the boat deck; for some reason he was wearing the curious rig that was of his own particular invention: a white Number Ten tunic with immensely long shorts that flapped about stockinged legs that were overly thin for a short, fat man – a most curious sight beneath the glory of his gold oak leaves. He still carried his telescope, not beneath his arm but in his right hand as though ready to strike. Two minutes later he came back. He had lost his way and was being convoyed by an obsequious steward. He vanished again, into the proper alleyway. Ten minutes later Halfhyde went down as ordered to 'A' Deck and found Captain Watkiss supervising his unpacking and stowage of gear. He looked remarkably out of place: Captain Watkiss did not fit aboard a liner, in a community where another man was God. He was now a post captain without a command. . . .

'Ah, Mr Halfhyde.' Watkiss turned upon the steward, who was a Goanese. 'Get out.'

'Sahib?' The innocent, helpful face was puzzled. 'Sahib, it is my – '

'Don't argue, just do as you're damn well told and get out. Don't come back till I send for you. Mr Halfhyde, kindly do not stand about like a lily in a pond. Get rid of that black man at once.'

Halfhyde opened his mouth to speed the Goanese with tact, but the man was already on his way. Watkiss simmered for a while, then ejected his monocle and said, 'A man named Petrie-Smith is aboard and will report here shortly. Foreign Office wallah . . . came post-haste overland to brief me. I don't like it. Feller's coming back with us.'

'You say to brief you, sir. Am I included?'

13

'Yes, you are. We're going on a mission together and I'm damned if I know what. There's some jiggery-pokery afoot. Ever heard of the *Meridian* battleship?'

'I have indeed, sir. Improved *Inflexible* class, launched in '77, thickest armour and biggest muzzle-loaders of any British ship. Sailing rig replaced with pole masts and fighting tops in the mid eighties – '

'Yes, quite. Well, she's no damn use and she's going to the Chilean Navy. And we're taking her to Valparaiso. I shall be in command. You will be my Executive Officer, since we shall carry no one of commander's rank. You'll also take watches – ship's company's to be only of steaming party complement. You'll be given no extra rank or pay,' Captain Watkiss added sourly, then, after a pause, spoke again. 'I smell trouble!'

Halfhyde shrugged. 'A routine job, sir.'

'Oh, rubbish, Mr Halfhyde, a Post Captain of my seniority and experience to be employed to command a damn steaming party? And what about Mr Petrie-Smith? Or do you *expect* the Foreign Office to take an interest in every obsolete battleship for delivery to some damn dago port? I – ' Captain Watkiss broke off as a discreet knock came at the door of the stateroom. 'Come in,' he called. The door opened. A man with a domed head, completely bald save for sprouts of white over the ears, entered; a tall, stooping man of immense leanness dressed in a frock coat and black trousers with a high starched collar, and wearing gold-rimmed pince-nez.

Watkiss replaced his monocle in his eye and stared at his visitor. 'Do I take it you're Petrie-Smith?' he asked distantly.

The tall man inclined his head. 'Indeed I am, Captain. How d'you do.' They shook hands; Halfhyde was introduced. With the air of a conjuror producing a rabbit, Petrie-Smith released the information, presumably relevant, that he held the equivalent rank of Senior Clerk in Her Majesty's Foreign Office. Captain Watkiss was well enough aware that a senior clerk in the Foreign Office was not by any means as lowly as a clerk in lesser spheres – in bank or office, insurance or indeed anywhere else: in the Foreign Office Senior Clerks were but one stage removed from the godliness of the Permanent Under-Secretary of State, and as such were senior to post captains of the Royal Navy, an unwelcome thought. However, Captain Watkiss was able to pounce on the word 'equivalent', and he did so. He was given to understand that Petrie-Smith was no ordinary diplomat such as would be appointed openly to an overseas embassy but was rather a functionary who kept his ear to the ground in certain quarters at home and abroad and in whom certain matters, unknown to the general public, reposed. Watkiss' accusation, angrily uttered, that in plain language he was a damned spy, was met with a gentle but reproving smile. Spies did not exist in the Foreign Service although from time to time intelligence came to hand or was diligently gathered in. On this occasion, certain intelligence had been received that all was not well in regard to British interests in South America. A jealous eye was being cast by the German Emperor upon the availability of the Falkland Islands to the British fleet. Germany, who wished to establish increasing trading relations with the South American states, and Chile in particular, had no corresponding availability or coaling stations that could be depended upon for her use. It was believed that a squadron of the German Navy was about to be despatched to South American waters in an attempt to put matters right and sway the Chilean Government towards the best interests of the Fatherland. Thus there would be a clash of interests.

'War,' Watkiss stated firmly and plainly.

'Not *war* – '

'Oh, stuff and nonsense! I dislike circumlocution and I dislike mealy-mouthed persons, dislike 'em intensely. If a clash of interests isn't war, then I should like to know what you call it, Mr Petrie-Smith!'

'I repeat, I do *not* call it war. There is no reason for war to develop, and I assure you it had better not. Her Majesty has no wish to go to war with her own grandson, nor has Lord Salisbury for that matter. You, Captain, are being despatched under cover of a ship-delivery appointment to guard our British interests and to see to it that war does not result from your success. Should you bring about a state of war between Great Britain and Germany

. . . then, I fear, you would incur Her Majesty's displeasure and would find yourself upon the unemployed list for a very long time indeed.' The smile was still gentle but the steel of the Foreign Office had shown rudely through. Captain Watkiss was speechless.

TWO

When Petrie-Smith had had his say, which was a long one, a number of questions still remained in the air : one of them being, in Halfhyde's mind at any rate, why choose Captain Watkiss for a semi-diplomatic mission? Captain Watkiss was an impetuous officer at the best of times, a man of sudden temper who was possessed of an ingrained dislike of all foreigners, a man as different from the suave, silken-tongued gentry of the Foreign Office as it was possible to imagine. Pondering, however, made the problem simple : much of Captain Watkiss' impetuosity, and no doubt all of his errors of judgment in dealing with foreigners, would have been nicely concealed when in the past he had compiled his reports to his superiors in the fleet and in the Admiralty. And it had to be admitted that the recent past had in fact encompassed no less than two successful exploits in the semi-diplomatic field : first with his flotilla in Russian waters, and then again with his flotilla in the waters of Spain, Captain Watkiss had brought high and important missions concerned with throne and state to a more or less triumphant conclusion. At any rate, his reports would thus have indicated, and the actual results had of course been plain for all to see and wonder at. St Vincent Halfhyde, pacing the liner's boat deck after leaving Watkiss' stateroom, permitted himself a moment or two of conceit : he himself had not been uninstrumental in securing honour and glory for his senior officer, and, though Captain Watkiss in his reports would not have stressed this assistance too far, it had been plain that Petrie-Smith was aware of Halfhyde's part and that the conclusion had been drawn in Whitehall that Captain Watkiss and Lieutenant Halfhyde made a good team.

And there had been another point that revolved round Halfhyde: Petrie-Smith had mentioned that it was no less a person than Vice-Admiral Paulus von Merkatz who was believed to be under orders to stand by with the German Special Service Squadron for duty in southern waters. Halfhyde had crossed swords with von Merkatz already and had outwitted the German Admiral to the extent that the Special Service Squadron had been led willy-nilly from South-West Africa into Plymouth Sound to have a highly-placed but reneging British Civil Servant, Sir Russell Savory, with the blueprints of future naval construction in his possession, laid bare to the exploring fingers of Her Majesty's Customs and Excise before he could decamp to Germany. . . . Where Halfhyde had succeeded once, said Petrie-Smith, he might well succeed again; he now had the advantage of personal contact with von Merkatz, contact that would have led to some understanding of how the German's mind worked.

Halfhyde paced on reflectively. The orders were far from precise, but such was not at all unusual. Whitehall in general and the Admiralty in particular preferred always to leave the initiative to the officer on the spot. On the rock of what constituted initiative, and what constituted failure to observe imprecise instructions, many a seafaring career had been blasted with a charge as effective as the broadside of a battle squadron. Thus had the Lords of the Admiralty and the politicians preserved their own reputations and appointments. This time the vagueness of the orders left gaping holes through which the whole Mediterranean Fleet could sail: Captain Watkiss and himself were to prevent the Emperor of Germany from establishing coaling bases and trade lifelines with Chile, no guidance whatsoever being given as to how this might best be achieved.

Halfhyde snorted, and stopped his pacing. He stopped perforce: a liner's boat deck was a more cluttered space than a warship's quarterdeck, if longer, and Halfhyde had reached an impasse formed by a very obvious Anglo-Indian colonel and his lady, reclining in deck chairs and rug-covered in some attempt to recapture the warmth of the sub-continent. Both were asleep; Halfhyde forbore to disturb them and turned instead to look over the starboard rail towards the Spanish shore. The liner was coming up now towards Cape Trafalgar where some ninety years earlier Vice-Admiral Lord Nelson had struck his decisive blow for England.

'"Here and here did England help me",' Halfhyde quoted aloud with some feeling; and beside him the sleeping colonel stirred.

'I beg your pardon?'

Halfhyde turned politely. 'And I beg yours, sir. I was thinking aloud.'

'About Trafalgar? I see you're a naval feller, so it's natural.' The soldier hacked at his throat, clearing it of phlegm. 'Been past many times myself, of course. A great victory. You fellers must be proud.'

Halfhyde nodded. 'I had an ancestor there with Nelson. My great-grandfather.'

'Really? That's interesting. Nothing like a tradition of service in a family I always say. May I ask the name, my dear sir?'

'The same as mine. Halfhyde.' It was plain enough that the gallant soldier expected to hear of a Collingwood, or a Hardy, or a Pascoe. 'Daniel Halfhyde . . . gunner's mate in the fighting *Temeraire*.'

'Ah? Gunner's mate . . . really. Interesting.' The colonel's interest faded abruptly on a sniff that was very nearly imperceptible, and, catching the eye of a steward, he snapped his fingers and demanded *chota pegs* for himself and his lady wife. Halfhyde turned away and paced aft. The Army had always been a more aristocratic affair than the Navy, aside from a few younger sons who, not having the family honour at stake in so positive a way as their elder brothers, had been permitted – along with the traditional fool of the family – to take up midshipmen's berths. But none had gone to sea on the lower deck, to live rat-infested lives of near starvation in constant terror of the cat-o'-nine-tails, to die in the red hell of shot and cannonball as the broadsides raked the gun-decks or brought down the masts and yards upon breaking backs. Halfhyde went below and, in obedience to an order given before leaving Watkiss' cabin, removed his uniform in favour of plain clothes. In the protuberant blue eyes of Captain Watkiss, a need for a degree of secrecy had already begun. The next few days passed peaceably enough. At mealtimes Captain Watkiss, dressed in a black frock coat or tails according to the time of day, ate at the Captain's table, brandishing his monocle in place of his telescope, laying down nautical law to the unfortunate ship's master and the passengers who appeared to hang upon his every word. When the master was absent from his place at table as the liner entered the coastal waters of the English Channel, Captain Watkiss by some personal process of natural inheritance took over from him and acted as host. For his part Halfhyde ate his meals monosyllabically in the company of four elderly spinster ladies who had been visiting a brother on the staff of Southern Army at Ootacamund and who talked endlessly of their exotic experiences, of *chota pegs* and *amahs*, *chaukidahs* and *mem-sahibs*, generals and colonels met, and which were the best regiments. It was with a high degree of thankfulness that at last Halfhyde, standing with Captain Watkiss on the embarkation deck as the liner slowed her engines off St Catherine's Point, saw the Commander-in-Chief's steam picquet-boat coming round the headland out of Spithead.

Watkiss strutted up and down impatiently. Soon, decreasing sound and vibration indicated that the engines had been stopped. A party of Lascar seamen, who had been unsecuring the liner's port-side accommodation ladder under the direction of the Second Officer, now winched it down to the waterline and set the lower platform in position to continual loud criticism from Captain Watkiss, Royal Navy.

'Damn poor. Should have been done in half the time. What can you expect of niggers, Mr Halfhyde? And that Second Mate – cuffs are dirty.' Watkiss shot his own cuffs from the sleeves of the civilian frock coat: secrecy was still all. 'Comes down from the top, of course. I, for instance, would never permit a gravy stain on my mess dress,' he added, inferring that the liner's master had been guilty of this sin. 'I'd have someone's guts for garters first, Mr Halfhyde, you may be sure!'

Halfhyde gave no answer. The picquet-boat came alongside, smartly and in accordance with naval drill. The two officers' baggage was carried down the ladder and embarked efficiently, then Captain Watkiss stood aside for Halfhyde to go down first. In the Royal Navy, junior officers by custom entered boats first and left them last so as not to keep their betters waiting. As Captain Watkiss strutted importantly down to the lower platform and stepped aboard, salutes were given and returned and the Commander-in-Chief's coxswain placed a silver whistle in his mouth and blew. The picquet-boat was borne off from the liner's hull fore and aft; bowman and sternsheetsman lifted their boat-hooks high after this manoeuvre, then lowered them to waist level as one man before placing them up-and-down before their bodies as their bare toes nimbly held the deck. The whistle blew again, smoke issued from the polished brass bell-mouthed funnel, the wheel went over, and the picquet-boat turned its stern towards the liner and its bow towards Spithead. As she headed away, the crest of the Portsmouth Naval Command was clearly seen upon the bows; and from the liner's boat deck Mr Petrie-Smith of the Foreign Office, voyaging on to Tilbury, waved a tall hat at Captain Watkiss, who responded with a formal salute as though he were in uniform. The liner had taken a slight list to port under the press of curious passengers crowding the rails to witness the naval ceremonial. Thus was Captain Watkiss' concept of secrecy adhered to. As distance was put between him and the liner, Watkiss spoke to the Admiral's coxswain.

'Have the cabin cleared. Mr Halfhyde and I will clean into uniform before arrival in the dockyard.'

*　　*　　*

'A damn waste of time, Mr Halfhyde.' Watkiss was looking sour; Halfhyde had not been required after all to report in person to the Commander-in-Chief and had kicked his heels in an ante-room aboard Nelson's *Victory* while Watkiss had been ensconced.

The ensconcement had been short; rudely so, said Watkiss' expression and tone. 'Nothing that that feller Petrie-Smith hadn't already told me. Except for one thing, and I'm pleased enough about that, certainly.'

Halfhyde coughed. 'Am I to be told, sir?'

'Yes. After *Meridian*'s been handed over to the Chileans, I'm to join Rear-Admiral Daintree as his Flag Captain.'

'Rear-Admiral Daintree, sir?'

'Didn't you know,' Watkiss said disagreeably, 'Admiral Daintree commands the Detached Cruiser Squadron, operating largely from the Falkland Islands and with responsibility, jointly with the Pacific Squadron, for southern South American waters?'

'I did not, sir – '

'Then you do now. I'm appointed in the room of a Captain Harris, who has died after eating a poisonous fish in some filthy dago river.'

'I see, sir. And I?'

'Oh, goodness me, I don't know about you, Mr Halfhyde, I didn't ask.' Disembarked now from the *Victory*, they walked through the dockyard towards the berth where the old battle-ship lay. Halfhyde's thoughts were cynical: an appointment as Flag Captain was a step towards flag rank for the holder himself, and a Rear-Admiral Watkiss might well emerge from the cocoon of Chile. Halfhyde smelled a degree of nepotism: Watkiss was not unconnected. He had two sisters, one being married to the Permanent Secretary to the Treasury, the purse-strings of power, the other to no less a person than the First Sea Lord. It was an interesting thought. As they moved through the clutter of the dockyard, with Watkiss returning salutes from junior officers and working parties of seamen, and responding to the doffed bowlers of civilian foremen, Halfhyde's mood grew pessimistic. The clamour and dirt of the dockyard, the haphazard piles of old rope, the tar and the paint, the rusting heaps of discarded machinery, the figureheads from old sailing men-o'-war, the broken masts and spars from the same – it all pointed towards the gloomy dereliction that they must expect aboard the *Meridian*.

She would be a sad ship to sail in; no one liked the last voyage under British colours of any brave ship that in her time had served her country well in many seas, a ship that once had been smart and trim and fully manned. The reality was the equal of the expectation: both Watkiss and Halfhyde stopped in dismay as they rounded a long, high shed and came upon the basin where the battleship was lying, forlorn at her berth in foetid water that was covered with a film of filth, oil and coal-dust and with floating segments of wooden packing-cases and other harbour impedimenta.

'By God!' said Captain Watkiss, fixing his monocle in his eye.

'A sorry sight, sir.'

'Very. But cleaned up she will be, Mr Halfhyde.'

'Not in time for sailing, sir.'

'Oh, balls and bang me arse, Mr Halfhyde,' Captain Watkiss said in a long-suffering tone, 'it's your job as my First Lieutenant to clean ship and do it fast. I will *not* take my ship to sea looking like a hen coop that's been descended upon by a haystack.' Watkiss moved closer, then stopped again and looked appalled, staring upwards at the foretop. 'Excreta, Mr Halfhyde, and I *won't have it*, d'you hear me?'

'Yes, sir. Seagulls will be seagulls, sir.'

'Oh, don't argue with me, Mr Halfhyde, it's a habit I detest. Rig hoses – scrub down the whole damn ship! Painting parties. Plenty of disinfectant needed below in the heads, I wouldn't be surprised. See to it.'

'Aye, aye, sir.' The battleship was due to sail on the morning flood tide in two days' time and the task was probably impossible – yet it had to be done even if they saluted the Commander-in-Chief outwards with the hoses still gushing excreta down the washports and hawse-pipes. Captain Watkiss advanced up the gangway to the shrill whistle of a single boatswain's call and the salutes of a depleted gangway staff: no corporal of marines, no sideboys. The Officer of the Watch, a midshipman, looked as miserable as the old ironclad itself.

'Name, boy?' Watkiss asked.

'Perrin, sir.'

'Well, Mr Perrin, you're a disgrace to your ship and to the service. That's fact, I said it.' Captain Watkiss lifted a hand and his telescope, which he had unpacked aboard the steam picquet-boat, aloft. 'The foretop, Mr Perrin! A few years ago I'd have flogged any man who allowed it to get to such a state! See to it – turn out the watch immediately!'

Watkiss passed pompously on towards the door in the after screen, pondering on painters and shipwrights who would be required to construct signs for ladders. Perrin, looking dead scared and puzzled, caught Halfhyde's eye. Halfhyde winked. 'Seagull shit, Mr Perrin. Take my advice and have all dockyard seagulls fitted with knickers of the best quality canvas.'

'Aye, aye, sir.' The youth, pimply, pale and fat with a voice high from sheer nerves, seemed more flummoxed than ever. 'Sir, the dockyard stores – the indents for canvas – the Pay-master – '

'Oh, for heaven's sake, Mr Perrin, I didn't intend to be taken literally.' Halfhyde moved on, catching up with his Captain. Mr Midshipman Perrin looked like having an appalling time of it under the good Watkiss.

*   *   *

During the afternoon Captain Watkiss cleared the lower deck and spoke to his assembled ship's company or what there was of it. Besides himself and Halfhyde the officers consisted of two lieut-enants, one sub-lieutenant and three midshipmen of the executive branch; plus a paymaster and an engineer, the latter being the only acting departmental head with a full complement, for engines were engines whatever the rest of the ship might or might not be. The upper-deck warrant officers were represented by a boatswain and a gunner; Halfhyde encountered Mr Pinch, the boatswain, with much pleasure. Benjamin Pinch had served with him aboard the *Viceroy* in the Pacific some years before, and was a solid, dependable seaman of the old hardy school, trained in sail. Of the lower deck, there were some forty petty officers and seamen plus a variety of cooks and stewards and supply ratings in addition to the engineroom staff. The complement of a steaming party was always pared to the bone, but Captain Watkiss addressed them as though he commanded a full battleship's company and was about to steam into glorious action against England's foes mustered in Spithead.

'Because my ship is old, it does not mean a lowering of standards. I wish the best and I shall have it. Slackness will be most severely dealt with. Master-at-Arms?'

A portly person wearing a frock coat and with a face empurpled by rum wheezed a pace forward and saluted. 'Yessir?'

'Your name?'

'Titmuss, sir.'

'Well, Master-at-Arms Titmuss, the discipline of my ship will be as tight, the routine as tautly run, as the flagship of the Mediterranean Fleet from which I come. Do I make myself clear, Master-at-Arms?'

'Yessir.'

Watkiss nodded. 'Then we shall get along well enough. I would be reluctant to remove your frock coat from your back, Master-at-Arms, but I am not known to shrink from unpleasant measures in the line of duty.'

'Nossir.'

Watkiss lifted his telescope, releasing the colourful snake from the constriction of his uniform sleeve. 'Then lose no time in seeing what's going on behind your back, and take the name of the man who is picking his nose over there, a disgusting habit. Chief Boatswain's Mate?'

'Sir!' A grizzled chief petty officer saluted as the frock coat pushed through towards the nose picker.

'Chief Boatswain's Mate, as soon as you're dismissed you shall see to the overhauling of all boats' falls. They are in a deplorable condition, a damn disgrace. *Dirty*! Aboard my ship, all boats' falls will be pipeclayed when in harbour. Mr Halfhyde?'

Halfhyde saluted. 'Sir?'

'Carry on, if you please, Mr Halfhyde.'

Again Halfhyde saluted. Captain Watkiss turned, jumped

down from the bitts upon which he had been standing, and bounced his way aft along the deck, importantly. He was the Captain of a battleship, a post captain's pinnacle of seagoing appointment, and the *Meridian* was going to live up to him whether or no pipeclay clogged up the free running of the falls. At his retreating footsteps his ship's company dispersed about their various duties, duties that had been interrupted by the clearing of the lower deck; and the *Meridian* grew slowly and painfully cleaner as the traces of seagulls and the dust of a recent coaling were sluiced away by the hoses. Below in the boiler-rooms the troglodytes of the black gang toiled in dirty singlets to prepare for the raising of steam in due course. On the signal bridge the yeoman of signals overhauled his bunting and his tack-lines, padding barefoot round the flag lockers. The dark came down and the 'watch below' of a weary ship's company, cursing captains and Chileans alike, cleaned into night clothing while the duty watch toiled on and on. Next day's dawn came unpropitiously, bringing a fine but soaking drizzle under which the litter of the dockyard lay bleak and cold and dreary like the premises of a dealer in old iron; and bringing more work. The next dawn after that brought something else: it brought a brougham which, directed through the main gate from the Hard by one of the Metropolitan Policemen who guarded all the Royal Dockyards, stopped behind a weather-mournful horse alongside the *Meridian*'s gangway. A man got down on the coachman's arm: Mr Petrie-Smith. Halfhyde, who from the now excreta-free foretop had witnessed this arrival, hastened down to warn his Captain.

'Oh, damn the man!' Watkiss said in exasperation. 'What the devil does he want at this stage?'

The conundrum was soon solved: Mr Petrie-Smith, brought to the cuddy by Mr Midshipman Perrin in person, announced that he was under orders to accompany the *Meridian* into Chilean waters.

'Why?' Captain Watkiss demanded.

'One moment, Captain.' Petrie-Smith lifted an admonitory hand and Captain Watkiss, reproved aboard his own ship and in his own cabin, reddened dangerously. 'First, I must make it quite plain that I am voyaging incognito. I shall not be known as Petrie-Smith. All arrangements have been made with the Admiralty through the good offices of the Second Sea Lord. I am joining your ship, Captain, as an assistant paymaster.'

'Are you indeed?' Captain Watkiss sounded incredulous but icily polite.

'Yes. I shall be known as Assistant Paymaster Luckings, Royal Navy, and I have been provided with uniform appropriate to that rank.'

'Ah-ha.'

'Now you'll wish to know the reason for my presence, Captain.' Petrie-Smith, alias Luckings, waved a hand. 'Do sit down, I require no ceremony.'

'You don't? Well, I'm glad.' Captain Watkiss, his face a picture, sat. 'And now the reason, if you please.'

Petrie-Smith produced a cigar case and without offering it round proceeded to light up. He blew smoke thoughtfully towards the deckhead. 'Rear-Admiral Daintree. He took his flagship into Valparaiso . . . without precise orders to do so, but apparently to show the flag in British interests. Commendable – no blame should lie in my view, even though he was in fact somewhat off his proper station. But he went ashore to call upon the port authorities and he has not returned aboard. It's all very awkward, as you'll appreciate – '

'I don't see why. Captains of Her Majesty's vessels – '

'If I may be allowed to finish, Captain. The point is this: word from our consul by the telegraph suggests that Daintree is actually being held in restraint – '

'*Held in restraint*, did you say? By God, I've never – '

'Yes. And we also have positive news now that Vice-Admiral von Merkatz has left Bremen and is believed to be directing his course southward through the Atlantic Ocean. Frankly, a definite link is suspected between the German movement and what's happened to Daintree – of which latter we have at present no details. Doubtless our trading position is involved also.' More smoke was blown. 'We must use extreme caution upon arrival, Captain – but

27

I should make one point quite plain at this stage : I do not in any way take over your command – '

'No?'

'No. I shall not interfere, merely act in an advisory capacity . . . principally, of course, to preserve the all-important diplomatic requirements.'

'Oh, good. No interference. I'm still to be Captain aboard my own ship.' Watkiss had got to his feet and was rubbing his hands together and his face was nearly purple. 'In that case, Mr Luckings, you are dismissed. I have to take my ship to sea in half an hour and I'm busy.'

'But I – '

'You'll report to my ship's office wearing your uniform and carry out any duties ordered by my Paymaster, and carry them out properly and to my satisfaction.'

'Really, this isn't what – '

'Get out, Mr Luckings, before I kick you out with my own foot.'

'But – '

Captain Watkiss advanced with telescope lifted. Halfhyde placed a tactful hand beneath Petrie-Smith's elbow and propelled him out of the cabin. From behind the Captain's door as it closed came a torrent of strong language, a good deal of it rhyming with an ill-chosen pseudonym. The gentleman from Whitehall was conducted to the ship's office, introduced to his superior, and set in place at a ledger concerned with the issue of items of uniform from an entity known officially as the Slop Chest. Fifteen minutes later Captain Watkiss climbed the ladders to the compass platform and under still-wet skies received the reports that indicated HMS *Meridian* was ready to proceed. The main engines were rung to stand by and looking somewhat smarter than two days previously the old ship went to sea. Her wires and ropes were cast off and hauled inboard as the eyes were lifted free of the shore by a miserable-looking dockyard unberthing party, huddling in thin garments against the drizzle's penetration. Slowly the iron-clad moved off the berth in the care of the attendant steam tugs. Halfhyde, on the fo'c'sle, felt an immense sadness. The battleship had known splendid departures, moving off the South Railway jetty beneath an Admiral's flag, with the band of the Royal Marine Light Infantry playing on her quarterdeck . . . *Rule Britannia, A Life on the Ocean Wave, Heart of Oak, Auld Lang Syne, Will Ye No' Come Back Again* sounding out from the brass and the drums and fifes. Today, when at least the last two tunes would have been appropriate – nothing. Nothing but the unberthing party with running noses and sniffs, and the ever-wheeling seagulls, and the rain over Portsmouth Town, and cloud rolling down from Portsdown Hill. Just an old, worn-out ironclad of England slipping silently out from her home port, cheap at half the price as the saying went, a bargain-basement offer from the Queen of England to the President of the Chilean Republic. She deserved something better. As she moved out into the fairway and was pulled round by the tugs to head past the South Railway jetty and make her departure signal to the Commander-in-Chief, Halfhyde, hands clasped behind his back, moved aft past the great 16-inch twin turrets, two of them set *en echelon* in the waist. They, too, looked forlorn as though their throats would never open again to hurl their thunder against the enemy. But there was a curious pricking in Halfhyde's thumbs . . . a day might yet come! *Meridian*, if matters went wrong as so often they could, might feel again the din and recoil of her guns, for England rather than for Chile. The South Americans were a weird bunch, and a British admiral would not, whatever the consequences, be left to moulder in Chilean hands.

*　　*　　*

They moved out from Portsmouth Dockyard, past the Round Tower and the steps where King Charles II had received Catherine of Braganza as his bride, past the jetty where Lord Nelson had taken his own last leave of England before Trafalgar; past Fort Blockhouse and along the buoyed channel for the starboard turn into Spithead, past the sea forts built by Lord Palmerston to keep out the French back in the fifties. Around St Catherine's Point into the Channel and back on their tracks for the Western

Approaches and the passage into the wide waters of the North Atlantic for the island of Madeira, which would be their first coaling port, after which they would head across towards the coast of South America to drop down by stages on Cape Horn and the terrible ice of the South Polar fringe. A south-westerly wind came up strong as course was steadied for the Lizard, and the sea grew choppy, with spray coming back from the bows to sweep the fo'c'sle and the guns and the compass platform. Captain Watkiss, who could have gone below and left the ship to his First Lieutenant, did not do so: he had not commanded a battleship before and he liked it. He hummed a little ditty in his simple pleasure and then prodded his telescope into Mr Midshipman Perrin, Midshipman of the Watch. 'Backside's too damn fat. Like a damn paymaster – all sit and no do. Get some exercise at the first opportunity, that's an order.'

'Aye, aye, sir!'

'And don't squeak. The voice of command does not squeak.' Captain Watkiss leaned over the guardrail of the compass platform, searching for faults. Below, the black gang sweated in the red glow of the furnaces and under the voice-lash of the stoker petty officers. In the ship's office Mr Luckings stared forlornly at rows of figures concerning socks and vests and tried to arrange himself handily for the porthole as the onset of nausea seized him. His head was in fact through the scuttle when a little later, off Portland Bill, a despatch vessel was seen coming off and signalling with every appearance of urgency at the *Meridian.*

THREE

'What's the signal, yeoman?' Watkiss' telescope was to his eye.

'Request you to heave to, sir.'

'Why?'

'Coming through now, sir.' The yeoman of signals read off the message and reported to the Captain, 'Passenger to put aboard, sir, on instructions from the Admiralty.'

'Who?'

'Doesn't say, sir.'

'Then find out.' Captain Watkiss snapped his telescope shut and rounded on the Officer of the Watch. 'Mr Lamphorn, engines to slow ahead.'

'Aye, aye, sir, slow ahead.' Lieutenant Lamphorn passed the order to the quartermaster at the helm; bells rang below in the engineroom and were repeated on the compass platform. 'Engines repeated slow ahead, sir.'

'Thank you, Mr Lamphorn. Mr Perrin.'

'Sir?'

'My First Lieutenant to the compass platform immediately.'

'Aye, aye, sir!' Midshipman Perrin turned away and doubled for the starboard ladder to the upper deck, but was stopped in his tracks by a shout from the Captain: the signpainter had been busy.

'Not that ladder, boy! Can you not read? Do you wish to be confined aboard the ship should leave be piped in Valparaiso?'

Perrin halted, turned, stammered an apology, went red, saluted, and ran for the port ladder, sliding down the rails on his hands. Watkiss brought up his telescope again and studied the approaching vessel. He saw uniforms : policemen, he believed, and a naval officer – a commander. There was also a civilian. He lowered his glass. 'Mr Lamphorn, stop engines.'

'Stop engines, sir – '

'And have the watch make ready a jumping-ladder, starboard side aft.' Hearing footsteps on the port ladder, Watkiss swung round. 'Ah, Mr Halfhyde. Somebody appears to be coming aboard.'

'Yes, sir. I fancy I know who it is.'

'Oh?'

Halfhyde, who through his own telescope had recognized the figure wearing a bowler hat secured with a cord toggle to the lapel of a dark blue suit, grinned and said, 'Detective Inspector Todhunter, sir, of the Metropolitan Police.'

'I'll be damned!' Watkiss looked scandalized. 'What the devil does he want?'

'Passage to Valparaiso, at a guess, sir.'

'Fiddlesticks! What does a London bobby want in South America, may one ask, Mr Halfhyde?'

'He – '

'All right, Mr Halfhyde, you may tell me later. Go aft and see to the embarkation, if you please. I don't yet know what my seamen are capable of and we don't want a catastrophe.'

'Mr Pinch and the chief boatswain's mate – '

'Oh, don't argue, Mr Halfhyde, just do as you're told.' Watkiss turned his back. Halfhyde descended to the upper deck and walked aft; there was a fair wind blowing now, coming up, he fancied, to gale force. White horses were forming on the sea, their tops blown off in sprindrift that brought the stickiness of salt to the skin and clothing. Overhead the clouds sped swiftly, streaky white against the blue. Mr Todhunter, Halfhyde remembered, had been a poor sailor and one who carried his own remedy since the day he had once accompanied his late mother on a voyage from the Clarence Pier at Southsea to Ryde in the Isle of Wight. Halfhyde's recollections crowded back: under Captain Henry Bassinghorn in the *Prince Consort* had sailed Detective Inspector Todhunter on the mission against Vice-Admiral Paulus von Merkatz, the policeman's task being to arrest the British traitor with the blueprints of Britain's naval construction programme. History was repeating itself with a vengeance: Halfhyde himself, von Merkatz, and Detective Inspector Todhunter sailed again. It was intriguing to say the least. As the familiar bowler hat, now blown from its owner's head but safely held by its toggle, emerged from the deep by way of the swaying rope ladder, Halfhyde gestured to two seamen. They went forward and grappled Detective Inspector Todhunter aboard and set him breathless upon his feet, the shiny knees of the blue suit damp with spray and the high starched white collar a trifle soggy.

'Why, Mr Halfhyde, I do declare!'

'Well met again, Mr Todhunter.' Halfhyde shook the policeman's hand, which was as fish-limp as ever. The black walrus moustache appeared to have grown longer since their last meeting, giving the man an even sadder look, and was touched now with grey. 'If I may make a guess, mine is not an unexpected face?'

'To tell you the truth, Mr Halfhyde, no, it is not.'

'And you're coming . . . how far are you coming, Mr Todhunter?'

The Detective Inspector put a finger to his lips, bent towards Halfhyde, and whispered in his ear. 'All the way to Valparaiso, Mr Halfhyde, between you and me and the gatepost so to speak.' Todhunter looked about him in some agitation, then gave a sound of relief as a bulging straw-sided hamper and a Gladstone bag were drawn up to the deck on the end of a rope. His luggage was safe and of that at least he was glad; already his long, pale face was a trifle green. Halfhyde ordered his effects to be taken below and a cabin made ready, then he escorted the policeman to the compass platform as the despatch vessel, last link with England, turned and made its way back into Portland harbour behind the great bluff of the Bill. Captain Watkiss received his unexpected passenger with ill grace and an affronted manner.

'Someone at the Admiralty must have gone mad. I can't see what use policemen are at sea. What's your name, I didn't get it?'

'Todhunter, sir, Detective – '

'Yes, yes, yes. Todhunter.'

'And I'm only in the singular, not the plural, if I may make so bold – '

'What?'

'One police officer, sir, not police*men*. I shall be unobtrusive.'

'I trust so.' Watkiss' eyes went to Mr Todhunter's boots: they were large, serviceable and hobnailed, not good for holystoned wooden decks. 'What is your purpose?'

'Only to be revealed in private, Captain.'

'Sir is more appropriate, Todhunter. And this is private.'

'No, sir, it is not. I shall speak in your cabin – '

'Get off my bridge this instant, damn you.'

'Captain – '

'Get off.' Watkiss waved his telescope and bounced up and down on the balls of his feet, his face a deep red. 'Mr Halfhyde, remove this person instantly.'

*   *   *

'Alas,' Mr Todhunter said gloomily.

'What?'

'My task is to prove a hard one, I fear, Mr Halfhyde.' Todhunter raised a hand and pushed his pearl-headed tiepin deeper into his cravat. 'Captain Bassinghorn was a gentleman.'

'Good heavens, so's Captain Watkiss – '

'Yes, sir, all naval gentlemen are gentlemen in a sense, but there are stages if you follow my meaning.'

'I think I do, but you'll not lead me into any disloyalty to my Captain, Mr Todhunter. God is God, and is to be obeyed, and if you find that a somewhat large statement, then you've never been trained aboard the old *Britannia* or had your backside kicked by a petty officer instructor. You must take things as you find them aboard a Queen's ship, Mr Todhunter, as indeed you did under Captain Bassinghorn.'

'Yes,' Todhunter said in an aggrieved tone, then split his face into a mournful smile. 'I was at Bow Street once. We had a Chief

34

Super who thought he was Jesus Christ. He got taken down a peg – '

'Well, Mr Todhunter, I'd not suggest to Captain Watkiss that there's any similarity between himself and a Chief Super if I were you, or you'll not live to round Cape Horn.' At the mention of Cape Horn, Mr Todhunter's eyes grew glassy and the involuntary upsurge of bile was almost visible in the hue of his complexion. 'Captain Watkiss will send for you presently,' Halfhyde went on. 'In the meantime, can you be at all forthcoming to an old comrade-in-arms as it were?'

'It's kind of you to say that, Mr Halfhyde, but no, I'm afraid I am permitted to speak only to Captain Watkiss in the first instance.'

Halfhyde nodded. 'I understand perfectly, Mr Todhunter. But perhaps you know the name Petrie-Smith?'

'Goodness gracious me, sir, most certainly I do not. I have no knowledge of the name whatsoever!' Todhunter was shocked.

'Of course you haven't, Mr Todhunter,' Halfhyde said smoothly, and took the policeman's arm. 'A perambulation of the deck, I think. Aboard the *Prince Consort* you made some progress towards your sea-legs, and it would do no harm to recapitulate.'

*   *   *

Mr Todhunter had to wait; Watkiss would not leave the compass platform until his ship had left both the Lizard and the Bishop Rock away on the starboard quarter. The conference was not called until well into the following day. In the meantime the Detective Inspector lay horribly in his allotted bunk and eschewed all meals in the warrant officers' mess to which, on account of his rank, he had been attached for accommodation, sharing it, when making one brief appearance, only with Mr Pinch and the gunner, and the artificer engineer who ranked as a warrant officer. The sea was a cruel thing and was acting in a rough manner as the *Meridian* began to shudder towards Ushant for the dreadful

35

Bay of Biscay. Alarming thuds crashed against the deadlight outside Mr Todhunter's porthole, and now and again from the deckhead above came sounds of running feet, horrendous and alarming sounds that spoke with eloquence of crisis and disaster and a possible projection of a police body into a lifeboat to face as it were naked the dangers of the deep. From time to time Mr Todhunter gushed into a chamber-pot handily placed at his bedside by his steward. At breakfast time the dreadful smells of frying eggs and bacon from the warrant officers' mess reduced him to a palpitating pulp, so later did the smell of roast beef and Yorkshire pudding. During the afternoon following his embarkation the summons came from Captain Watkiss. Manfully, Mr Todhunter pulled himself together, washed, and proceeded on wobbly legs to the Captain's day cabin which Watkiss found more spacious than his sea cabin for the holding of a conference.

*　　　*　　　*

'Good God,' Watkiss said, staring as at an apparition.

'I apologize, Captain – sir. I am unwell.'

'Yes, you look it. Been skulking in your bunk, I don't doubt. Worse thing you can do. The very worst. It's fresh air you want, and food, that's fact, I said it. No one can vomit on an empty stomach, it needs something to grip on. I should have thought you'd have known that, any fool does. All you do otherwise is strain the stomach lining till it comes up like – like a shroud.' As Todhunter, eyes huge in the green of his face, conveyed something from a bottle towards his mouth, Watkiss stared harder. 'What the devil's that, may I ask?'

'A remedy, Captain. Sir. The Four D's.'

'God give me strength.' Watkiss closed his eyes.

'Doctor Datchet's Demulcent Drops. My late mother's recommendation. If I might have a glass of water, sir?'

'As much use as a fart in a frying pan,' Watkiss said in disgust, but nodded to Halfhyde to ring for his servant. 'Had the stuff been any damn good, you'd not have remained so long on the flat of your back. However, I suppose it's your affair.' The Captain's servant appeared and water was brought; Mr Todhunter placed two pills in his mouth and swallowed while Watkiss looked angrily impatient. 'Well, now that performance is over, Mr Todhunter,' he said as his servant disappeared, 'you may give me your explanation of why you're aboard my ship – we are now in private, I trust you've observed. One moment, though.' Watkiss turned to Halfhyde. 'We'd better have Petrie-Smith, I suppose – '

'Captain – '

'Kindly do not interrupt, Mr Todhunter, it's a habit I detest. Mr Halfhyde, I say again, we had better have Petrie-Smith.' Captain Watkiss pressed a bell-push beside the roll-top desk in his day cabin, and his servant appeared.

'Yessir?'

'My compliments to Mr Luckings, and I want him here immediately.'

'Yessir.'

'He's required to take notes,' Watkiss added with an eye to the preservation of secrecy. An expression of relief vied with illness on the Detective Inspector's face as the Captain's servant departed. 'Now, Mr Todhunter, while we wait you shall expound.'

'Very well, sir. Perhaps Mr Halfhyde has told you, I was involved in the pursuit and arrest of the traitor Sir Russell Savory a year or two back – '

'Yes.'

'In which Admiral von Merkatz was also concerned, of course. Which is why Mr Halfhyde was taken on the strength of this vessel – '

'Naval officers are not taken on like tradesmen, Mr Todhunter, they are appointed.'

'Yes, well,' Todhunter said in an aggrieved tone. 'The constituent parts of the affair now come together, is what I was intending to say, sir.'

'Be more precise.'

'Very good, sir, I will be.' Mr Todhunter's face became almost transparent as the *Meridian* lurched to a wave that slid beneath her bottom plating, and he emitted a horrible noise but, his stomach being mercifully empty, nothing else. Sweat poured down his face and his hands trembled. 'Sir Russell Savory may be involved in South American matters – '

'Why?'

It was Halfhyde who answered: 'Savory arrived in German South-West Africa from South America, sir. From Chile, in fact.'

'When?'

'At the time of the scandal over the purloined blueprints, sir – you remember – '

'Yes, yes, yes. But that is not *now*, is it?'

'It is not, sir,' Halfhyde answered patiently, 'but I must confess I see a possible link. Perhaps Mr Todhunter would explain?'

'I shall, sir,' Todhunter said, and once again addressed himself to Watkiss. "As we know, Savory had useful friends in Chile – '

'Who?'

'That we don't know, sir. That never did emerge, despite the most patient and diligent enquiries undertaken largely by myself.' Todhunter paused, as if for approbation. None came. 'Savory was not hanged, sir, if you recall. He in fact, in the event, committed no treason, he merely attempted to do so.' Todhunter glanced at Halfhyde briefly. 'I made my arrest in time, you see. Savory was committed to penal servitude for life. He has now escaped.'

'*What*? When?'

'Four days ago, sir, from Dartmoor Prison.'

'Why was I not told?' Watkiss demanded.

Todhunter said, 'I can't answer that, sir.' Watkiss was about to utter again when there was a knock at the door and Assistant Paymaster Luckings appeared.

'Ah, Petrie-Smith – '

'Luckings,' Petrie-Smith said with reprimand in his voice.

Mr Todhunter clambered to his feet and stood swaying. Watkiss snapped at him to sit down. Sleuth and pseudonymous diplomat shook each other by the hand: their paths had crossed before now. Mr Todhunter was obsequious, his 'sirs' to Petrie-Smith carrying an audible capital letter.

'I have revealed our suspicions of Savory to Captain Watkiss, sir.'

'No you haven't,' Watkiss said rudely, and turned to Petrie-Smith. 'What, precisely, is Savory's present involvement, may I ask?'

Petrie-Smith shrugged. 'Precise is what I cannot be, Captain. We know he has escaped from prison, and we know too that he went to Liverpool, since he was seen there. That was four days ago . . . he's not been seen since, though the port and town of Liverpool and Birkenhead have been searched most thoroughly and the area has been cordoned off. The prognosis is fairly obvious, I think: he has taken ship, either as a stowaway or as a member of a crew, signing articles under a false name, most likely as a steward, or he could even – '

'All ships in Liverpool have been searched, I take it?'

Petrie-Smith glanced at Todhunter, who answered, 'Yes, sir, that has been done, with no result. But in the interval between the sighting in Liverpool and alerting the authorities, many ships left the Mersey. And Liverpool's seaborne trade, sir, is largely with South America. So many companies . . . Iredale and Porter's sailing ships, the steamers of the Pacific Steam Navigation Company to name but two – '

'Yes, yes, Mr Todhunter, your point is made and taken. Savory may have decamped to South America. Again I ask *why*?'

Todhunter spread his hands. 'A nefarious purpose, sir. A nefarious man. It is feared that – '

'But those damn blueprints – they're out of date by now! Any naval officer could have told you that. We live in fast-moving times, Mr Todhunter. A ship is obsolescent almost before it has left the fitting-out basin.'

'Indeed, yes. But it is not the blueprints – they were recovered, I am proud to say. Nor is it Savory's inner technical knowledge, the content of his brain – or at any rate we don't believe so.' The Detective Inspector gulped and sweated more. 'Perhaps Mr – Mr *Luckings* will explain further.'

'Oh, damn this nonsense,' Captain Watkiss said angrily, 'we're all *British* in my cabin, and none of us is a traitor. Petrie-Smith?'

Petrie-Smith stroked his jaw. 'It's the contiguity,' he said. 'Whitehall fears that Savory may act together with von Merkatz against the wider British interest in South America. He's already branded as a traitor – '

'Nothing more to lose – yes, I see that,' Watkiss said, looking sage. 'But what precisely can he do?'

'One cannot be precise,' Petrie-Smith answered. 'We are working on conjecture, on an interpretation of known facts, which are simply that Savory made his escape, curiously, at the very time that von Merkatz was despatched to Chile, and that he is known to have gone to Liverpool, a port with many connections with South America – '

'And other places.'

'Yes, indeed – world-wide, of course. I concede the point, but do not relinquish my own.'

Watkiss lifted his head and scratched reflectively beneath his chin. 'How would Savory have known von Merkatz' movements and intentions, may I ask? Breaking stones on Dartmoor is an occupation far removed from diplomacy and international intrigue, I fancy?'

Mr Todhunter pounced on that. 'As a Detective Inspector of the Metropolitan Police, sir, I must disagree up to a point. That is to say, felons have their ways and means of obtaining information even inside Her Majesty's prisons and other corrective establishments. I remember – '

'Yes, yes, Mr Todhunter, thank you. One would still not connect the German Emperor with Dartmoor Prison.'

'Via the grapevine, Captain,' Petrie-Smith said, 'I would see no inconsistency. I agree with Todhunter. I have a good deal of experience of such matters. And Savory is known to have developed a more marked Anglophobia since being sentenced. Before his attempted defection to Germany with the blueprints, he was intensely devoted to his own aggrandizement and advancement. Circumstances have intensified his self-seeking desires. He may see a way to accomplishing his wishes via von Merkatz. If he can be of service to the Emperor – '

'Yes, exactly,' Watkiss broke in. 'We come back to my original

40

question: what the devil use can he be to Germany – he's out of date and he's totally discredited, isn't he?'

Petrie-Smith nodded. 'That's agreed, Captain. Certainly his technical knowledge is out of date – that's to say, he can release no useful secrets of a constructional nature. Savory, however, is not a mere technician or naval architect. He had advanced to high places, remember. He had contacts with a number of governments – '

'You're hinting at the Board of Trade, Petrie-Smith?'

'Among others, Captain. The Committee of Privy Council for Trade includes the Commercial Intelligence Branch – the people who deal with information affecting British and Colonial trade. Foreign interests also tend, unofficially at any rate, to come within their scope. Savory had many friends in the Department and much information rubbed off on him. Secret trading agreements . . . under-the-table arrangements in the British interest . . . names of persons, South Americans among them, known to favour Britain, and names of persons known to favour other powers such as Germany. Persons both high and low who could be useful to one nation or another. I prefer not to be too specific, Captain, but I think you will understand that Savory can be most useful to the Emperor's designs.'

Watkiss blew out his cheeks. 'I am a simple sailor, Petrie-Smith, accustomed to fighting the elements and the Queen's enemies cleanly. I dislike chicanery, and I dislike people who are not gentlemen. Savory, I understand, was not a gentleman by birth – that came out, did it not, at his trial?'

'Yes. A common man who made good – until he went bad.'

Watkiss nodded and sat straighter in his chair. His shoulders braced and a proportion of his stomach was drawn flat and forced up into his chest. Halfhyde recognized the signs: metaphorical anti-Savory swords were flashing from their sheaths. A man of the common people who had dared act against Her Majesty was to be pursued and caught and vengeance was to be exacted. This Watkiss and the old *Meridian* would achieve in glorious selfless service to the Crown of England. All those present, including even Mr Todhunter, seemed to sense that Captain Watkiss was enjoying his moment of projection to success and honour; Halfhyde knew that in his mind's eye was a picture of Her Majesty Queen Victoria staring across the Great Park from the windows of her drawing-room in Windsor Castle, receiving most welcome news from Lord Salisbury and reflecting moist-eyed upon the devotion to duty of the Post Captains of her Fleet. No one seemed inclined to break the curious spell; and it was Watkiss himself who did so.

'Tell me, Petrie-Smith: you used the words, "among others". What other departments of state were involved? I ask because it appears likely that the Foreign Office itself could have been at risk. If so, I require you to tell me at once.'

There was a brief interchange of looks between Petrie-Smith and the Detective Inspector, then Petrie-Smith, his face icy and withdrawn, said, 'There was an involvement, but one that did not come to light – '

'It was hushed up at the trial?'

'The Foreign Office, Captain, does not *hush up* anything. It deals with its own. Certain persons were retired – that is all. I cannot, and will not, say more.'

Captain Watkiss rose to his feet and seized his telescope from the desk. 'Another thing I dislike intensely: damn inefficiency leading to an inability to appoint trustworthy persons to high positions in the Foreign Service! The whole blasted lot of you would benefit from a two-year commission on the lower deck of a man-o'-war.'

Petrie-Smith went pale with anger. 'Really, my dear sir – '

'Thank you, Mr Luckings, that will be all.' Captain Watkiss jabbed at him with his telescope. 'Back to the ship's office and mind your P's and Q's or I'll have your reasons in writing and your balls for breakfast.'

*   *   *

The weather deteriorated sharply as the *Meridian* entered the Bay of Biscay and headed south towards Cape Finisterre for the run down the coast of Portugal. The ironclad laboured, dipping her head under the waves as they dropped upon the fo'c'sle, lifting her stern in a horrible pitching motion. Great mountains formed alongside and then by some mysterious process transferred themselves below the bottom plating and made the battleship slide sideways in a stomach-draining swoop into a valley. Pitching and rolling combined to make a corkscrew motion. In the ship's office Mr Luckings sought mercy from his superior the Paymaster and was despatched to lie upon his bunk before he could bring ruination to the ledgers and stores lists. In the warrant officers' mess Mr Todhunter, who had begun to improve as a result of his self-administered remedy, had a wicked relapse that left him paralysed and totally unable to retreat to his cabin and avoid the horrid smells of dinner. Mr Pinch surveyed him anxiously. A kindly man, the boatswain had no wish to worsen his situation, or to seem unsympathetic, but he had his messmates to consider in his capacity as Mess President, and the Detective Inspector was certainly no adjunct to a well-served meal. Mr Pinch addressed the corpse.

'Mr Tod'unter, my best respects, but wouldn't you be better off shifting to your bunk?'

There was no response and for a moment Mr Pinch suspected actual death. He prodded with a finger stained with tobacco and calloused from many years of hard work along the upper decks of warships. 'Mr Tod'unter, if you please. This'll never do.' He was joined by Mr Mottram, the gunner, a slow-moving man of much bulk, little hair, and the despotic manner of all seamen who have made the long haul by way of the gunnery branch from able-seaman via chief gunner's mate to the exalted rank of Gunner, RN.

'Leave 'im to me, Ben, right?'

'He's a copper, Guns, not one of your turret crews.'

'Once a bloody copper tried to run me in for drunk and disorderly, when I was a young leading 'and,' Mr Mottram said with relish, and spat upon his palms. He stood to attention and shouted in the Detective Inspector's ear. 'Now, Mr Tod'unter – hup-hup-hup! On yer tootsies, sharp.' He reached out and yanked the policeman from the settee upon which he lay. Mr Todhunter swayed and groaned, and the gunner called up the mess steward.

'Starboard side o' Mr Tod'unter, Bates, then the lee side o' the upper deck for 'im to unload, after which 'is cabin. All right?'

'Yessir.'

'Off you go, then.' Mr Mottram raised his voice again. 'Lef', right, lef', right and I advise a bath before you turn in.' As the Detective Inspector lurched out of the mess Mr Mottram spoke to the boatswain. 'Fat look o' good 'e's going to be, Ben, when we catch up with this Savory. What's the bettin' Savory's aboard von Merkatz' squadron, eh?'

'Don't see how.'

'Why not? Transfer at sea.'

Mr Pinch jeered. 'Likely! No British shipmaster would have a part o' that. No, he'll turn up in Valparaiso if he turns up at all, you mark my words.'

Dinner that night in the warrant officers' mess was accompanied by much speculation; so was supper along the messdecks. The Captain's steward had ears enlarged and made attentive to detail by many years spent in his calling, and one of the time-honoured if unofficial duties of a Captain's steward was to keep all hands informed upon matters affecting their future.

* * *

Passing Finisterre, the weather showed improvement; and by the time the *Meridian* was in the latitude of Cape St Vincent and coming down upon the Portuguese island of Madeira to coal ship, Mr Todhunter was in better shape and able to sway along the upper deck to take the air, clutching for support at stanchions and davits and guardrails as he went. The wind blew kindly and warm now, and refreshed rather than buffeted him. His bowler hat remained in place, the toggle that secured its brim to the miniature ringbolt on his lapel blew gaily around one ear as he surged along to the now gentle plunge of the bows, and ground to a halt as they rose again. He was hailed peremptorily from behind.

'You there, that policeman.'

Mr Todhunter turned: Captain Watkiss was strutting up with

his First Lieutenant. 'Good morning, Mr Todhunter, I see you are alive. I've been talking to Mr Halfhyde.'

'Yes, sir?'

'And I've been thinking. Mr Halfhyde tells me – I'd forgotten the details of that damn feller's trial – you made the arrest upon a German warship – '

'That is correct, sir.'

'I know it is, I didn't ask for your confirmation. Keep your mouth shut, if you please, until bidden to open it. Also that you first *attempted* to make an arrest ashore in what was it, German South-West Africa.' Watkiss paused expectantly. 'Well, am I right or am I wrong, Mr Todhunter?'

'Oh, right indeed, quite right – '

'Then why didn't you damn well say so?' Watkiss demanded irritably, shaking his telescope. 'The point is this: in my view you violated every concept of international law and diplomacy, or intended to, and that won't happen this time, that's fact, I said it.'

Todhunter's mouth gaped. 'But – '

'No buts, Mr Todhunter, this is my ship and you're under my command and I won't have it, d'you hear – '

'Sir, my Chief Superintendent – '

'Oh, balls to your Chief Superintendent, Mr Todhunter,' Captain Watkiss said distantly, 'I am a post captain of the Royal Navy and that's that. I am not to be compromised, I am under orders not to break diplomacy and I don't give a fish's tit what Mr Petrie-Smith says either. If Savory is to be arrested, he must be arrested aboard my ship, which is British sovereign territory.'

'But really, sir, I simply must – '

'Kindly hold your tongue, Mr Todhunter, and don't argue with me.' Captain Watkiss strutted for'ard and climbed his ladder to his bridge. Halfhyde gave the Detective Inspector a sympathetic wink as he passed on behind the Captain. A fat lot of help that was, Mr Todhunter thought in extreme bitterness of spirit, a bitterness intensified by the fact that he was a dedicated member of the Salvation Army and as such regretted the use of strong language. . . . A matter of minutes later he found himself almost overwhelmed by a mass of seamen rushing barefoot along the deck like the tide amid a shrilling of boatswain's calls and the strident shouts of Mr Mottram. Captain Watkiss, it appeared, had decided to exercise his guns' crews in case action should come. Action would fracture diplomacy a blooming sight more than a mere arrest on foreign soil, Mr Todhunter thought acidly, but there was obviously no accounting for Captain Watkiss' mental processes. Clinging to the guardrail the Detective Inspector watched and listened in acute anxiety as men shouted incomprehensible words mixed with profanity. Metal objects banged and clanged, and the great mouths of the 16-inch guns swung with their turrets to bear dangerously upon either bow.

FOUR

At Madeira, with coaling completed and the decks hosed down and scrubbed to gleaming whiteness under Halfhyde's eye, a curious contraption was seen approaching along the berth, a horse-drawn vehicle containing a bench seat beneath a fringed and tasselled canopy once white but now filthy with coal dust. From it descended a fat man in a gaudy uniform, dark with sweat stains beneath the arms and down the back, accompanied by a thinner, cleaner person in a plain white suit and a Panama hat. Disembarking, these persons approached the *Meridian*'s gangway and climbed aboard. Audience of Captain Watkiss was requested. The gentlemen, one of whom was the British consul in the port, remained aboard for half an hour and took gin. On their departure Halfhyde and Assistant Paymaster Luckings were summoned to the Captain's quarters, where Watkiss sat in a wicker chair on his sternwalk enjoying warm sunshine and a view of blue calm waters beyond the port installations.

'Work for you, Petrie-Smith. In your capacity as one of my clerks . . . the consul brought a cabled message in naval cypher. To be broken by an officer only. The Paymaster has the decyphering tables.' Watkiss handed over the message. 'Off you go and don't take too long.'

Petrie-Smith demurred. 'I should have thought the Paymaster himself might be more adept and therefore quicker.'

'But you are of the Foreign Office, my dear sir, and thus more suitable to receive what may prove to be secret information, and almost certainly will in the circumstances.' Watkiss had spoken

47

in a lofty tone, and Petrie-Smith went off with the flea lodged in his ear. Watkiss turned to his First Lieutenant. 'I don't care for that feller, Halfhyde. Sly. I couldn't find him in Burke's *Landed Gentry*, either.'

'Nor me for that matter, sir.'

'I know. But you don't give yourself airs and graces and stick hyphens in your name. I've a damn good mind to call him Smith in future. However, let us consider more important matters.'

'Yes, sir.'

Watkiss scratched beneath his arm. 'The cheese has gone off. That's happened before as you know – in *Venomous*. My Camembert . . . you'd think a damn battleship would have room to carry more ice.'

'*Can* Camembert go off, sir?'

'I don't know, but mine has. I've a good mind to put the damn Paymaster in arrest, it's his job to see that I'm decently fed. Now to von Merkatz.' Captain Watkiss got to his feet and gestured to Halfhyde to follow him into his day cabin, where charts of the South Atlantic were laid out on his dining table and held flat by the strategic positioning of bottles of ink and Plymouth gin, a heavy brass ashtray and a Connemara marble pig. The charts covered the sea expanses across to the coasts of Brazil, Uruguay and the Argentine, including the area of Cape Horn and the Drake Strait running between the stormy Cape and the Antartic. 'I have been arriving at an estimation of von Merkatz' position, Halfhyde. If we assume his course to be for Cape Horn, which it obviously must be if our overall premise is correct, and assuming also that he left Bremen on the day indicated by Petrie-Smith, then I believe him to be about *there*.' Captain Watkiss brought a finger down upon an area of sea to the south of the Azores. 'I expect him to have coaled at the Azores.'

'Rather than here?'

'The dago who boarded said no German squadron had entered recently. This was corroborated by our consul and is therefore to be believed.'

'No doubt, sir. What do you intend to do?'

'Remain as it were in his wake, Mr Halfhyde, what else?'

'And leave the initiative to him, sir?'

'Not exactly. If I had the bunkering capacity to use more speed, I might well have decided to overtake von Merkatz, but I have not.' Watkiss became patronizing. 'Free your mind of sail, my dear fellow . . . the more the speed, the more the coal burned.'

'I am not unaware of that, sir,' Halfhyde answered coldly. 'Am I to understand that you propose to make a virtue of necessity, and allow von Merkatz to arrive first in Valparaiso and thus – '

'And thus be forced to show his hand – precisely! After that, you see, I can formulate a plan.'

'Always assuming von Merkatz enters Valparaiso, sir.'

Watkiss stared truculently. 'What the devil d'you mean, Mr Halfhyde?'

'There are other ports in Chile, sir.'

'Rubbish.'

'A glance at the chart, sir – '

'Oh, don't be impertinent, Mr Halfhyde. What I meant to say was that Valparaiso's the only one he'll enter, surely that's obvious. If you were some blasted foreigner wishing to enter into intrigue with the British Government, you'd not be likely to take your squadron into – into Littlehampton or Polperro, even if there was depth of water enough for you to do so.'

'But the Germans are devious people, sir.'

Watkiss nodded. 'True.'

'And if von Merkatz showed his hand where you were not in a position to see, sir – '

'*If.* I've dealt with that, Halfhyde, thank you. If you're suggesting that I should aim to overtake von Merkatz, then my answer is no, I shall not.'

'With respect, sir, I suggest that he who strikes the first blow seizes the initiative – '

'Kindly – '

'If I may be allowed to state a point of some importance, sir. I am not in fact suggesting you overtake the German squadron – if you did so, von Merkatz might slip into some other port and in effect deviate behind you. In any case, you have not the speed. What I am suggesting is that you enter the first practicable Chilean port after rounding Cape Horn, leaving von Merkatz to steam on – so that before he reaches Valparaiso you can communicate by the telegraph with the authorities who are holding Admiral Daintree.'

'Why?'

'Because, sir, he who first communicates has in effect arrived first – and also because in my view the safety of Admiral Daintree is of paramount importance, not only to the Admiralty and the British people, but also to the success of our mission.'

Captain Watkiss blew out his cheeks and got to his feet, in an obvious huff. He strutted the length of his day cabin and back again, half a dozen times, holding his telescope like a club. Then he faced his First Lieutenant. 'I suppose you have a point. I don't know, though. The White Ensign, flaunted in the faces of the Valparaiso authorities, would have a far better effect than a telegraphed message.' He paused. 'Which port do you suggest?'

Halfhyde said, 'Puerto Montt, to the north of the Gulf de Ancud, at the head of Reloncavi Bay – '

'I'm aware of its position, Mr Halfhyde, thank you. An impossible place to enter! So far as I know, it's little more than a fishing port.'

'Reloncavi Bay is used by the liners of the Pacific Steam Navigation Company, sir, and we would not actually need to enter the port. There is plenty of water for us to lie off, and send a boat inshore. Or there is Puerto de Coronel, thirteen miles south by west of Concepción, but – '

'Yes. Well, I shall give the matter my consideration.'

'Sir, if I may – '

'You may not, the matter is closed for now. I have a ship to command in the meantime, Mr Halfhyde, and as my First Lieutenant you have it to run for me. The men are to be smartened up. They are fat and lazy like that youth Perrin. Gun drill before arrival here was a damn disgrace. The ship is still filthy – this morning I found brasswork with polish that had not been rubbed off! I shall require the cable on deck to be burnished before arrival in any Chilean port, and the freshly exposed links burnished after I anchor, if that is what I do. I insist upon a smart ship, Mr Halfhyde, and you shall provide me with one.' Captain Watkiss went at some length through his list of what constituted a smart ship and was approaching the end of it when there was a knock at his cabin door and Petrie-Smith entered.

'I've decyphered the cable, Captain.'

'Ah.' Captain Watkiss reached out and took the proffered sheet of paper. Placing his monocle in his eye, he read. He was pleased by his reading: his back straightened and the glint of war came to his eye. 'By God, I'm being given a squadron! Parity with Admiral von Merkatz!' He waved the transcribed cable. 'I am to rendezvous off the Falklands, Mr Halfhyde. Her Majesty's ships *Biddle* and *Delia* are to join my command as – as escorts,' he ended a little lamely.

'Escorts, sir? From what you said, I understood –'

'The word is immaterial,' Watkiss snapped. 'You'll ginger up my ship's company, Mr Halfhyde, in no mean fashion. The flagship will set an example, by God!'

*　　*　　*

According to the Navy List, which Halfhyde lost no time in consulting in the ship's office, *Biddle* and *Delia* were elderly 6-gun sloops, wood built in the sixties, carrying direct-action trunk engines as auxiliary power to sail and commanded in each case by an officer of lieutenant's rank. Their sisters had all gone either to reserve or conversion into store hulks around the Empire. The wonder was that *Biddle* and *Delia* had managed to reach the Falklands at all; most probably, Halfhyde thought, they had been unable to make the passage back to England and had remained to end their careers with the Detached Cruiser Squadron by maintaining some sort of armed presence to defend the islands when Daintree had taken his main units to sea. Whether or not they would stand up to the weather off Cape Horn would be revealed in due course. 'Parity with von Markatz' was a large claim: besides his flagship, the second-class battleship *Friedrich der Grosse*, Vice-Admiral Paulus von Merkatz flaunted the German naval ensign from the first-class cruisers *Kaiser Wilhelm, Nürnberg* and *Königsberg*. The difference in fire power, in sea-keeping qualities and in total complement was vast. If things should go wrong, the *Meridian* herself could be blown out of the water by a single broadside from the *Friedrich der Grosse* alone. . . . Later, as the old battleship proceeded to sea from Madeira with her bunkers filled, Halfhyde could not help but admire the sheer gall of Captain Watkiss. And his courage too, for that matter: if the guns should fire, Watkiss would not be found wanting. If necessary, he would steam his command straight into the gun-muzzles of the German ships, standing himself four-square upon his navigating bridge, as open to danger as any man aboard.

Moving along the upper deck, Halfhyde heard his Captain shout from the compass platform: 'Mr Halfhyde!'

'Sir?' Halfhyde looked up.

'You will clear lower deck, men on watch to stand fast, as soon as special sea dutymen are fallen out. Hands to muster in the waist. I shall address my ship's company and inform them myself of the great honour that has been conferred upon their Captain.'

'Aye, aye, sir.' Halfhyde, grinning inwardly, saluted. When the men had been mustered, Captain Watkiss descended from his lofty position and spoke as if symbolically from atop a gun-turret: England expected, and his squadron would not be found hanging back when the call came. An enemy might await them after they had rounded Cape Horn, which was why the Admiralty had strengthened his hand. . . .

'*Stop that damn talking*!' Captain Watkiss shouted, waving his telescope. A seaman gunner among *Meridian's* company had once served in a sister ship of *Biddle* and *Delia*, and word of their senility was spreading like lightning through the interested muster. Grins were concealed, and Captain Watkiss proceeded with his harangue, breaking off again to address his First Lieutenant.

'Mr Halfhyde, that man. That loafer.' Captain Watkiss

pointed to a group of cooks and stewards, persons who, along with other non-watchkeepers, were known officially as daymen or loafers. 'Cap's crooked. Have him put in the report.'

* * *

Mr Todhunter, blossoming next day in the peaceful calm of the South Atlantic as the battleship thrust through the blue towards the South American coast to take more coal in Monte Video, returned to an already well-aired complaint.

'But how am I to effect the arrest, Mr Halfhyde, supposing I do apprehend the traitor Savory?'

'As I remember, you carry a warrant in your Gladstone bag.'

'That was last time, Mr Halfhyde, and that is not my point. Warrant or no, am I expected to approach the traitor Savory and say, Mr Savory, beg pardon, Sir Russell, would you be so kind as to step aboard a British man-of-war so that I can serve you with a warrant of arrest in due course?'

'Difficult.'

'Do you imagine he would comply, Mr Halfhyde?'

'It would be unlikely, Mr Todhunter, but the Captain's word is law. Not, perhaps your law – '

'Then – '

'But certainly mine. And you, too, must obey.'

'Not once I'm on the shore, Mr Halfhyde, in a foreign land.'

'Where, as in German South-West Africa, the British fiat does not run. I fancy, should you arrest Savory ashore, Captain Watkiss will permit neither you nor he to board his ship afterwards.'

'But this is lunacy, Mr Halfhyde!' The Detective Inspector lifted his bowler hat and fanned his face with it; as he did so a flying fish skimmed across the deck, narrowly missing him before plunging back into the sea to leave only a memory of its shimmer. 'I have my duty to do when all's said and done.'

'Patience, Mr Todhunter, and first catch your traitor. Once you've nabbed him, other ways must be thought of.'

'What ways, Mr Halfhyde?'

'You'll not find me uninventive when the moment comes. In the meantime, bear well in mind that Captain Watkiss remains God.'

Todhunter pulled a face. 'I think that's blasphemous, to be frank.'

'Your thoughts, Mr Todhunter, are your own concern but facts are facts. In a sense, Captain Watkiss has now become Commodore Watkiss, and on that you'd do well to ponder.'

'Oh?'

Halfhyde kept his expression austere. 'Now he ranks senior to God. Cross him at your peril, Mr Todhunter!'

'My Chief Super,' Mr Todhunter said bitterly, 'would *never* put up with this, never!' Halfhyde left him to reflect on the ways of senior naval officers and proceeded for'ard for a conference with the boatswain. Mr Pinch was at his wits' end: during the forenoon, the Captain had ordered the calm to be taken advantage of and a seaboat lowered, to pull round his hove-to ship for exercise with Mr Midshipman Perrin in command to reduce his fat. The evolution had taken far too long, as Mr Pinch was the first to acknowledge: Captain Watkiss' insistence on pipeclaying the falls had contributed to this delay, but Watkiss had been in no mood to agree.

'Nonsense, Mr Pinch, and don't presume to tell me what to do. Slackness is slackness and is not to be blamed on pipeclay. You will exercise the lowerers throughout the rest of the day until Evening Quarters.'

'Aye, aye, sir.'

'Send Mr Perrin to me.'

The result of Mr Perrin's visit to the compass platform met Halfhyde as he walked towards the bows: Perrin was moving rapidly around the deck, from aft to for'ard along the port side and back again on the starboard side, his face red with effort and his body sweating profusely into his uniform. Halfhyde raised an eyebrow at the boatswain.

'How many times round, Mr Pinch?'

'Not times, sir, hours. Four hours to be precise . . . poor little bugger.'

Three nights later Halfhyde had the middle watch, from midnight to four o'clock in the morning: the graveyard watch. It was a balmy night, with no wind at all to move sails if they had had such. The beat of the main engines grew monotonous, as did the swish of the water past the iron hull; Halfhyde kept on the move in order to remain awake, pacing the compass platform back and forth with hands clasped behind his back, exchanging an occasional word with the yeoman of the watch, the midshipman, or the helmsman via the voicepipe to the steering position below the compass platform. At intervals hot cocoa came up from the galley and was thankfully taken; at intervals the midshipman was sent below to make rounds of the messdecks and flats, to stalk behind a ship's corporal bearing a lit lantern and to bend beneath the hammocks that contained the sleeping bodies of seamen and stokers, daymen and signalmen. Halfhyde breathed fresh air, glad that it was not his duty to make rounds. In tropical waters, at night with all ports closed in accordance with damage control requirements, the stench along the messdecks was quite indescribable. Sweat that had soaked into hammock-canvas and blankets, bodies improperly washed, feet, human breath, often hundreds of men in a small and enclosed space where no air moved save that consciously or unconsciously emitted from bodily apertures . . . God alone knew how the sailors could put up with it when it was as much as an officer could do to walk quickly through it and back again to the upper deck! Halfhyde carried on with his pacing, found his thoughts moving away from an easily-steaming ship in good weather, towards the Yorkshire Dales where his childhood had been spent on his father's farm. Wensleydale . . . a good place to be with its changing seasons, and the wind blowing fresh from atop distant Ingleborough and Great Whernside, the right and proper place for a sailor to be when not aboard a ship. There was much similarity between farmer and seaman, poles apart though their lives might seem to be: the weather eye, the good fresh air, the need for instant readiness for an emergency, be it for a sick sheep on the fells, a cow in calf, or the sudden squall that could catch even a battleship unbattened down. . . .

'Mr Halfhyde, sir!'

Halfhyde swung round on the starboard lookout. 'Yes?'

'Sternlight ahead, sir, fine on the starboard bow.'

'Thank you.' Halfhyde brought up his telescope and steadied it on the faint white light, by his estimate some two miles distant. Black bulk loomed above it, and he believed he saw a trail of smoke, and beyond it, though he could be mistaken, another sternlight. Lowering his glass, Halfhyde turned away to the chart table behind him and studied the chart in the light of a candle lantern, dim and flickering between the canvas screens. On their westerly course they had already come due south of the Azores and had on the Captain's order altered southwards some two hours earlier. Halfhyde frowned, measured off the distance from his last star sight back northward to Ponta Delgada in the Azores. Then he withdrew from the screen and used the voicepipe to the Captain's sea cabin.

'Captain, sir.'

Watkiss, a light sleeper, was swift to answer. 'Oh, what is it, Mr Halfhyde, for God's sake?'

'I believe we have von Merkatz in sight ahead, sir.'

'What? Oh, rubbish, Mr Halfhyde, he can't possibly be, my estimate places him much further to the south!'

'Your estimate could be wrong, sir –'

'Kindly don't be impertinent.' There was a long-suffering pause. 'Oh, very well, I'll come to the compass platform but woe betide you if you're wrong.'

FIVE

The ships ahead remained obstinately, irritatingly beyond identification distance in the darkness. Captain Watkiss grew angry.

'Mr Halfhyde, when did you first raise the sternlights?'

'Just before I called you, sir.'

'Then we must have the legs of them!'

This was obvious: otherwise the unknown ships, which were on the same course as the *Meridian*, would have been in company since the southward alteration. Halfhyde acknowledged the point, but added, 'At the time of sighting they were steaming slowly. I believe they've increased speed now.'

'After sighting us astern?'

'Yes, sir.'

'I call that impertinent.' Captain Watkiss strode the compass platform, a ghostly blur in the night. 'Quite clearly they must be warships – merchantmen don't go about the seas in company, do they, Mr Halfhyde?'

'No indeed, sir.'

'Inform the engineroom, Mr Halfhyde, that I require maximum revolutions.'

'Aye, aye, sir.' Halfhyde bent to the voicepipe and below the telegraph handles were pulled back twice and sent ahead again. At the same time the Captain's order was passed verbally to the engineer on watch on the starting platform in the bowels of the ship. Soon, the increased thrust of the screws was felt in the immense vibration that shook the old battleship's plates and seemed almost to make the compass platform hum. But very little extra speed appeared to result. There was no closing of the gap between themselves and the ships ahead; indeed, the gap seemed to be increasing. Watkiss grew agitated.

'Inform the engineer of the watch that I shall place him in arrest if he fails to obey my order to produce more speed.'

Halfhyde coughed. 'The engineer of the watch is only human, sir. The engines are old and – '

'You will do as I say, Mr Halfhyde, or you'll be in arrest yourself.' Watkiss turned away and for the hundredth time, as Halfhyde passed the message down, lifted his telescope towards the vanishing glow of the sternlight. The warships, and never mind his earlier estimate of relative positions, must be those of von Merkatz. Watkiss fumed: the damn German was getting away from him, cocking a metaphorical snook at him with each revolution of his propellors while the old *Meridian* wallowed along like an egg-bound duck. More minutes passed in anguish; the threat of arrest failed to produce more speed and Captain Watkiss swore roundly.

Halfhyde tried to smoothe troubled waters. 'I think little is being lost, sir. The – '

'Only the British trading interest, and my reputation with the Admiralty, God damn you, Mr Halfhyde.'

'You can scarcely be blamed, I fancy, sir. Your spirit is willing, but your ship is old and weak.'

'True, certainly.' There was grudge in Watkiss' tone, but he was already receptive to excuses. Halfhyde followed up the advantage, remarking that in any case there would have been no positive action that could have been taken against the German squadron at sea. This was a mistake.

'You may be lily-livered, Mr Halfhyde, but I am not, and that's fact, I said it. I would have made a signal demanding that von Merkatz heave to and submit to a boarding-party, and I would have carried out a search for the man Savory – just in case.'

'You may still do so, sir. We are still within visual signalling distance by lamp.'

'Oh, don't be so stupid, Mr Halfhyde, he wouldn't take the

slightest notice since he has more speed than I. I have no intention of making myself a laughing-stock for the damn Germans. I only wish,' Watkiss added vigorously, 'that I was able to use my guns on his blasted backside. As a matter of fact, I've a damn good mind to!'

'And cause an international incident, sir?'

'Not international, Mr Halfhyde, an affair between Great Britain and Germany.'

'If the ships are German, sir.'

Watkiss, his face truculent in the dim glow from the binnacle, stared. 'What d'you mean, *if* they're German?'

Halfhyde shrugged. 'Just a thought, sir. We may have an Argentine squadron ahead, or even a Chilean – '

'Stuff and nonsense! Dagoes, as far to sea as this? They still believe the world to be flat most probably. I am quite positive we have the Germans ahead of us.' Watkiss paused, then bounced a little on the balls of his feet. 'Matters are going reasonably well, my dear Halfhyde. I have brought my ship up behind von Merkatz as I intended. You'll remember it was never my intention to overtake the bugger . . . I shall shadow, and hold myself in readiness to strike when the time is ripe, the iron hot. You will maintain your course and speed, if you please, Mr Halfhyde, and in the meantime I shall return to my sea cabin.'

'Aye, aye, sir.' Halfhyde, familiar as he was with his Captain's chameleon-like qualities, was as ever intrigued by his infallible ability to turn every circumstance to his advantage in his mind. 'The engines, sir. They'll not keep up maximum revolutions for long.'

'Oh, yes, they will, Mr Halfhyde, for as long as I require them.' With dignity, Captain Watkiss left the compass platform. Halfhyde reflected sourly on the propensity of holding-down bolts to sheer away from their moorings in the engineroom if pressed too far, and upon the huge quantities of valuable coal that the furnaces consumed at high and uneconomical speeds. Captain Watkiss, left to wallow with broken engines or cold boilers in the middle of the South Atlantic Ocean, would be an uncomfortable shipmate and one who would cast blame. Halfhyde made a prudent decision and spoke to the engineer by voicepipe.

'This is the Officer of the Watch, Mr Duffett. Revolutions to normal full speed, if you please, but bring them down slowly if you value my life.' What Captain Watkiss didn't know about, he didn't grieve over, and a gradual reduction in the vibration might even lull him back to sleep. 'And if you're worried about being placed in arrest, set your mind at ease.'

'I gave you enough speed, then?'

Halfhyde chuckled. 'No, but I've a working knowledge of Captain Watkiss.' He replaced the voicepipe cover and looked out ahead : the sternlight was still there, but distantly, and within the next half hour it had gone. At 4 am the watch on deck was relieved and Halfhyde went below to his cabin. When he emerged for breakfast in the wardroom the day was clear and bright, the sky was blue and the sea stood utterly empty of ships beyond the old *Meridian* herself, forging south until the time came to alter in again for the River Plate for another coaling, her engines intact and her bunkers not seriously depleted. Captain Watkiss, emerging after breakfasting on porridge, kedgeree, fried eggs and bacon, toast, marmalade and masses of coffee in his sea cabin, emerged onto the compass platform to find Mr Midshipman Perrin's back-side protruding from the chart-table screen.

He prodded with his telescope and Perrin backed out.

'Improving your knowledge of navigation, I see, Mr Perrin.'

Perrin saluted hastily. 'Yes, sir.'

'Where are we, Mr Perrin?'

Perrin's mouth opened.

'Mr Perrin, kindly do not stare at me as if you've never seen me before in your life. Where are we?'

'Sir, we're in the South Atlantic, sir!'

'I know that, Mr Perrin. *Precisely* where?'

Perrin's face was as red as a beetroot. 'I – I don't know, sir.'

'Find out. When you've done so, I am to be informed.'

'Yessir!' Perrin saluted again.

'And when you are relieved from your watch, you'll eschew your breakfast and run round my upper deck again until you are next due on the compass platform. Exercise increases the speed of the mind, Mr Perrin, and the intelligence, whereas food clogs it.'

'Yessir!'

Captain Watkiss turned for'ard and surveyed the seas, returning the salute of the Officer of the Watch. 'Mr Lamphorn,' he said, 'you may tell the engineroom to reduce to normal revolutions now. I shall not strain my engines unnecessarily.'

'Aye, aye, sir.'

'And my compliments to those responsible for tending my engines throughout a prolonged period of maximum power. They responded nobly.'

'Yes, sir.' With all faces straight, the messages were passed and received: the camaraderie of conspirators held, and Captain Watkiss basked in the giving of praise. It never did any harm to be expansive when such was called for; afterwards, the men put their best feet forward in the interest of a considerate captain. In the meantime Mr Perrin struggled with mathematical calculations, a pencil, a pair of dividers and a parallel ruler and in due course approached his Captain diffidently and with a sinking heart.

'Captain, sir.'

'Yes, what is it, Mr Perrin?'

'I know where we are, sir.'

'Good. Where are we?'

Perrin stated the ship's position in terms of latitude and longitude.

'And that is precise?'

'Yessir!'

'Rubbish, Mr Perrin, it is not precise. You will not be taking a sun sight until noon, therefore your position is mere dead reckoning from the position found by the last sight. Dead reckoning is by its very nature imprecise, Mr Perrin, and what are you?'

'I – I don't know, sir!'

'You are a liar, Mr Perrin, a damn liar to approach your Captain with false information. Mr Lamphorn?'

'Sir?'

'Mr Perrin is to be relieved immediately and sent aloft. He's to stand upon the foretopmast crosstrees until I order him down personally.'

*　　*　　*

The sun was strong and Perrin burned; blisters formed as his skin grew red and his thoughts grew antagonistic towards his Captain. He was ordered down from aloft at three bells in the afternoon watch to begin, unnourished, his marathon run round the upper deck; he was on the point of descending when he spied something in the far distance ahead.

He called down to the compass platform, where once again Halfhyde was on watch. 'Smoke on the horizon, sir, dead ahead.'

'Can you identify?'

'No, sir, but I believe there are three ships.' There was a pause. 'Four, sir.'

'Hull down, I take it?'

'Yes, sir.'

'Then say so, Mr Perrin. Remember the Captain likes precision or you'll be aloft again around the Horn!' Halfhyde, hearing a step behind him, turned and faced Captain Watkiss. He repeated Perrin's report.

'I heard it, thank you, Mr Halfhyde, I am not deaf. You did right to warn Mr Perrin of inattention to his duty. He's too fat by half, and thick-headed. He's to report instantly when he has identified the ships ahead. Tell him that.'

Halfhyde did so. Fifteen minutes later, Perrin called down again. 'Four warships, sir, a battleship and three cruisers, I think.'

'Think, think! Thinking, Mr Perrin, is stinking. You do not think in Her Majesty's Navy, Mr Perrin.' Watkiss turned upon the yeoman of signals. 'Aloft with you, yeoman, join Mr Perrin and report instantly when you see an ensign.'

'Aye, aye, sir.' Nimbly the yeoman of signals, a small dark man with a mass of wrinkles around his eyes, went down the port ladder and moved at the double for the fiferail alongside the foot of the foremast. He was aloft in a twinkling, climbing the shrouds like a monkey. Watkiss bounced up and down impatiently, his monocle jingling on its toggle. Another five minutes and the yeoman, his glass to his eye, sang out.

'Battleship *Friedrich der Grosse*, sir, wearing a vice-admiral's flag and the German naval ensign, sir, in company – '

'All right, yeoman, you may come down. And Mr Perrin.' In much excitement Captain Watkiss prodded his telescope at Halfhyde. 'Mr Halfhyde, we are overtaking them! Sound for action – beat to quarters!'

'*Action*, sir?'

'Oh, for God's sake, Mr Halfhyde, must I repeat my orders?'

'Do you mean to open fire, sir?'

'Probably not! But I intend to impress von Merkatz with my strength and determination.'

'Sir – '

'Do as you're told or I shall relieve you of your duties.'

Halfhyde shrugged and passed the order. Bugles sounded, but no drums: without marines embarked, the ship could not beat to quarters despite Watskiss' bombastic order. There was a rush of activity as the ship's company doubled to their stations at the gun-turrets and the six 20-pounders and at the submerged and carriage-borne torpedo tubes. Captain Watkiss watched impatiently, uttering criticism as the guns' crews closed up – too slowly, in his view. To the compass platform came Mr Mottram, the gunner, in vest and trousers, straight from his customary afternoon nap.

'Sir, I'd like to know the orders.'

'Mr Mottram, you are improperly dressed.'

'Action stations, sir – '

'Yes, Mr Mottram, action stations, but how dare you face your Captain in your damn vest?' Watkiss shook his telescope in the gunner's astonished face. 'As one of my warrant officers, you shall set an example to the common seamen. Go below and dress in the rig of the day.'

Mr Mottram, scarlet with anger and mortification, took a step backwards and almost fell down the ladder. Proceeding aft with murder in mind he encountered Detective Inspector Todhunter staring in some alarm towards the great gun-turrets aswing as the captains of the guns tested the machinery.

'Are they going to shoot?' Mr Todhunter enquired.

'With any bloody luck at all,' the gunner said, 'they'll shoot the bleedin' skipper.' He went on his way, leaving the policeman confused and uncertain. Mr Todhunter continued for'ard, keeping carefully out of the menacing arc of the 16-inch guns. He hovered at the foot of the starboard ladder to the compass platform, wishing to ascend and ask questions but not daring to do so: Captain Watkiss might well be occupied and would not welcome intrusion, and there was that proprietorial notice. . . . As Todhunter hovered, the *Meridian* began to close the German ships, bringing them full in sight ahead and a little on the starboard bow so that Mr Todhunter could see them clearly: four great men-of-war, with tall upperworks and many funnels and abristle with guns from stem to stern, and over all the flaunting ensigns of the German Emperor. . . . Mr Todhunter stiffened towards his duty, which could well be approaching. Although Savory was unlikely in Todhunter's view to be aboard any of the ships, the galley wireless already had it that Captain Watkiss intended to send a boarding-party to the flagship with his demands for search. It would be his, Todhunter's, duty to accompany the boarding-party, and God alone could tell what he would be expected to do should he after all encounter the traitor Savory who was not to be arrested other than aboard a British ship. Mr Todhunter, sweating now with apprehension, turned and made his way down to his cabin: he must have his Gladstone bag with him. In that Gladstone bag had at one time or another reposed all Mr Todhunter's directives and warrants and authorizations from his Chief Superintendent, documents that had covered every imaginable crime from rape and prostitution and pickpocketing to murder and treason and stealing from the gentry. It was part and parcel of him. As he left the upper deck and burrowed into the iron innards of the battleship, he was visited suddenly by hell. A tremendous explosion rocked the ship and a terrible clang echoed right through her plates and a moment later a tremendous thud came from above Mr Todhunter and a mass of water flowed through the hatch which he had left open, knocking him from the ladder in its apparent haste to flood the ship. Then there was closer hell: from immediately, it seemed, over his head, a greater explosion came and the ship lurched through the water, flinging him sideways. Falling to the deck of the cabin alleyway, he was trodden upon by Mr Mottram, re-emerging to the upper deck in the rig of the day.

'Sorry, Mr T.' The gunner dragged him urgently to his feet.

'W-what's happening?'

'Skipper's gorn berserk.' Mr Mottram vanished up the ladder. On the compass platform Captain Watkiss, far from berserk, wore an expression showing a mixture of pleasure, anger and mortification. The pleasure was due to the apparent fact that he had caught von Merkatz with his trousers around his ankles – with his ships steaming in circles for no known reason. The anger was due to the fact that the German's reaction to his presence had been remarkably fast and very unexpected – von Merkatz' guns, in opening upon *Meridian* as appeared to be the case, had put a shell into the water close enough to drench the battleship with a gigantic spout of sea. Watkiss' mortification was due to the sad inaccuracy of his command's return fire: the fall of shot had been noted well short of the nearest cruiser and Mr Mottram reached the compass platform in good time to bear the brunt.

'Poor gunnery, Mr Mottram – poor ranging, and it's your job to give me accurate gunfire. What have you to say?'

'Inaccuracy's your salvation, sir,' Halfhyde said, butting in. 'The – '

'Hold your tongue, Mr Halfhyde. Mr Lamphorn, I gave no orders to cease firing – '

'I did, sir.' Halfhyde again, to Watkiss' fury. 'The Flag has signalled, sir. Admiral von Merkatz is exercising his guns' crews.'

'What?'

'With no hostile intent, sir.'

'I'll be damned! No hostile intent indeed! The man must be mad! He could have hit my ship.'

'But did not, sir. He was not aiming at us.'

'Then what's he doing? What's he up to, Mr Halfhyde? Why

is he steaming in circles as though all his damn ships have lost their damn rudders?'

'I don't know, sir.'

'Find out, then! Make a signal.' Captain Watkiss thought for a moment. 'Yeoman, make to the German flagship: I demand an explanation in the name of Her Majesty.'

'Aye, aye, sir.'

Once again, Halfhyde interposed himself. 'Diplomacy, sir – '

'Oh, balls to diplomacy, Mr Halfhyde, kindly hold your tongue and send for Mr Pinch. I want boarding-parties to stand by to go across. I shall not be insulted by a damn German popinjay and you can put that in your pipe and smoke it.'

SIX

Whilst waiting for the German Admiral to respond to his demands, Captain Watkiss had more to say to Mr Mottram about poor shooting and loafing gunnery rates who would not match up even to the standards required of a ship's cook. 'You shall chase them, Mr Mottram, if you value your warrant. It's a pity the lash has been done away with. When I was a snotty – ah, Mr Pinch.' He broke off to address the boatswain. 'I trust your seamen will prove more efficient than Mottram's men. I wish boats and boarding-parties immediately.'

'Aye, aye, sir. I'll see to the boats' crews and lowerers, sir.'

'Yes, Mr Pinch. Mr Mottram, see your boarding-parties properly armed. The chief gunner's mate will provide a cutlass, the remainder will take rifles and side-arms.'

'Aye, aye, sir. And the orders, sir?'

'The orders will be promulgated shortly, Mr Mottram, and in the meantime the policeman is to report to the compass platform.' Captain Watkiss turned away abruptly and lifted his telescope towards the German squadron. A string of flags flew from the Admiral's signal yards, and in the other ships the answering pennants were being sent aloft. With an apparently total disregard of the *Meridian*'s peremptory signal demanding explanations, the Germans were re-forming into Line Ahead behind the *Friedrich der Grosse*. Captain Watkiss' face reddened dangerously and he hitched at his overlong shorts. 'Yeoman!' he called.

'Yessir?'

'Repeat my signal to the Hun and say I'm waiting his reply with such patience as I can muster.'

'Aye, aye, sir.' The yeoman of signals turned to his mechanical semaphore and worked the twin arms. An acknowledgment came from the flagship, but the insolent manoeuvre continued, the South Atlantic foaming up below the counters to the thrust and turmoil of the screws. A moment later Mr Todhunter reached the compass platform and politely lifted his bowler hat to the Captain.

'Good morning, sir,' he said.

'Good morning, Mr Todhunter. You will be going across to the German flagship presently. All ships will heave to.'

'Oh, dear,' Todhunter said anxiously, his worst fears now confirmed. 'In a boat?'

'In a boat, Mr Todhunter, unless you prefer to swim. Or would you like me to lay my ship alongside the Flag for your greater convenience?'

Recognizing sarcasm, Mr Todhunter prudently refrained from any reply. He asked, 'What am I to do upon my arrival, sir?'

'You will use your discretion and your initiative,' Watkiss answered promptly. 'The man Savory is not really likely to be aboard, I admit. Even if he is, he'll undoubtedly be kept out of sight and Admiral von Merkatz will make no admissions.'

'Do you intend a search to be made, sir? I would hardly think – '

'To enforce a search might be unwise, Mr Todhunter.' The Detective Inspector looked much relieved. Watkiss went on, 'I am instructed by the Admiralty to use discretion, and here upon the high seas discretion I shall use. My purpose will be to impress Admiral von Merkatz with my presence, my ubiquitousness if you like, and with my strength and my determination, and to show him who is master, by God! The question of an arrest will not arise – that follows from what I said just now – '

'Not necessarily, Captain.'

'What? What d'you mean?'

'The traitor Savory is an unprincipled man, and a cocky one too as I understand from the prison authorities at Dartmoor. Once aboard a German ship – if that is where he is – then he may feel perfectly safe to treat all Britishers with contempt. Should he flaunt himself, sir, I would welcome your advice as to how I should proceed . . . bearing in mind your wishes – '

'Orders.'

'Pardon?'

'A Captain's wish is his order, Mr Todhunter,' Watkiss stated flatly, 'and that's fact, I said it. Pray go on.' He swung round as a disturbance was heard at the foot of the ladder to the upper deck. 'What's that, Mr Lamphorn?'

'Mr Luckings, sir. He wishes words – '

'Good God, I'd forgotten all about him.' Watkiss blew out his cheeks. 'Petrie-Smith! Oh, very well, tell him to come up.'

Lamphorn coughed in some embarrassment. 'He was asking for you to go down to him, sir.'

'The devil he was! Tell him to go to hell, Mr Lamphorn.'

'Sir – '

'Hold your tongue, Mr Lamphorn, and do as I say.' Watkiss' eye was caught by the waving arms of the German flagship's semaphore. Impatiently he waited for the yeoman to read the message. 'Well, yeoman?'

'From Vice-Admiral von Merkatz, sir, commanding – '

'Yes, yes, yes!'

'Admiral says, sir, 'e's already passed the explanation. Exercising guns' crews, sir, in the interest of 'is Imperial Majesty the Emperor of Germany, sir, and 'e 'as no more to say, sir.'

'By God! That's all, is it?'

'Well, sir – '

'Is it or isn't it?'

''E adds goodbye, sir.'

*   *   *

Watkiss, for once, was speechless. The rude goodbye was acted upon swiftly. The sea boiled up below the counters, below the Admiral's sternwalk, the funnels belched smoke and the German ensigns streamed back in the wind made by the ships' passage

69

as they showed a wonderfully clean pair of heels to the wallowing British battleship. Captain Watkiss bounced down to the upper deck in a huff and Mr Pinch, anticipating the obvious order, restowed his boats. Carefully Mr Todhunter replaced his Gladstone bag in the wardrobe in his cabin. It would be needed, but not yet. Going back again to the upper deck, he met Petrie-Smith, and almost tied himself into a knot as he cringed before the representative of the Foreign Office.

'A fortunate ending, I believe, sir.' He held his bowler hat before his chest in an attitude of subservience. 'I feared that Captain Watkiss might – er – '

'Quite. A forthright man.'

'Very forthright, sir, indeed. I would appreciate your overall guidance in any future and similar encounter, sir.'

'You must be guided by your own past experience, Todhunter, and use your initiative.' Carefully, Petrie-Smith passed on along the deck, his bald head reflecting the strong South Atlantic sunlight like a heliograph. Mr Todhunter clicked his tongue dolefully: for the second time that morning, his initiative had been invoked and it was being borne in upon him that when a man became involved willy-nilly in great affairs of state it behoved that unfortunate man to walk very, very warily indeed, for help there would be none. Important heads would never be allowed to roll. . . .

The old battleship steamed on in the wake of the fast departing German squadron. The ships were hull down by the time the pipe had been made for the rum issue and along the messdecks the sailors mustered with tin mugs for filling with the standard three-parts-water grog. When the hands were piped to dinner the seas stood empty but for a windjammer heading down under all sail for Cape Horn. Another nasty thought came to Mr Todhunter: Captain Watkiss might decide upon another attempt at search, and once again initiative and the putting of his head upon the block might be called for. But a moment's further thought suggested that even Captain Watkiss would take it in that the traitor Savory had not escaped in time to leave the Mersey and sail this far south in a windjammer. The sailing ship, after an exchange of polite, routine signals, was left behind and the *Meridian* in due course altered westerly towards the South American coast to take coal in the Plate and then, with full bunkers for the Horn passage, to drop south for the Falkland Islands and her rendezvous.

*   *   *

'Ships ahead, sir. Two sloops, sir.' The call came down from the masthead lookout, who had been sent aloft as dawn broke.

'My fleet!' Captain Watkiss preened and felt a sense of relief: however small the sloops were, they were undoubtedly some extra strength and he had pondered much on the signal in which the German had made reference to having exercised his guns' crews in his Emperor's interest. That might mean little or much, all depending; it could have been a very pointed warning. From above, the man on lookout glanced down sourly as he caught the Captain's loudly uttered words; he muttered blasphemy under his breath, likening the approaching 'fleet' to his own backside. Watkiss in the meantime rounded upon the Midshipman of the Watch. 'Mr Perrin, my compliments to my First Lieutenant. He's required to attend upon me immediately.'

'Yessir.'

'And at the double, Mr Perrin, you are still too fat.' Up came Watkiss' telescope. He studied the horizon and in due time the mastheads of his fleet came into view. Then the bridges and funnels and a good deal of thick black smoke. As this latter manifested itself Halfhyde reached his Captain's side and saluted.

'Ah, Mr Halfhyde, good morning. *Biddle* and *Delia* are joining my command.' Watkiss swept a hand ahead. On the port bow, land could be seen: the Falklands, some three hundred miles east of the Magellan Strait, with Port Stanley abeam of the approaching sloops. 'Smoke, Mr Halfhyde. Dirty! I dislike smoke, dislike it intensely. Yeoman?'

'Yessir!'

'Make, *Biddle* and *Delia* from Senior Officer in *Meridian*:

71

Welcome to my command. You are making too much smoke and will stop it forthwith.'

'Aye, aye, sir.' The yeoman hesitated. 'Sir, the sloops aren't in visual signalling range, sir, yet – '

'I'm not blind, yeoman,' Watkiss said distantly. 'Pass the signal as soon as you're able. And while you're about it you can add the formation signal. *Biddle* to take station four cables on my port bow, *Delia* the same to starboard.'

'Aye, aye, sir.'

Halfhyde asked, 'You'll not steam in Line Ahead, sir?'

'No, Mr Halfhyde, I shall not, had I wished to do so I would have damn well said so, and it so happens I can keep an eye on both of them better if they're on the bow, can I not?'

'You can, sir.'

'Untried commanding officers – unknown quantities – never heard of either of them and they're not in Burke's *Landed Gentry*.'

'You've tried the Navy List, sir?'

'Don't be impertinent, Mr Halfhyde, that is where I found their names.' Watkiss turned away and bounced along the compass platform. Lieutenants Barber and Forbes-Forrester would need to be assessed as to their seamanship, ship-handling capabilities, general obedience to orders and so on. Forbes-Forrester at all events sounded as though he might be a gentleman but one never knew. Barber had a very common ring. Fortunately Forbes-Forrester was the senior of the two, which was why he had been accorded the starboard bow. As *Biddle* and *Delia* closed, Watkiss studied them closely through his telescope, seeking faults. *Biddle*, commanded by the common fellow Barber, was still making too much smoke. Peremptorily by signal, Captain Watkiss said so. Following upon his signal, *Biddle*'s semaphore started waving, but not in apology, as the yeoman reported.

'From *Biddle*, sir, may I have permission to approach your lee side to transfer passengers for Valparaiso.'

'Passengers?' Watkiss was furious. 'I've been told nothing about damn passengers and I don't want 'em! Who are they?'

'Don't say, sir – '

'Find out.'

'Aye, aye, sir.' The yeoman busied himself once again, then reported, 'Canon Rampling and servant, sir.'

'Good God! A damn parson! I don't like parsons, I dislike 'em intensely and the answer's no, he can stay aboard *Biddle*.' Watkiss looked sideways as Halfhyde coughed in his ear. 'What is it, Mr Halfhyde?'

'The Navy List, sir. Do you not remember the name . . . Canon Rampling is Admiral Daintree's chaplain.'

'By God, you're right. Yes.' Watkiss scowled. 'What's he doing, then, skulking in the Falklands?'

'I don't know, sir, but it seems he's now rejoining his Admiral. If I may make the suggestion, I think Admiral Daintree might prefer him to make the passage of Cape Horn aboard a battle-ship rather than a sloop.'

'Possibly. But I don't like parsons, Mr Halfhyde, they always bring bad luck to any ship. Parsons and corpses, they're both the same, birds of ill omen.'

'All the same, sir – '

'Yes, yes, yes, I take your point, you don't need to labour it. Unnecessary verbiage, Mr Halfhyde – verbal diarrhoea. Damn! Tell *Biddle* to approach me on the port quarter and warn Mr Pinch to provide a breeches buoy for the damn parson.'

More signals were made and on the upper deck the boatswain and a party of seamen began rigging a breeches buoy for sending across on its ropes to the sloop. When this was in position aboard *Biddle*, the parson would sit in it and would be drawn by pulley-hauley over the gap of deep blue water. It all took time, and since the engines had to be stopped it caused delay. Watkiss, with his mind on the speeding German squadron ahead, grew more anti-clerical in his attitudes. 'Oh, balls and bang me arse, Mr Halfhyde, if clergymen act as preventers against my doing my duty, how the devil do they hasten people's passage into heaven?'

Halfhyde smiled. 'I suggest you ask the canon, sir.'

'I'll do no such thing. Snivelling little curates, all airs and graces and lily-white hands.'

'Not, I think, Canon Rampling.'

'What d'you mean?'

'Look, sir.' Halfhyde pointed.

Watkiss looked down at the tiny sloop that seemed to cower in the great shadow of the battleship, a cockleshell against an iron monster. On *Biddle*'s fo'c's'le Canon Rampling was being eased with difficulty into the confines of the breeches buoy. He was an immense man, a bull in a cassock, with a heavy firm face rising above the clerical collar, the kind of face given to thunderous utterances from the pulpit, and big capable hands that could well be imagined thumping upon lecterns. Watkiss looked bleak: the parson could prove troublesome and might need to be put down with a firm display of authority. Canon Rampling was hauled safely across the water, and deposited upon Watkiss' quarterdeck to be met by Halfhyde. He seemed a jovial man, one who smiled much, a man of bluff manner. He was followed by his servant, then his gear was sent across, and while he went with Halfhyde to the compass platform the breeches buoy was dismantled and stowed and *Biddle* hastened to take up her allotted station on Watkiss' bow. On the compass platform as *Meridian* once again proceeded on passage for the Horn, introductions were made.

'It's good of you to take me aboard, Captain Watkiss, very good. I'll try not to be a nuisance.'

'Yes.'

'You don't carry a padre of your own, I believe?'

'My ship is for disposal – for delivery. I have only a steaming party.'

'Quite. If you wish me to take divine service, you've only to say.'

'Yes, I know. If I see fit to give you the order, then I shall do so. This servant of yours. I failed, when observing his embarkation, to find uniform upon his back.'

'He wears none, sir. He is not enlisted – I obtained a special dispensation from the Admiralty when I was first appointed to the fleet. I was previously rector of a country parish in Yorkshire, and Tidy was rector's warden – '

'A churchwarden, aboard a battleship at sea!'

'A loyal friend, one who would not hear of leaving me . . . a gardener by profession, sir, and a servant by his own will.'

'God give me strength.'

'When needed, sir, He will. In the meantime, I would appreciate a word in private as soon as you have the time to spare.'

'Good God, Canon Rampling, I have a ship to command and a landfall to make off Cape Horn, a most notorious area. What do you want?'

Rampling smiled pacifically. 'Not affairs of the cloth, I assure you. Matters that you would currently consider of more pressing urgency, I think.' He paused, and thereafter gave his words a certain weight and emphasis. 'From time to time many secular duties fall upon a simple chaplain to Her Majesty's Fleet, sir. Late yesterday a vessel entered Port Stanley from Cape Town . . . bringing from the telegraph there certain advice from London. I act as a messenger and perhaps as an intermediary. I crave your indulgence.'

*   *   *

'Crave my bottom,' Captain Watkiss remarked to Halfhyde when the clergyman had been sent below to the cuddy to await an audience. 'The feller's oily. Slimy. A wolf in Bible binding. Crave my indulgence indeed, never heard such a mealy-mouthed statement! What's he an intermediary for? God?'

'A purpose to be hereinafter divulged I don't doubt, sir.'

Watkiss breathed hard down his nose. 'H'm. Well, you'd better come with me while he divulges it, Halfhyde. Who knows, I may need a witness later. I presume his presence is to do with Admiral Daintree.'

'Perhaps, sir. If that's the case, do you not think Mr Petrie-Smith should be present also?'

'No.'

Captain Watkiss, with his ship on a south-south-westerly course to take him straight down for Cape Horn, turned for his starboard ladder and made no complaint when Halfhyde came down the same ladder behind him. He was clearly anxious: to some extent Halfhyde shared his perturbation. No seagoing officer welcomed the cloth aboard a ship at sea; it could not be denied that they, the holy wearers of it, created problems, the more especially, of course, in the minds of officers of Watkiss' vintage – and when a captain was upset it tended to affect the whole ship's company. Proceeding aft, Watkiss said suddenly, 'I remember a parson, a shore-side one . . . Missions to Seamen. I believe it was off Deal, or perhaps Dover. It was years ago. I was in a sloop at the time, and there was a merchantman at anchor off the port. This parson decided not only to pay a visit to the merchantman, but to demonstrate the power of God at the same time.'

'Indeed, sir?'

'Yes. He decided to walk, like Christ on the Sea of Galilee or wherever it was. He wore floats on his feet. Quite lunatic.' Watkiss sniffed. 'Naturally enough, the bugger turned upside down and sank.'

'Poor fellow . . .'

'Yes. Because of the floats, he couldn't turn right way up again and he drowned – rescue came too late since all hands were beside themselves laughing.' Captain Watkiss reached the hatchway leading to his quarters below, and went pompously down the ladder followed by Halfhyde. As the two officers entered the day cabin, Canon Rampling rose from a leather armchair. 'Now, Canon,' Watkiss said. 'You have complete privacy and you may speak freely in front of my First Lieutenant.'

'Yes indeed. As for me, sir, I am entrusted with the facts, or such as are known, of my Admiral's present predicament.'

'His arrest. His arrest by the dagoes.'

'The Chilean authorities – yes. And I may be instrumental in securing his release.'

'Who says so, pray?'

'The Foreign Office.'

'Oh.' Captain Watkiss dropped somewhat heavily into a chair and, hitching up his long shorts, gestured the canon and Halfhyde to be seated also. 'How are you supposed to be of assistance, may one ask?'

'Having been close to the Admiral – '

'Yes. But I am to be his Flag Captain after handing over my ship to the dagoes. I shall be closer to Admiral Daintree than you.'

'Yes indeed. But not yet.'

Watkiss glared. 'So long as it is clearly understood that upon my taking up my appointment, you shall come under my orders, I am prepared to listen further.'

'Thank you, sir. It is not merely that I have been close to Admiral Daintree, you understand . . . there is the important matter of my cloth. It is believed in London that the Chilean authorities will not deny me access to Admiral Daintree even though he is being held incommunicado.'

'Because you're a parson?'

Rampling nodded. 'Certainly. As a priest –'

'Ah – there you have it!' Watkiss pounced. 'A priest, precisely, which you are not. I understand the dagoes are Catholics, whereas you are Church of England, I take it?'

'I am.'

'Then you'll cut no ice at all, my dear fellow! They'll regard you as a heretic.'

'I think not, sir, I think not. The cloth is respected by Catholic and Protestant alike, and the fact that I am a priest of Admiral Daintree's religion will also be respected.'

'Well, time will tell,' Watkiss said disagreeably, 'and you'll do nothing without first seeking my approval, is that clear?'

Rampling nodded, but a curious and somehow formidable expression crossed his face briefly. 'It's quite clear. I take full note of your views, sir.' He paused, and stroked his boxer-like chin reflectively. 'I understand you have a Mr Petrie-Smith aboard?'

Watkiss raised his eyebrows and glanced at Halfhyde. Then he said stiffly, 'The matter is supposed to be secret, Canon. I –'

'And secret it shall remain with me, I promise you. But I am to speak to him . . . and I understand I am to take his orders in regard to Admiral Daintree.'

'Rather than mine?' Watkiss had reddened dangerously.

Rampling spread his hands in a conciliatory gesture, and smiled. 'Not rather than. As well as, perhaps? You, sir, are the

77

Captain of this battleship, and being also of the Navy I appreciate the position of a post captain at sea. There need be no inconsistency of orders, no conflict.'

'H'm,' Watkiss said dubiously, but seemed mollified by Rampling's words and manner. He glanced at the clock on the bulkhead above his roll-top desk and asked, 'You'll take a drink, Canon? or are you – '

'Teetotal?' Rampling laughed, a loud and jovial sound. 'By no means! To be teetotal in the wardrooms of the fleet is a harder task than I would care to undertake!'

'Harder than acting as an intermediary in a dago port?'

Rampling laughed again. 'I think so, sir.' Watkiss gestured to Halfhyde, who rose and pressed a bell-push near the desk. Almost on the heels of it, the Captain's servant entered from the pantry.

'You rang, sir?'

'Gin.'

'Yessir.' The steward went back to his pantry; while he was gone little was said. When the gin came it oiled the wheels of conversation and Watkiss enquired what, precisely, Canon Rampling would seek to achieve when visiting Admiral Daintree in his confinement.

'Chiefly his release, sir. I shall make representations to the authorities, earnestly requesting consideration of the fact that he is an elderly man and that his constitution has been weakened by many years spent at sea – '

'Oh, stuff and nonsense!' Watkiss snapped, moving restlessly in his chair. 'Utter rubbish! The sea strengthens the constitution, it doesn't weaken it. Tell that to the dagoes and you'll be branded a liar straight away!'

'I venture to disagree, sir. Admiral Daintree has spent much of his service in unwholesome waters – '

'Unwholesome my arse – '

'An unwholesome expression if I may say so.' The clergyman's face had hardened, a touch of temper showing through at the oblique insult to his cloth inherent in coarse language. 'West Africa . . . the white man's grave as it is known. China with its

78

many diseases and debilitations. South America itself is not the healthiest of naval stations, Captain Watkiss.'

'Well, there was that fish, certainly, the one that killed my predecessor – Captain Harris. What happened exactly?'

'He turned blue,' Rampling said with deliberation and a glint in his eye.

'Good God, did he?'

'Yes. Convulsions, then rigor, then he turned blue and died. My point about health will be a good one, sir.'

'I hope so, for your sake.' Watkiss was looking almost pale. 'It wouldn't wash with me, but there we are, I suppose. Well, that's your chief aim, you said. What are the others?'

Rampling didn't answer immediately: he stared down at his large, capable-looking hands, apparently studying the fingernails with a concentration that precluded his looking Watkiss in the face. He said slowly, 'I can bring back tidings of Admiral Daintree . . .'

'Tidings?'

'The state of his health and so on. Messages for his family. In return I can take him, shall we say, tidings of his squadron?'

'And of Admiral von Merkatz?'

Rampling looked up briefly. 'Yes, possibly. Very possibly . . . there can be valuable exchanges, such as may well enable you to, ah, gauge the position vis-à-vis the Chilean authorities and to interpret those tidings that are exchanged. To put no finer point upon it, the Foreign Office sees a certain value.'

'Tidings, eh?' Captain Watkiss fixed his monocle in place and stared hard at the cleric, his head tilted a little backward. 'I'll agree you could be damned useful as a spy, Padre, and I don't decry that use since, to a fighting officer at any rate, all's fair in love and war. But by God, you're a curious parson, are you not?'

*   *   *

Seeking more space in which to walk off his dudgeon and his antipathy, Captain Watkiss strode with his First Lieutenant to the quarterdeck. He detested all parsons more or less cordially,

79

but those who manifested unparsonlike qualities were the work of the devil. Parsons should be above reproach in their character and conduct; and moreover – and never mind what he had said about not decrying the use of spies – Captain Watkiss, a simple sailor as he liked to think of himself, had no love of intrigue and dirty dealing. By the very nature of their horrible work spies could not be gentlemen. (But here he had struck a snag: Hereward Charles Montagu Rampling had been found listed in Burke's *Landed Gentry* as a younger son of a squire residing at Berralton Hall in the North Riding of Yorkshire. However, that made it worse.) Captain Watkiss had further distractions upon his mind: there was Petrie-Smith, masquerading as Assistant Paymaster Luckings, Royal Navy, and evidently to join forces with the wretched parson . . . Watkiss saw difficulties ahead. Whatever Rampling had said, there was bound to be a conflict of orders sooner or later. Captain Watkiss was in command of the *Meridian* and he would not take orders from a Foreign Office clerk allied to a bloody parson and that was that. Nevertheless he had to face facts and recognize that in certain circles at home the Foreign Office was regarded as ranking above the fighting services of the Queen – the parson, of course, didn't come into that; in rank's respect he was unworthy of any consideration at all outside his church. Watkiss scowled as he bounced along his holystoned quarterdeck clutching his telescope. The blasted man, when peremptorily confronted with his essential baseness, had retreated towards his God: God would understand that he was acting for the right, and God would not only forgive, His mercy being infinite, but would actively assist him in gaining access to Admiral Daintree, being urged by prayer to put kindly and chivalrous thoughts into the heads and consciences of the dagoes, the latter being Captain Watkiss' own word.

Above his sternwalk, right aft by the ensign staff, Watkiss halted. He looked for'ard and he looked aloft at his masts and yards, at his funnels, and then down at his great guns. He took a deep breath. 'Thank God, Mr Halfhyde, for the sea.'

'Sir?'

'It's clean,' Watkiss said with feeling, 'and it's a place for men, not mice. I am mouse infested, Mr Halfhyde, and I don't damn well like it!'

'I'm sorry, sir. I don't quite understand.'

'Don't you?' Captain Watkiss brandished his telescope. 'Just look at what's been foisted on to me! A damn pimp from the Foreign Office, a London policeman in a bloody stupid bowler hat who looks as though he's about to arrest every man-jack aboard my ship – and now a blasted bible-boatswain and a churchwarden! It's too bad.' Watkiss grabbed the guardrail for support as the battleship lurched to the beginnings of a heavy sea. Already the skies had begun to lose their blue brilliance, passing into the grey and the cold and the general overcast of the southern latitudes as the engines thrust them on towards Cape Horn and the northern fringes of the icefields.

SEVEN

Von Merkatz and his heavy squadron had vanished as though they had never been. Halfhyde, on the compass platform with the terrible Cape Horn just visible abeam to starboard through the spindrift, shrugged himself deeper into his bridge coat and oilskins. God preserve the merchant mariners whose continuing task in life was to take their wind-blown ships back and forth round this dreadful cape at the world's purgatorial bottom. They were welcome to it! Never before had Halfhyde rounded the Horn, nor had Watkiss nor any of the battleship's officers; from this time forward they would each be permitted by naval custom to place one foot upon the wardroom table when taking their ease in the armchairs. Halfhyde hoped devoutly that the time would never come when he would be entitled to place both feet on the table – and then remembered with a shudder that he would need to come back this way when the mission had ended in success, though as yet he knew not in what ship the passage would be made.

He stared ahead through the spume that covered the long greybeards, torn and battered by the howling wind, holding on for support from anything handy and firmly anchored as the battleship lurched and rolled, dipped beneath the seas and rose again with green water rushing and tumbling along the decks. Life was hell: gone were the balmy days and the off-watch comfort of cabin and wardroom. Now, with everything battened down, there was an appalling fug below, and despite lashings to secure the furniture the ship was a shambles inside, and of comfort there was none. The galley fires had been allowed to die down as the weather worsened, in the interest of preventing calamity, and all food was cold and unappetizing. In the boiler-rooms the black gang, sweat-soaked and burned, fought the coal with huge steel shovels, somehow keeping it from showering out from the furnace-mouths as they laboured before the great red openings licked with flame, or skidded on raw backsides across the steel deck as the *Meridian* was tossed like a cork by the raging water. Out on the bows the little sloops *Delia* and *Biddle*, largely invisible, were suffering far worse torment as the huge crests, long and high, reared above them and threatened every moment to fall and submerge them totally. But they kept going, manfully reappearing and streaming green water as they fought their way through.

Some faces were seen no more : a temporary release according to Watkiss. Assistant Paymaster Luckings, grieving for Whitehall's wonderfully immovable buildings, lay in his bunk under heavy lashings set to prevent his being shot out as from a catapult, and lay perforce amid his own vomit, smelling like a personal mess-deck. Mr Todhunter, similarly situated, lay as white as death itself, trying to fix his thoughts upon his Chief Superintendent and the doings of his fellow detectives at Scotland Yard, a very haven of peace and stability. By his bedside, safe but slighted in a drawer, lay Doctor Datchet's Demulcent Drops, now rejected as totally useless : efficaciously assisting his late mother on passage across Spithead to the pier at Ryde, they had failed him off Cape Horn. Doctor Datchet was unthroned. Another victim was Mr Tidy, late rector's warden from Yorkshire, swinging in a hammock in the vicinity of the petty officers' mess : Mr Tidy had posed a problem. As chaplain's servant he was, of course, a mere junior rating; but no one could be quite sure of the relative rank and precedence of a churchwarden afloat. The title had the ring of petty officer status, but the petty officers had objected to messing with a mere steward, so a compromise had been reached by the slinging of the churchwarden's hammock as near as possible to the petty officers' mess without being actually in it. Apart from a certain explosive danger when the battleship lurched, which necessitated a good deal of nippiness when coming and going, the petty officers seemed satisfied; while Mr Tidy himself cared not a jot where he was so long as he was flat on his back and allowed to moan and groan his way around Cape Horn, wishing only that he had succumbed to the sexton of the parish before being foolish enough to leave Yorkshire.

But Canon Rampling was undefeated. Having breakfasted as amply as a fireless wardroom galley permitted, he climbed to the compass platform to pass the time of day with the Officer of the Watch, an oilskin over his cassock and a sou'wester tied beneath his chin.

'Good morning, Mr Halfhyde. Boisterous!' Rampling rubbed his hands together and brought in the trailing end of a long woollen scarf.

'Very boisterous.'

'The wind blows from the west, I see.' Canon Rampling turned his back to it: it was so strong as to make breathing difficult. 'My first passage, you know.'

'Of Cape Horn?'

'Yes. Also my first real sea voyage – my appointments to date have been on shore. The barrack hulks in Portsmouth, the base at Bermuda . . . while presently, under Admiral Daintree, my duties are confined to the Falklands.'

'Then I congratulate you on your sea-legs, Padre,' Halfhyde said, and meant it. At that moment a figure cocooned in oilskins and sou'wester, the latter lashed down like a tarpaulin on a cargo hatch, fought its way on to the compass platform by way of the starboard ladder: Captain Watkiss, recently emerged from his sea cabin and red-faced from the sheer effort of lifting his body.

'Good morning, Mr Halfhyde.'

'Good morning, sir.' Halfhyde lifted a hand to the brim of his sou'wester.

Watkiss heaved himself for'ard against the pitch of his ship and gained the guardrail. His voice was swept back by the tearing wind. 'Canon Rampling has no business upon my compass platform, Mr Halfhyde, and I'm astonished at your condoning his presence.'

'I'm sorry, sir,' Halfhyde shouted in the Captain's ear.

'I never permit parsons on the bridge, the buggers are likely to sink the damn ship, Mr Halfhyde.'

'Yes, sir.'

'Then get him off. Wait a moment, though. Since he's here . . . bring him alongside me and I'll have a word.'

'Aye, aye, sir.' Halfhyde gestured to the canon who, taking the hint, pushed his tall frame into the wind and gripped the guardrail beside the Captain.

'Good morning, sir. You wished to – '

'Yes. Those dagoes in Valparaiso. Do you happen to know anyone in authority there, know anyone personally?'

'The Chilean authorities, sir?'

'Yes, the dagoes.'

'If I may advise it, Captain, I'd not refer to them as dagoes.'

'Don't argue with me, Canon Rampling, if you please. *All* foreigners are dagoes. Kindly answer the question.' Watkiss stared ahead into the wind and sea, without so much as glancing at the cleric, who was towering over him like a lamp post, which he found irritating. 'Do you, or do you not, know any of the dagoes?'

Rampling said, 'Some months ago, a certain General Codecino paid a visit to Port Stanley.'

'And you met him?'

'Yes. A pleasant enough man . . . I had the honour of showing him something of the islands, and – '

'What was his job, his position in Chile?'

'I understand he is the Governor of the province of Llanquihue.'

'He is, is he? And you were friendly with him?'

'Reasonably so,' Rampling answered.

'I see. Thank you, Canon Rampling, that will be all; you may go below.' Watkiss remained in his position at the for'ard guard-rail, allowing the parson time to clear his compass platform; then he turned and jerked his head to indicate that he wished Halfhyde to join him. 'Mr Halfhyde, I am reaching certain conclusions as to how the forthcoming mission should be handled so as to achieve success. There will be a conference in my *sea* cabin at four bells in the afternoon watch – I shall not leave the vicinity of my bridge in these waters. Kindly inform Mr Petrie-Smith and the policeman, and be there yourself.'

'Aye, aye, sir.'

'But not that parson, I don't trust him.' Captain Watkiss turned to starboard and lifted his telescope to survey the grey, forbidding eminence of Cape Horn across the storm-tossed waste of sea. 'A moment to be remembered, Mr Halfhyde, one to speak of to our grandchildren in years to come. How we rounded Cape Horn on duty for Her Majesty and her far dominions that stretch from the Shetlands down to here, from – '

'Her Majesty has no fiat upon Cape Horn, sir.'

Watkiss stared. 'I never said she had, Mr Halfhyde.' He swung an arm to port. 'But down there she has! British Antarctica, Mr Halfhyde, the *South* Shetlands – King George Island — Graham Land! There is nowhere in the whole world that has not seen the Flag of England, Mr Halfhyde, and it is that which annoys the damn German Emperor! It would not surprise me if von Merkatz might one day cast his eyes southwards.'

*   *   *

The conference that afternoon was an uneasy one : Halfhyde had pointed out to the Captain that both Todhunter and Petrie-Smith were virtually moribund, but this Watkiss had totally rejected as an excuse for non-attendance. They could, he said, bring utensils. This they did, and the chamber-pots reposed on the deck of the sea cabin while green and mournful faces stared like ghosts as Watkiss laid down the law. He announced his decisions, arrived at after much thought.

'I intend taking my fleet into Reloncavi Bay to lie off Puerto Montt,' he said without indicating that this had been Halfhyde's earlier advice. 'From there I shall send messages by the telegraph to Valparaiso, announcing my presence and demanding that Admiral Daintree be released and returned to his flagship which must then be allowed to sail peacefully and rendezvous with me outside Puerto Montt. From there I shall accompany him to the Falklands. Yes, Mr Petrie-Smith, what is it?'

'I thought the *Meridian* was to be handed over to the Chileans.'

'Exactly. But I shall make no hand-over until after the Admiral is released. If he is not released I shall, of course, refuse to hand over my ship. If and when I hand over it will be off Puerto Montt and I shall distribute my ship's company between *Biddle* and *Delia*, and in them shall rendezvous with my Admiral outside the port, and take up my duties as Flag Captain, boarding the flagship with all men from *Meridian*. Is that clear? I repeat, no release, no hand-over.'

Petrie-Smith put his head in his hands, somewhat distractedly. 'This is not in accordance with Foreign Office instructions – '

'Oh, balls to Foreign Office instructions, Mr Petrie-Smith,' Watkiss said wearily. '*I* am in charge here, not the Foreign Office. Matters must be left to the judgment of the man on the spot, must they not? Speaking of the Foreign Office, however : that parson Rampling. I don't like him. Have you had words with him yet, or have you been too damn sick?'

'He came to my cabin,' Petrie-Smith answered, 'and was so well and hearty that I – I – '

'Told him to go away again, Mr Petrie-Smith?'

'Yes.'

'I don't blame you,' Watkiss said sourly. 'But I wish matters to be clarified in his respect. Has he proper authority?'

'He says so, and I have no reason to doubt him.'

'Then you were not informed about him before leaving Portsmouth?'

'No. But I can see a very positive use for him – '

'As a spy?'

Petrie-Smith gave a slight shudder. 'It's not a word we use in the Foreign Service, Captain – '

'No, but I do. You can call him what you damn well like. Yes, Mr Todhunter, what is it?'

'Sir, the traitor Savory. I trust your plans include his apprehension?'

'Of course they do, but at this moment I have formulated nothing precise. We must watch developments, Mr Todhunter, and we must watch Admiral von Merkatz, who is the person most likely in my opinion to be contacted by Savory.'

'But how do we watch Admiral von Merkatz, sir, when we don't know where he is?'

'Don't be impertinent, Mr Todhunter, that is my concern, not yours. Admiral von Merkatz will be found, never fear. We know he is ahead of us and that he must be bound for Valparaiso, do we not?'

'Yes, sir,' Todhunter said faintly, and for a few dreadful moments occupied himself with his utensil. 'But if he's bound for Valparaiso, sir, and we enter this other place, Puerto Montt, are we not –'

'Leave the broad conduct of affairs to me, if you please, Mr Todhunter, I have plans to cover all eventualities,' Watkiss said with dignity. He did not, in fact, go into any detail regarding these plans and as the conference proceeded Halfhyde formed the impression that his Captain had been thrown off balance by the Detective Inspector's pertinent observations. The remainder of the conference was devoted to discussion with Petrie-Smith of a theory formed by Watkiss that von Merkatz might, as he had mentioned to Halfhyde during the forenoon, have designs upon Antarctica. Captain Watkiss had some notion, derived from glancing through some scientific magazines a long while ago, that Antarctica might one day become a fruitful trading area for the world's powers to quarrel over. Crops might be made to grow there, not inconceivably, and farming made to vie with the whaling industry. Was this not so?

'Only if the ice can be overcome, Captain.'

'Overcome?'

'Made to melt. This would take very many decades, if it were possible at all.'

'Oh.' Captain Watkiss lost interest in Antarctica. 'Well, these damn people who scribble in magazines do write a lot of drivel, of course.'

With Cape Horn away behind and the ships into the South Pacific Ocean and proceeding north up the coast of Chile, the weather improved. *Biddle* and *Delia* steamed serenely on *Meridian*'s bows, fully visible once again. The sun came out and the sea grew smooth and friendly, and the galley fires were relit. Mr Todhunter emerged from recumbency with Mr Petrie-Smith, the latter to work again in the ship's office. Mr Todhunter trod the decks in his bowler hat and shiny blue serge suit, handcuffs metaphorically ajingle as the clustered Chilean islands backed by distant mountain peaks were seen on the starboard beam of the battleship, bringing promise of eventual arrest for the traitor Savory. Mr Todhunter had a reputation to live up to.

'Like the Royal Canadian North-West Mounted Police, sir,' he remarked to Halfhyde, 'I always get my man. I shall not fail this time.'

'I shall mark your words, Mr Todhunter,' Halfhyde said gravely. 'As a matter of fact – between you and me and the gatepost if there were one – someone else has marked them already and I congratulate you.'

'Who?' Todhunter looked bewildered.

'Captain Watkiss. Your comment on the whereabouts of Admiral von Merkatz. We're not to enter Puerto Montt after all, but are to head for Valparaiso.'

Mr Todhunter gave a whistle of relief. 'My Chief Super will be very relieved, Mr Halfhyde, very relieved.'

'Good. But if I were you, I'd not say so to Captain Watkiss.'

The battleship steamed on placidly. Watkiss, in critical mood, strutted his compass platform, carefully watching *Biddle* and *Delia*, laying his telescope upon them frequently and being frustrated every time: he could find no fault at all in either of the sloops. No lines were hanging judas, the funnels emitted only a normal quantity of smoke, the wakes streamed back straight as a ruled line, indicating punctilious steering by the quartermasters; each ship remained dead in station when checked by the bearing indicator. Soon the great peaks of the Andes reared huge to starboard. As watch succeeded watch the *Meridian* came up towards the latitude of Puerto Montt with her face set towards Valparaiso, still distant to the north. As the outer approaches to Puero Montt began to be raised on the starboard bow Captain Watkiss came again to the compass platform; and half an hour later a fishing boat was reported ahead, issuing from behind Chiloé Island.

'I shall speak to her,' Watkiss announced; and Halfhyde felt an odd premonition in his bones. As the *Meridian* came up to the fishing boat, bringing her on to the starboard beam, Captain Watkiss took up his megaphone and shouted: 'You there, that boat. Ahoy!'

Dark Chilean faces stared back and chattered in Spanish. Watkiss glared. 'Damn dagoes, why can't they speak English?' He roared again, spacing out his words: 'Are there foreign ships in Reloncavi Bay, and if so, what nationality?'

'Allow me, sir,' Halfhyde said. 'I have some kitchen Spanish that may pass.' He relayed the Captain's question and raised an acknowledgment and an answer. Waving his thanks, he reported to Captain Watkiss. 'Four ships, sir, and they're German.'

'By God! Von Merkatz!' Watkiss swung round upon the Midshipman of the Watch. 'I don't trust damn dagoes. Aloft with you, Mr Perrin, and see what you can see. Then report. And at the double, or I shall have the skin off your backside.'

'Yessir!' Perrin lost no time in dragging his podgy form up the shrouds to the foretopmast crosstrees. He levelled his glass from the platform and took a good look: his skin was tender, and the cane was a harsh instrument when wielded by the sub of the gunroom. Having looked searchingly, he reported in a shout to the Captain. 'I can't see anything, sir, there's high ground – '

'Oh, come down, Mr Perrin, come down for God's sake.' Watkiss turned to Halfhyde. 'I don't trust damn snotties any more than dagoes, Mr Halfhyde. I've made up my mind. I shall enter Reloncavi Bay after all and confront von Merkatz and defeat his nefarious schemes, by God! Take my ship inwards, if you please, and man and arm the guns.'

EIGHT

The *Meridian* came round to starboard and approached the entry, with the cable and side party standing by on the fo'c'sle and the anchors being prepared for letting go if required to bring her up short, and the guns' crews doubling to their positions under the lashing tongue of Mr Mottram. Already Halfhyde had informed the Captain that the Sailing Directions indicated that it was normal to take the services of a pilot; Watkiss had stated flatly that he had no time for delay, that to make signals for a pilot would alert the damn Hun and ruin the element of surprise, and that he was a post captain of the Royal Navy and thus competent to take a ship anywhere.

'Nevertheless I distrust charts, *and* the Pacific Steam Navigation Company whom you once quoted at me, as well. You will take soundings, Mr Halfhyde, if you please.'

'Aye, aye, sir. Perhaps after all you'd prefer to take the ship in yourself, sir?'

'Oh, don't argue everything, Mr Halfhyde, I have given my orders and I have every confidence in you.'

Halfhyde, sending away the seaboat with a sounding party as the battleship approached the narrows, was not particularly grateful for the trust implicit in his Captain's letting him take the ship in: if the truth be told, Watkiss was probably reluctant to risk besmirching his own reputation. If under Halfhyde they should touch bottom, or strike the shore, Captain Watkiss would not of course escape without court martial, but at least he would be able to point to ineptitude on Halfhyde's part. In the meantime Watkiss watched like a hawk as his command moved in and came between the arms of the land, her engines moving dead slow behind the boat under oars with the sounding party. Again and again the lead was heaved in an overhand cast, but nowhere could bottom be found, such was the depth. Watkiss, however, was still in some agitation.

'Where are you taking me, may I ask, Mr Halfhyde?'

'Into Reloncavi Bay, sir.'

'Don't be impertinent. I require to know my route, and the leading marks.'

'Yes, sir.' Halfhyde indicated the chart: from the end of the narrows the track ran between Abtao and Carba Island, to the north of the Lami Bank, and then between Calbuco and Quenu Islands: a nasty looking passage on the chart, all shoals and a tide-rip.

'Are you sure you're right, Halfhyde?'

'I am, sir – '

'What's the rise and fall, and state of the tide?'

'Fifteen feet, sir, and we have low water now, but water enough. Had the tide been full, the track would have been between Calbuco and the main – '

'It's no place for one of Her Majesty's ships of war, Mr Half-hyde. I suggest you alter – '

'Sir, I am following a precedent. In '64 a German pilot – '

'German!'

'– took H M S *Shearwater* into Reloncavi Bay by the track I am following, and shall continue to follow so long as I have the ship.' Halfhyde turned his back upon his Captain and conned the *Meridian* onward beneath the great peak of Hornopiren standing 5,479 feet above the water as later they came past Calbuco Island. Moving along the north-western side of Puluqui they entered Reloncavi Bay below the island of Huar, and as they came into more open water they saw the German squadron tucked away behind a promontory and apparently lying at anchor.

Watkiss waved his telescope.

'There he is, the bugger! Thought he'd hide, I suppose. He

won't get away with it, Mr Halfhyde, I'm damned if he will!'

'No, sir.' Halfhyde coughed. 'We should ask permission to enter, sir, indeed we should have done so earlier – '

'Oh, balls and bang me arse, Mr Halfhyde, I know what I should do and I'm not going to do it, damned if I am. It's time the Navy had another Nelson. I have entered Reloncavi Bay *without* permission, that's fact, and the dagoes can make what they like of it.'

Halfhyde shrugged. 'Very good, sir – '

'I know my orders are very good, Mr Halfhyde, kindly try to sound seamanlike. Port ten. Inform *Biddle* and *Delia* that I am proceeding through to the anchorage.'

'Aye, aye, sir. Port ten, sir.' Halfhyde passed the orders and as the bows swung to starboard in response to the port helm, he asked, 'Are you taking the ship now, sir?'

'No.' Captain Watkiss stood facing for'ard and gripping the guardrail. His back was straight, his head, with the gold-rimmed cap-peak low over his eyes, was high. His monocle, dangling at the end of its black silk toggle, flashed fire reflected from the sun, which also brought fiery gold from the four stripes of his rank on either cuff of his blue monkey-jacket. The one note of incongruity was struck by the curious long white shorts flapping about his knees in a gentle breeze, shorts that were good enough to wear in front of Huns and dagoes; his officers were in conventional half-whites – blue jackets with long white drill trousers. Watkiss' telescope was pointed towards the German flagship and when he lowered it he held it like a gun aimed at Admiral von Merkatz. 'Yeoman!' he called suddenly.

'Yessir?'

'Make to the Admiral: What are you doing in these waters? In English.'

'Aye, aye, sir.'

Halfhyde was about to utter words of caution when Petrie-Smith appeared, prudently using the port ladder. Watkiss stared at the Foreign Office man. 'What do you want, may I ask?' he demanded.

'Your signal, Captain. I overheard – '

'Well?'

'The tone was peremptory. I advise conciliation.'

'Do you, Mr Assistant Paymaster Luckings, do you indeed?'

Petrie-Smith flushed; he still looked ill and wan, but he stuck to his point. 'I think you understand my rank well enough, Captain. I shall say no more on that score, but must insist that it is my duty to ensure that no feelings are exacerbated unnecessarily. Quite apart from von Merkatz, it so happens that since 1853 there has been a sizeable German colony in Puerto Montt.' He dabbed at his face with a linen handkerchief. 'I suggest you cancel your signal, Captain.'

'I shall do nothing of the sort,' Watkiss stated flatly.

'But I must insist – '

'You are impertinent, my dear sir! Impertinent!'

'In this instance, Captain, I outrank you, and – '

'Get off my compass platform!' Watkiss advanced with telescope upraised and his face beetroot red. 'Get off this instant or I shall show you that a post captain has the authority to clap you in irons below!'

'I beg of you – '

'Mr Halfhyde, Mr Perrin. Remove this person.'

Halfhyde, who had ordered opposite helm to meet the starboard swing and had now steadied the ship on course for the anchorage, left the binnacle and advanced upon Petrie-Smith. 'You must obey the Captain's order,' he said austerely. 'Aboard a ship, the Captain is the law. You will leave the compass platform instantly of your own volition, or I shall have hands piped to take you down.'

'The man's insane!' Petrie-Smith said viciously, but turned and went down the ladder. Halfhyde breathed a sigh of relief: the moment had been tricky, but fortunately Watkiss had failed to hear the slur cast at him. He was otherwise occupied, with his telescope once again raking the German ships for signs of hostility. A few moments later his signal received its answer.

'Admiral says, sir,' the yeoman of signals reported, 'my ships have entered to land a sick man.'

Watkiss blew out his cheeks. 'Sick man, indeed! Oh, a likely story, a likely story! Damn it to hell, Mr Halfhyde, each of those ships must have leeches aboard, and sick berths! Anyway, why bring all four heavy ships in to land one man sick?'

'I can't say what's in the Admiral's mind, sir.'

'Can't you, well I can. Chicanery – that's what! He's up to no good.'

'Possibly, sir. In the meantime, what do you wish to do with your own ships?'

'What?'

'Your fleet, sir, is standing into danger.'

'Do something about it, then. You still have the ship, or are you incapable of handling her in inshore waters?'

Halfhyde compressed his lips. 'Do you wish to anchor, sir?'

'Yes, yes, so long as there's water and room enough, of course I do! Consult your chart, Mr Halfhyde, and bring me up eight cables'-lengths clear of the nearer Hun.'

Halfhyde passed the necessary orders preliminary to letting go an anchor and made signals to *Biddle* and *Delia* indicating the Captain's wishes. The three vessels crept on and when cross-bearings showed that the *Meridian* was nearly in position Halfhyde, who had already checked for depth, put his engines astern to bring her up and lifted the green flag preparatory to passing the executive order to let go the starboard anchor. Watkiss, whose particular prerogative it would normally be to bring the ship to anchor, was too busy: his roving telescope eye was everywhere, seeking out, considering, summing up. As the bearing came dead on Halfhyde roared out, '*Let go*!' and at the same time brought his green flag sharply down. On the fo'c'sle the slip was knocked away and, with the cable-holder already out of gear, the anchor, veered to the waterline earlier, smashed down to the harbour bottom, pulling behind it the great links of the cable and a cloud of rust-red dust amid an almighty clattering and banging. Halfhyde stopped the engines and the ship, still with some headway on, drifted ahead to lay the cable in a large bight leading from hawse-pipe to anchor shackle.

'Third shackle on deck, sir.'

'Secure at that, if you please, Mr Halfhyde.' The telescope shifted. 'What, pray, is *Biddle* up to?'

'Anchoring, sir.'

'I know that. Making a hash of it, too. Inform Mr Barber he's to report the name of his cable officer and to regard himself as reprimanded also. I will not be made to look a fool in front of Huns and dagoes.' The telescope moved on, but appeared to find nothing of special interest and after a few more minutes Watkiss lowered it and snapped it shut. 'Well, there we are, Mr Halfhyde, and you've made a fair job of bringing my ship in.'

'Thank you, sir.'

'Remember you've yet to take her out again.'

'Normally an easier manoeuvre than entry, sir.'

'I was not referring to pilotage problems, Mr Halfhyde, but to the Huns.'

Halfhyde lifted an eyebrow. 'And also, perhaps, the dagoes?'

'Perhaps.' Captain Watkiss, after another all-seeing look around the anchorage, which was some considerable distance from Puerto Montt itself, proceeded towards the starboard ladder. 'Set an anchor watch, Mr Halfhyde, and keep the guns manned. Full alertness, and my Officer of the Watch to report at once should anything untoward seem about to occur. When you've made your arrangements, come to my day cabin. I shall hold a council of war.'

'War, sir?'

Watkiss placed his monocle firmly in his eye and stared. 'Yes, Mr Halfhyde, war.'

'Aye, aye, sir.' Halfhyde saluted and Watkiss vanished down the ladder. Lieutenant Lamphorn was sent for to take the first anchor watch, and, duly briefed by Halfhyde, settled himself down to prophesy untoward occurrences before they happened, an uphill task. Halfhyde strode the upper deck, hands behind his back, tall body bent beneath davits and other overhead impedimenta, to check on the readiness of the guns and torpedo tubes. War in the circumstances had an ugly sound: the bay with its islands was somewhat restricted, not a place to afford much manoeuvrability should von Merkatz be provoked by stupidity into opening with his massively superior armament. Mr Mottram was equally apprehensive.

'I hope, Mr Halfhyde, sir, that the Captain will not be hasty.'

'Do you doubt the effectiveness of your guns, Mr Mottram?' Halfhyde's tone was sardonic. 'We shall give a good account of ourselves, shall we not, before going down like heroes?'

'Aye, sir, we will that. And may have to! The Captain hasn't the look of a man who'll ever strike his flag, sir.'

'True.'

Mr Mottram extended an arm, and with his other hand tapped the brass buttons of his rank upon his uniform cuff. 'As a warrant officer's widow, sir, the pension paid to Mrs Mottram will be derisory.'

'Tut, tut, Mr Mottram, think of your duty, and of the Queen.' Halfhyde strode on, conscious of loud and obscene mutterings in his wake. Clearly the good gunner was as loyal as any man, but, also like any man, preferred to lay down his life to some purpose. There was a curious stir among all the ship's company and Half-hyde felt it strongly. Most of them were old hands who had not taken long to sum up their Captain, and there was a notable lack of confidence in the air, a doubting of the efficacy of the command. The petty officers were surly and uncertain, clearly expecting disobedience. Mutiny was perhaps too strong a word, though a small refusal by just one man could spread like a disease. If it started, it must be nipped in the bud without delay; the warrant officers of the seaman branch, Mr Pinch and Mr Mottram, could be relied upon to see to that. Never mind his widow's pension: in the last analysis, Mottram would act as his years of sea experience had taught him. And of Benjamin Pinch there was equally no doubt: he was married to the sea and the Navy.

Halfhyde went below to the council of war.

*   *   *

It was a full muster this time: Canon Rampling was present with Petrie-Smith and Todhunter, the latter clutching his Gladstone bag in case he was to be despatched immediately to the arrest of Savory. Watkiss, laying down the law on some point or other, broke off as his First Lieutenant knocked.

'Ah, Mr Halfhyde, come in. Is my ship ready in all respects for action?'

'All ready, sir,' Halfhyde reported, noting the look of extreme alarm on the face of the man from the Foreign Office. Bidden to sit, he sat opposite his Captain. He cleared his throat. 'If I may remind you, sir, with great respect, we are very heavily out-gunned.'

'Oh, stuff and nonsense, Mr Halfhyde, Her Majesty's Fleet is never outgunned, we are British. You have heard the saying, one volunteer is worth ten pressed men?'

'I have sir, but – '

'No buts, Mr Halfhyde, by the same token one British ship is worth ten foreigners. That means I have *thirty* ships. Now then. Where were we?'

'Cutting throats,' Canon Rampling said in tones of sharp disapproval. 'A proceeding that the church would deplore.'

Watkiss looked annoyed. 'Oh, ba–blast the church. I'm not commanding a pulpit, I'm commanding a battleship and if I say throats will be cut, then cut they will damn well be. A last resort,' he added, 'as my First Lieutenant will appreciate. Or an alternative, should I say.'

Halfhyde asked, 'An alternative to what, sir?'

'To opening fire.' Watkiss looked crafty. 'Sometimes a frontal assault may be unwise.'

'Or we may find ourselves outgunned, sir?' Halfhyde asked, his face straight.

'Hold your tongue, if you please, Mr Halfhyde, and don't be impertinent. What I have in mind is a nocturnal attack – an attack by boarding-parties under cover of night – an assault to cause havoc to von Merkatz' ships!'

'Yes, sir. And the purpose?'

Watkiss answered promptly, 'To show him that he cannot tweak the lion's tail with impunity, that's what!'

'He hasn't tweaked it yet, sir – '

'Oh yes he has, Mr Halfhyde, sending lying signals about sick men that any fool could see through, it's damn cheek and an insult through me to Her Majesty and I won't have it, d'you hear me?'

'Yes, sir. And the havoc . . . what form would this take?'

Watkiss waved his arms in the air. 'Slip his cables, lose him his anchors, put him at my mercy while he flounders adrift about the bay, unable to bring his guns to bear as he wishes! How's that?'

'A receipt for disaster,' Petrie-Smith said angrily. 'I can assure you HMG will give you no backing whatsoever. It is vital, quite *vital* that this affair be handled diplomatically and that is why I am here.'

'You may be here, Mr Assistant Paymaster Luckings,' Watkiss said with dangerous calm, 'but I happen to be your Commanding Officer as ordained by the Board of Admiralty and you will – '

'I – '

'Hold your damn tongue, sir!' Watkiss said loudly. 'Mr Half-hyde, what do you say about my plan?'

'A good one, sir, and likely enough to bring confusion to the German squadron – but also, I fear, to ourselves.'

'Why?'

Halfhyde gestured towards the sternwalk and the anchorage beyond. 'Narrow waters, sir. Four ships veering about the harbour out of control until von Merkatz is ready with his steam. I foresee much use of the collision mats.'

'Oh, balls . . .' Watkiss looked murderous for a moment, but then nodded sagely. 'Indeed . . . you may have a point, Mr Halfhyde.'

'Which I know you will have considered, sir, and concluded the risk worth while.'

'Yes, yes.'

'But if von Merkatz can be brought to book without damage to ourselves, so much the better.'

'Quite.'

'So I would suggest taking a leaf out of your own book, sir, bearing in mind how successful you have been upon earlier missions not dissimilar to this – '

'Yes.'

'The use of subterfuge, sir. To start with, make a conciliatory signal to Admiral von Merkatz – '

'I'm damned if I will.'

'But purely as a subterfuge, sir. To lull him so that in the end you win.'

'Ah.'

Halfhyde recognized the emergence of common sense and pressed his point home. 'Let us summarize, sir. Your objectives are firstly to secure the release of Admiral Daintree in Valparaiso, then to apprehend Savory – or allow Mr Todhunter scope to do so – and finally and in general to watch British trading interests and to circumvent any jiggery-pokery on the part of von Merkatz – '

'Jiggery-pokery, well said! Frankly I'm not too clear as to how I can be expected to watch trading interests, but – '

'You may leave that part to me, Captain,' Petrie-Smith broke in. 'If I'm afforded – '

'Oh, rubbish!'

'My dear sir, I happen to have the rank of Senior Clerk at the – '

'From what I've seen of you when free of your bunk, you're as much damn use as a whore at a wedding. Now, Mr Halfhyde: your plan, if you please.'

'Yes, sir. I suggest you invite Admiral von Merkatz aboard and give him hospitality . . . one moment, sir, if I may.' Halfhyde's voice rose over an angry interruption. 'That will give you the opportunity of assessing him – assessing his position, his aspirations, his intentions. To know one's enemy is half the battle won . . . I'm not sure if *you* said that, sir, or whether – '

'I may have done,' Watkiss said huffily.

'And after he has been lulled and probed – '

'Probed, yes, I like that. Go on.'

'Yes, sir. After that, I suggest a direct contact with the authorities in Valparaiso in order to establish your own presence and your urgent concern for Admiral Daintree – '

'And to tell the buggers of the concern of my sovereign and my government! Yes, By God, my dear Halfhyde, you're talking sense!'

Halfhyde inclined his head. 'As a result of your example on those earlier occasions, sir.'

'Oh, I don't know,' Watkiss said with an attempt at self-efface-ment, 'you were instrumental yourself as I recall.' He paused, scratching beneath an armpit. 'You did well. You proved a good emissary in Spain. In Sevastopol too . . . that damned Prince Whatsisname.'

'Admiral Prince Gorsinski, sir.'

'Yes. Well, you can do it again, damned if you can't! What?'

'You mean – '

'I mean the damn telegraph's unreliable even if there is one, and it can be read by dagoes and von Merkatz can be informed. A personal messenger is much better, Mr Halfhyde! You shall go with despatches to Valparaiso and put the views of Her Majesty's Government to the authorities there!'

'A long way, sir. A good six hundred miles at a guess.'

'Pooh, a mere step.' Watkiss waved his arms again. 'You shall hire a conveyance, a carriage. Or a horse. Perhaps there is even a railway.' He warmed to his plan. 'After nightfall – clandestinely – you shall be disguised – a British trader who must reach Val-paraiso to sell whatever it is the dagoes buy. In the meantime I shall prepare despatches in consultation – ' He broke off as a knock came at the door of the day cabin. Mr Midshipman Perrin stood revealed as the curtain was pulled back.

'Well, Mr Perrin?'

'A boat coming off from the port, sir.'

'Oh. Carrying whom?'

'I don't know, sir, but a person of some importance, sir, in a uniform with a lot of gold on it, sir.'

'*All* dagoes wear gilded uniforms, Mr Perrin, otherwise nobody takes any notice of them.'

'Yessir.'

'Well, don't stand there idling, Mr Perrin. Back on deck with you and see the person is properly received, and take care to stand with your back to a bulkhead – you never know the morals of dagoes, Mr Perrin.'

'No, sir.'

'Mr Halfhyde, you'll go too.'

'Aye, aye, sir. Full honours, sir?'

'Of course, Mr Halfhyde, we're guests in a foreign port, are we not?' There was never any knowing with Captain Watkiss, Halfhyde reflected, not for the first time. 'Depending who this person is, of course. If he's customs and excise there's no need to bother.'

*　　*　　*

The boat from the shore came alongside, cannoning into the lower platform of the accommodation ladder and causing the important person to drop heavily back on to a thwart. There was a period of acrimonious shouting, then, with immense dignity, much gold ascended the ladder to the quarterdeck. A uniform of mid-blue cloth came into view, with metal everywhere : gilt buttons, gilt collar, belt of silver thread, splendid sword, gold tassels from both shoulders, epaulettes, cocked hat with more gold. Behind the splendour came another person of lesser splendour but still with a good deal more gold than a British admiral in full-dress uniform.

Salutes were exchanged; the boatswains' calls sounded – the person looked important enough to warrant the piping party. Halfhyde brought his hand down and stretched it out.

'Lieutenant Halfhyde, Royal Navy. Welcome aboard, sir.'

His hand was shaken. The person, who was tall and heavy, gave a wide grin : the teeth were primitive. 'The Halfhyde?' he asked in poor English.

'Yes.'

'And the Watkiss?'

'Captain Watkiss is below, sir. You know of us?'

'Indeed yes – know, yes. Very great peoples, much. You will have courtesy given.'

'Good.'

'But no permissions to enter asked, this is a pity and I regret.'

'My apologies, sir.'

'Not matter now, I give ze permissions,' the gilded person said. Halfhyde thanked him, wondering about the Halfhyde and the Watkiss and reflecting that the information would most probably have originated from Admiral von Merkatz, whose intelligence might well have acquainted him with certain British naval appointments of a relevant nature. 'I am General Codecino. Here is Captain Santa Cruz, my aide-de-camp.'

Halfhyde shook the hand of Captain Santa Cruz. Codecino... Governor of the province of Llanquihue, and Canon Rampling's friend! There might be a need for circumspection below in the cuddy, and Halfhyde turned to the Midshipman. 'Mr Perrin, go below and inform the Captain that General Codecino is aboard with his ADC, if you please.'

*   *   *

Petrie-Smith had no need of the Captain's order to make himself scarce: as the undercover man, he must not be seen by the Chileans. Mr Todhunter was not so sanguine; he had his duty to perform.

'Sir, the traitor Savory – '

'Oh, balls to the traitor Savory, I'm more concerned about the Queen and Admiral Daintree. Your time will come, never fear – I shall not forget.'

'But – '

'Go instantly, Mr Todhunter, or I shall place you in arrest.'

'*Sir*!' Mr Todhunter was scandalized, shaken to the very soul. Arrest! Never in his whole life . . . detective inspectors of the Metropolitan Police . . . he gasped, but went. A protest was not worth the risk; his Chief Super would be livid and, not knowing Captain Watkiss, would assume he'd asked for it. To be frank, his Chief Super was . . . well, a word beginning with B, that Mr Todhunter could not bring himself to utter even to himself. As the Detective Inspector hurried from the day cabin with his Gladstone bag, Captain Watkiss turned to the canon.

'You'll stay and meet your acquaintance. He may be useful,

and his visit is most fortuitous. You may consider your duties to have begun, but remember you're not in the pulpit and this is not a meeting of the damn Dean and Chapter – you'll watch your words and say as little as possible, d'you hear?'

NINE

General Codecino, bringing a splash of colour to the day cabin, appeared delighted to renew his acquaintance with Canon Rampling. He took the clergyman in his arms and embraced him, a proceeding that fortified Captain Watkiss in his view that all dagoes needed to be treated circumspectly in regard to their morals; and Watkiss himself stood well clear of the ADC, whose face bore a predatory look.

'What a performance,' Watkiss remarked in a loud whisper to Halfhyde. When the General stepped back from the parson, Watkiss made his presence felt somewhat coldly.

'Ah, the Watkiss, yes.' Codecino beamed. 'To meet the Watkiss brings joy.'

'*Captain* Watkiss. I am not a clan chieftain in a kilt.'

'Not?' The Chilean looked puzzled.

'Not, but never mind, never mind.' Captain Watkiss cleared his throat importantly. 'I gather you and Canon Rampling have met before ... yes, Mr Halfhyde, what is it now?'

'The General,' Halfhyde said in a low voice, 'has little English and I don't believe he understood any of that, sir.'

Watkiss breathed hard down his nose and spoke thereafter in a louder voice. 'Sit down, General,' he said, doing so himself. Codecino followed his motion, as did the ADC after a lingering stare at Halfhyde. Watkiss, placing his monocle in his eye, began a kind of interrogation of the Governor of Llanquihue province designed to find out what the German squadron was doing in Puerto Montt and what the devil the dagoes thought they were up to in arresting Rear-Admiral Daintree. Fortunately, little of the Captain's harangue penetrated the Chilean's mind, as was soon obvious from his blank expression.

'Feller's thick-headed,' Watkiss grumbled. 'I'm making no headway at all, damn it!'

'If you'll allow me, sir,' Rampling said.

'What?'

'I am known to General Codecino, as you're aware, and also I have some Spanish. I was once attached to a legation in Uruguay.'

'Really.' Watkiss sounded discouraging: he had no wish to place himself in Rampling's hands, but saw no alternative. 'Oh, very well, but have a care – I warn you! For a start, ask him what he's come aboard my ship for.'

Rampling did so, gesticulating like a genuine Spaniard, and raising beaming smiles from the swarthy Chilean. He reported, 'A friendly visit, sir. General Codecino comes to ask how he can be of assistance.'

'He does, does he? Very well, then, he can tell me this: why have the damn dagoes arrested Admiral Daintree? What's the charge against him?' Watkiss looked truculent.

A further conversation took place in Spanish, a lengthy one, and after a while Watkiss showed signs of strain, fidgeting about in his chair. 'Oh, come on, come on, it's a simple question and it shouldn't take half a dog-watch to get an answer!'

'Patience, sir,' the parson said, frowning.

'Damn!'

More talk: Watkiss fumed. Then Rampling said, 'Admiral Daintree appears to have insulted the Chilean flag, sir.'

'Rubbish.'

'I gather it's not rubbish. According to General Codecino, Admiral Daintree . . .' Rampling paused, stretching his neck in the clerical collar. 'Let me put it this way, Captain: if a foreign admiral landed in Portsmouth and whilst attending a reception with civic dignitaries at the Town Hall shook his fist at the Union Flag because it had been hoisted superior to the flag of his own country, what would you do?'

Watkiss dropped his monocle into his lap, then replaced it. His face looked mottled. 'I dislike parables, dislike them intensely. If that's what Admiral Daintree did, then damn good luck to him, I say! But I don't believe for a moment that he did.'

'General Codecino – '

'Yes, yes, General Codecino. Do you really believe an admiral would allow his feelings to get the better of him to that extent, Canon Rampling?'

Rampling was grave. 'I believe Admiral Daintree would.'

'What!'

'A man of uncertain temper. Remember, I know him. It would be in character.'

'He wouldn't be *arrested* for that!'

Rampling shrugged. 'You don't know the Chileans, sir. Or any South Americans, come to that. They react differently from the British.'

'No damn right to. What a travesty of justice! How do they know he was shaking his fist at their damn flag?'

'He accompanied the gesture by uttering words, sir.'

'What words, pray?'

'Long live Her Majesty and . . . something or other to the bloody President of Chile.'

'Something or other?'

'I am remembering my cloth, sir.'

'Oh. H'm.' Watkiss was considerably disconcerted, but bounced back fairly rapidly. 'No doubt he was under much provocation. You say I don't know Chileans – by God, I don't damn well need to! Excitable buggers like all foreigners and high-handed with it. They've behaved damnably – damnably! When are they going to let Daintree go?'

'That hasn't been decided yet,' Rampling said, 'but General Codecino has a suggestion to make, and I myself think it's a very helpful one.'

'Well?'

Rampling looked as though he were well aware of forthcoming unpopularity. 'If an apology were to be offered – '

'Good God! An apology! By whom?'

Rampling spread his hands. 'Admiral Daintree has refused to apologize – '

'So I should hope.'

'President Errazuriz has asked that the British Government might formally apologize, but our Minister in Santiago has refused to pass on this request until he is in possession of a full report including Admiral Daintree's statement in his defence – '

'Very right and proper – I am surprised that he's shown such spirit.'

'General Codecino has more to offer, sir. A compromise – '

'Typical dago.'

'He suggests that an apology offered by another senior British naval officer of standing might possibly secure the release of Admiral Daintree – '

'Apologize my backside! An officer of standing – he means me, of course. I shall do no such thing and you may tell him so.'

Rampling pursed his lips. 'If I were you, sir, I would consider carefully. Admiral Daintree is an old man, and frail, as I've told you. He is reacting badly to being held in custody, but he's obstinate – '

'Naval officers are never obstinate!' Watkiss snapped.

'No, indeed.' The canon inclined his head. 'Determined, then. He will not, I repeat, apologize. An act of kindness to an old man, a touch of self-abnegation . . . it would go a long way and would, I am sure, be appreciated by Her Majesty's Government who would then not become directly involved.'

'Well . . .'

'And there's another point. General Codecino spoke of two more matters, sir: a trading agreement is currently being considered and may well be offered to Great Britain. On the other hand, if certain affairs are not settled with dignity, it may be offered elsewhere. I think you know what I mean, sir.'

Watkiss blew out his cheeks. 'The damn Germans?'

'Precisely. And General Codecino tells me that Admiral von Merkatz is in Chilean waters for the purpose of surveying ports suitable for use as bases and coaling stations for the German Navy . . . and that the two considerations may go hand in hand.'

Rampling paused. 'A simple apology, sir, offered on Admiral Daintree's behalf, could be of immense help. General Codecino offers further assistance, because he is personally friendly towards us and prefers a British alliance to a German one. The railway from Osorno is unreliable, dirty and uncomfortable and not fit for the Governor of a province – the General has business in Valparaiso himself, and will provide a carriage and relays of horses.'

*　　*　　*

Watkiss would come to no decision until he had consulted with the representative of the Foreign Office, for whom there was now a use; Rampling was left to entertain Codecino in the day cabin while Watkiss went with Halfhyde to the latter's cabin and sent post-haste for Petrie-Smith. When apprised of the situation, Petrie-Smith pontificated at some length. It would certainly be inadvisable for HMG as such, he said, to offer any kind of apology – to do so would at once and finally admit the British via Admiral Daintree to be in the wrong, and anti-British factions in Chile, to say nothing of the Germans themselves, would make fine capital out of that.

'Why the Huns, Petrie-Smith?'

'They have many friends in Chile, and many under-the-table accommodations could be arrived at, especially with a powerful German squadron in Chilean waters. Strength is strength as we all know, Captain, and the manifestation of it is impressive.'

'And if *I* were to apologize?'

Petrie-Smith shrugged and ran a palm over his shining bald head. 'As the Chinese have it, it would save face without being too committal.'

Watkiss pounced on that. 'You mean it leaves the door open for the government at home to disown my apology?'

'Oh, I certainly wouldn't go so far as that,' Petrie-Smith said smoothly.

'Perhaps not, but I would and I don't like it,' Watkiss said with much energy.

'Weigh the pros and cons, Captain. You have been offered the chance of retrieving a situation with honour. You cannot afford to cast it down. If you do . . .' Petrie-Smith paused.

'Well, out with it, man!'

'I would be the person who would have to make the report, Captain,' Petrie-Smith said, shaking his head sadly. 'As I've already told you, I have the rank of Senior Clerk in the Foreign Service . . . in the Navy the equivalent would be, I fancy, a vice-admiral. More than that, indeed – at this moment and in this place I represent Her Majesty's Government, the civil power – '

'*I* represent *Her Majesty*, thank you, Mr Petrie-Smith.'

There was a smile. 'I'm well aware of the table of precedence, Captain Watkiss, and the manner of thought of naval officers. Some of them, via Her Majesty as Head of the Church of England, have been known to consider themselves as representing God . . . but as for myself, I'd prefer to receive my unction from the hands of Canon Rampling – '

'You – you – '

'One moment, Captain.' Petrie-Smith raised a hand and with it the uniform cuff bearing two gold stripes unadorned with the curl of executive authority but bearing between them the white cloth of the paymaster branch, in Watkiss' eyes the colour of servitude. 'Her Majesty is accustomed by tradition and by the terms of constitutional monarchy to accept the advice of her ministers. And I advise you to accept the favour offered by General Codecino. I advise that very strongly indeed.'

*   *   *

'A rude bugger!' Watkiss said furiously. 'Blasted Foreign Office, who do they think they are?' The question was rhetorical; Half-hyde gave no answer. 'Well, I'm *not* going to apologize, you are.'

'I, sir?'

'Yes, you, sir! That is, you shall take my apology to Valparaiso for me. I'm damned if I shall prostrate myself before some damn mayor or whatever it is, I've never heard such a thing in all my life.'

'Sir, I – '

'Hold your tongue, Mr Halfhyde, I've had an idea.' Watkiss' eyes gleamed in the afternoon sun : he had decided to clear his thoughts by walking his quarterdeck before going back to face Codecino and the parson. He waved his telescope as he elaborated. 'I shall make the apology in writing, then those damn clerks in Whitehall won't be able to disown me afterwards – '

'Is that wise, sir?'

'Yes. Moreover, I'll sign it *Commodore* Watkiss. Damn it, I have three ships to command, and that warrants commodore's rank, does it not? No doubt I have in fact been promoted – being out of touch with the Admiralty, I naturally can't be informed. That gives the thing more weight and also acts as a let-out for Whitehall if they want one – without exactly going back upon my statement, if you follow.'

'I do not, sir.'

'Well, try to, then! I suppose you have a brain. Making the assumption I *haven't* been promoted, they can always say there's no Commodore Watkiss in the Navy List, which is true.'

'I still don't see – '

'What's that, by God?' Watkiss levelled his telescope across the sparkling blue water of the anchorage, then let out an oath. 'A boat from the German flag, Mr Halfhyde, a damn barge! It must be von Merkatz himself.'

'Did you ask him aboard, sir, as I – '

'No, I didn't, because that dago General came aboard before I could do so. Oh, well, it's an ill wind – we'll let the two of them confront each other and see what emerges, Mr Halfhyde. Have the side manned and piped.'

*   *   *

Halfhyde was convinced that von Merkatz had indeed been informed of his presence aboard the *Meridian* : the German was too ready with his recognition; their last meeting at sea aboard the *Friedrich der Grosse* had been not only some while ago but had been brief. Von Merkatz was courteous, giving Halfhyde a stiff bow from the waist upon reaching the quarterdeck and after exchanging formalities with Captain Watkiss.

'We meet again, Lieutenant Halfhyde.'

'A good memory, sir.'

'A memorable officer, Lieutenant Halfhyde, who last time bested me, I regret to say!'

'You have my apologies, sir.'

Von Merkatz laughed. 'It was the chance of war, Lieutenant Halfhyde, even though our countries were at peace. And are now,' he added, looking at Watkiss. 'Are your guns manned still, Captain?'

'Yes, sir, they are, and shall so remain until I decide otherwise. I trust your sick man is better,' Watkiss added tartly.

'He soon will be. The Chileans have excellent surgeons and the shore facilities are better than those of a warship when they are handily available.' There was a curious flicker in the German's eyes, which were cold and fish-like. 'I would like to know, Captain, why you consider it necessary to man your armament whilst at anchor in a foreign port?'

'My reasons are my concern, sir.' Watkiss glared upwards; von Merkatz was a tall man, as thin as a flagstaff, giving Watkiss the appearance of a ball at the foot of a cricket bat, stout, red and roly-poly. 'I suggest you come below to my quarters, where we may talk in privacy.'

Von Merkatz bowed again, stiff and formal. 'Thank you, Captain. I have one further observation to make, if I may be permitted, to Lieutenant Halfhyde.'

'Oh, very well.'

The German turned to Halfhyde, smiling slightly, a cold smile with no humour. 'When last we met . . . your Sir Russell Savory – you'll remember, of course. I am told he has escaped from your Dartmoor gaol. I see a connection between him and your presence here, I think.'

'Do you, sir?'

'If he has come to South America where, as I recall, he had friends, I wish you luck in recapturing him.' Von Merkatz turned away and followed Captain Watkiss below. Halfhyde wondered why the German should choose to bring up the subject of Savory. To disarm British suspicions in advance, to show an expected awareness of the facts – or to warn Halfhyde off? Certainly if Savory could be got aboard a ship of the German squadron he could become virtually untouchable . . . Halfhyde shrugged: something might emerge later, and in the meantime Admiral Daintree seeemed to be the more important figure. As the officers vanished below, a bowler hat came round the corner of the after screen, with a worried face beneath it. Mr Todhunter had caught the mention of the traitor Savory and his ears were acock-bill for more news of his victim. Sliding round the metal bulkhead, his hand contacted wet paint. Some adhered to his blue serge suit. 'Bother take it!' he muttered in exasperation. New suits were dear; a replacement would cost him all of thirty bob but you had to look smart to satisfy the Chief Super . . . forsaking the manhunt temporarily, Mr Todhunter hurried off in search of the boatswain and something to shift paint. The Navy and its passion for occupying every spare moment in touching up paint-work was a blooming nuisance.

*   *   *

'This is General Codecino – Admiral von Merkatz.'

'Thank you, Captain, we have met.' Von Merkatz bowed once more and clicked his heels at the Chilean. 'I have paid a courtesy call upon the port authorities. Have you, Captain?'

'No. You may take it that they've come to me instead.'

'A compliment indeed. I congratulate you.'

Watkiss nodded. 'The Union Flag, you know. The Chileans are good friends and allies of Great Britain.'

'Indeed.'

'Oh, very much so.' Watkiss was disconcerted by the German's cold, monosyllabic manner; conversation seemed to languish. The Captain's servant was rung for and gin was brought. After all, they were not at war. Ungraciously Watkiss lifted his glass and said, 'To His Imperial Highness the Emperor of Germany.'

Another Germanic bow, a tiresome performance in Watkiss'

view. 'And to Her Majesty the Queen-Empress . . . his grand-mother.'

Glasses were once again placed to lips. Watkiss glared across his cabin; the reference to the grandmotherly state had been made in an odd tone and somehow it detracted from majesty, as though Great Britain, in German eyes, were some sort of elderly matriarchy about to be nailed down in its coffin. Damn Huns. Well, they were going to be taught a lesson they wouldn't forget; Watkiss was thoroughly converted to the idea of an apology. Why not be magnanimous in the larger, wider interest? He puffed out his ample chest: it took a strong man to apologize – though, of course, one could understand old Daintree's reluctance to crawl. He, Watkiss, would not be apologizing on his own behalf, it would be a mere proxy affair. He downed his gin, and held his glass towards his steward for a refill; the other glasses had been dealt with already, Watkiss noted grudgingly: he was not a poor man but neither was he a rich one, and each gin represented one penny off his entertaining allowance. Exceed it, and his own pocket must be delved into, and besides, good Plymouth gin was wasted on foreigners. The dagoes probably drank some filthy wine, while Germans were more at home in beer gardens. . . . Meanwhile, it was time to get down to some business and the German might as well be put on the defensive from the start.

'The man Savory,' Watkiss said loudly, halting a conversation between von Merkatz and Codecino: von Merkatz, it seemed, spoke Spanish, which was a pity.

'Yes, Captain, the man Savory?'

'Naturally, I overhead your remark to my First Lieutenant. Have you any knowledge of the man's whereabouts?'

'I?' Von Merkatz spread his hands and smiled coldly. 'Why should I have knowledge of this person?'

'In the past – '

'In the past, yes. Let the past remain the past, Captain.'

'But he was attempting to sell secrets to your Emperor, sir!'

'And failed, as we know. Savory is of no further interest to Germany, Captain. He is out of date, he has been overtaken by the passing years, a fate to which we all succumb in the end.

Men – emperors – queens. Fleets and great empires. They wax, they wane – and then pouf!' Von Merkatz threw his hands in the air explosively, and gin descended upon Watkiss' monkey-jacket. 'Your pardon, Captain.' The German held out his empty glass to the Captain's steward.

'I trust,' Watkiss snapped, 'your remark was not intended to point insultingly at my country?'

Von Merkatz shrugged. 'If the cap fits,' he murmured, his eyes glinting, 'it may be worn by the person concerned. In Germany we have a strong and ambitious Emperor, and von Bismarck did much for the Fatherland before he retired from active politics. We are prospering, we are expanding, our army is of the finest, our Navy is in being in all the world's seas.'

'And in the end, my dear sir, you too will go pouf.'

'The time has not yet come.' Von Merkatz set his glass down on the roll-top desk. 'The time for something else, however, has come, and it is this: the reason why I decided to call upon you, Captain.' He waved an arm around. 'Your ship is old and worn out, already she has gone pouf – '

'By God, I'll not – '

'She is, I understand, about to be handed over to the Chilean Navy and then you will have no ship apart from the two rowing boats that accompanied you in, and which will take you out again. I suggest you accomplish the handing over very quickly, Captain, and depart from Reloncavi Bay before my inclinations get the better of me.'

Watkiss was almost speechless but managed to ask what the devil von Merkatz meant.

The German lifted an arm. 'Your Lieutenant Halfhyde once caused me to look foolish in the eyes of my Emperor and of your stupid excisemen in Plymouth, wretches who poked and probed into every nook and cranny of my squadron – '

'Yes, and found Savory – '

'I am a man of long memory, Captain, and one who resents insult. I do not forgive. As for you, you have armed your guns against me – a warlike act that in my Emperor's eyes would give me the excuse to avenge the past insult. Do you understand me?'

Watkiss snapped, 'I understand this, sir: you are on the verge of provoking war between Great Britain and Germany, and this your Emperor, I think, would not approve.'

'If you think that, you do not know my Emperor,' von Merkatz said flatly. 'However, as a gentleman, I am offering you a choice – I am warning you that your presence is exacerbating to my temper, and you would do well to conclude your business and leave the port and take Lieutenant Halfhyde with you. And now, if you please, you will have my barge brought alongside and escort me to your accommodation ladder.'

*　　　*　　　*

Captain Watkiss shook a fist from his quarterdeck towards the retreating German and then turned upon Halfhyde. 'It's all your damn fault!' he said bitterly. 'By God, what have I been given as a First Lieutenant I'd like to know!'

'I – '

'Hold your tongue, Mr Halfhyde. I would have thought you could have found a better way to protect those blasted blueprints than insulting an admiral!'

'That's in the past, sir.'

'Yes! And the past lives on, don't you see, to confound us in the present! You're a two-edged sword, aren't you, Mr Halfhyde? Oh dear, oh dear. Mr Lamphorn!'

'Yes, sir?'

'Fall out the guns' crews. See that it's done ostentatiously.'

Lamphorn stared. 'Ostentatiously, sir?'

'Yes, ostentatiously. Clean out your ears, Mr Lamphorn, and you won't need to repeat my orders back at me. Send Perrin, he's still too damn fat, send him round all guns personally. Mr Perrin!'

'Yessir?' The midshipman saluted nervously.

'You've failed to obey my orders, boy. Look at that stomach.' Captain Watkiss prodded hard with his telescope. 'Soggy, too much starch. You'll lose two stone before we leave for the Falklands, or I'll have your reasons in writing.' Watkiss turned away, and stared again towards Admiral von Merkatz. He shook his telescope violently towards the barge. 'The bugger's insufferable, Mr Halfhyde, quite insufferable, and I shall not put up with it. You'll leave with that dago forthwith for Valparaiso, or as soon as I've written that blasted apology. Once Admiral Daintree's released, the whole matter can be resolved.'

'And Savory, sir?'

'What's that policeman here for? I may decide to land him to execute his duty after we leave, and make his own way back to England.' Captain Watkiss, without more ado, bounced angrily towards the hatchway and descended to his quarters, followed by Halfhyde. Upon arrival he sent for Petrie-Smith and demanded assistance in the writing of the apology. When the task was accomplished, he turned to Halfhyde with the sealed document. 'There you are, Mr Halfhyde, for delivery to the authorities in Valparaiso, and you'll not go alone.'

'I'll not, sir?' Halfhyde was surprised.

'No. You'll take that damn cleric and relieve me of his presence. He speaks Spanish and he said he might be instrumental in securing Admiral Daintree's release, didn't he? Now he'll have his chance. Then we'll see if he's any use, or like the barber's cat – all wind and water. You'd better take the policeman too – he can liaise with the police authority in Valparaiso. I only wish to God,' Watkiss said vengefully, 'that I could also rid myself of that oaf from the Foreign Office, but being undercover, of course, he mustn't be seen . . . oh, what is it, Mr Halfhyde?'

Halfhyde raised his eyebrows to heaven and sudden realization came to the Captain. He looked over his shoulder, twisting from his desk. 'Damn,' he said crossly, 'I didn't realize you were still there, Mr Petrie-Smith.'

TEN

The carriage, rolling out northwards from Puerto Montt, was stuffy and uncomfortable, smelling of a mixture of leather and moth-balls. General Codecino sat with Halfhyde, back to the horses; he fell asleep soon after departure, and lolled heavily against Halfhyde in gilded somnolence. Opposite sat Canon Rampling, still in his cassock, with a travelling communion set in a box, Codecino's AD C, and Detective Inspector Todhunter with his Gladstone bag tucked behind his feet and his bowler hat upon his knees. The Gladstone bag now contained a revolver and ammunition provided by Mr Mottram. They travelled in some splendour : behind was a postillion, who exchanged constant loud talk with the coachman, to the discomfiture of Mr Todhunter.

The policeman spoke politely to Rampling. 'I wonder, sir, if you can interpret?'

'Why?'

'Because the Chilean persons may be discussing matters appertaining to ourselves, sir. As a police inspector – '

'Don't concern yourself, my dear fellow.'

'My duty impels me – '

'Consider my cloth, and *my* duty. Listeners seldom hear good of themselves, in any case.'

'Oh, I see,' Mr Todhunter said, and his long, sallow face reddened a little. As a Salvationist, he decried vulgarity as much as did Canon Rampling, naturally. He sat in silence thereafter, and jogged up and down to the motion of the carriage springs, thinking of the traitor Savory. Although much time would now be lost en route, and he would in some ways have preferred to consult the police in Puerto Montt first, he was grateful enough to Captain Watkiss for despatching him to Valparaiso which, while not Chile's capital, was a very cosmopolitan place where the police, like those of London, could be expected to be more aware of world events and so on than those in the provincial towns and ports. Mr Todhunter reflected : he had once worked on an out-of-town case, a murder enquiry into which the Yard had been called, and the provincial Chief Super had been a very different kettle of fish from his own Chief Super in the great metropolis. Nicer – much nicer – but rustic. He had called Mr Todhunter by his Christian name, which was a kindly touch and a democratic one. (Mr Todhunter had then been only a Detective Sergeant.)

However, to the present and the future : Chile was another kettle of fish again. Looking out through the carriage windows at Chile, Mr Todhunter's stomach began to react to the jogging motion and surreptitiously he ferreted in his pocket and brought a couple of Dr Datchet's tablets from a bottle and placed them in his mouth under cover of a yawn. There was nothing to drink, to help them down with, so he crunched. Tears came to his eyes : the taste was dreadfully bitter, just like poison. As he crunched and winced, General Codecino woke up and stared at the contorted, tear-wettened face of the Detective Inspector.

A pudgy hand was placed on Mr Todhunter's knee, which was at once jerked away. Todhunter sucked in his cheeks, horror-struck. In a kindly but hoarse voice the General said, 'Cry, so. Somezings ees wronk.'

'I am not crying, sir, thank you – '

'You mees ze friend, I zink. Do not lonely be, ve kom soon to rest and foods, and to bed.' The hand found the knee again, and patted. Mr Todhunter almost fainted, was saved only by catching sight of Halfhyde's wide grin accompanied by a wink. Mr Halfhyde, thank goodness, realized what was going on and would stand by him. What a country Chile was, to be sure. Mr Todhunter glanced sideways at Canon Rampling : the parson had noticed nothing untoward, being deep in a volume of religion that had the look of a professional *vade mecum*, the Church's equivalent perhaps of Harris' *Criminal Law*. The carriage jogged, swung, rolled and dipped upon its way. They passed through wild country, jungle country that would be full of animals, reptiles and snakes, a hostile place should they break a wheel. Bandits, too, without a doubt. Mr Todhunter, as night began to fall, indeed felt lonely, and was very glad when the day's journey ended at a hostelry in a small township. The horses were led away and the party was served a rather nasty supper, with wine, by the landlord's young daughter, who directed her attentions mainly towards Mr Halfhyde. The latter encouraged the girl who, in Mr Todhunter's eyes, was no better than she should be. Bed was provided in a long room below the eaves: six beds in all. Mr Todhunter entered his still wearing vest and long pants, and drew the blankets to his neck and never slept a wink all night, though General Codecino snored without cease. Come the dawn, Mr Halfhyde's bed still stood empty and Mr Todhunter, not un-possessed of imagination, pursed his lips in disapproval.

After an early breakfast, the party embarked once again and jogged, dipped and swung on for Valparaiso. No less than eleven further nights in hostelries en route, six hundred miles of terrible roads that climbed and descended, that forded occasional rivers, that detoured and sometimes disappeared into mere jungle tracks, with many changes of horses that enabled them to keep up a fair speed – all that, and then at last they rumbled into the outskirts of the great port of Valparaiso, a huge city of 104,000 persons lying below great cliffs. Mr Todhunter found it somewhat similar to an English city in its layout and construction, and he found this reassuring. Also, there were dozens and dozens of sailing ships out in the bay and at the berths, a veritable forest of masts and yards, some of which at least would be British, a link with the London River. Mr Todhunter felt close to his familiar past, to the spicy smells of the warehouses along the Thames: once, he had been stationed in Wapping, a salutary but interesting experience. The carriage rolled on, more comfortably now, past the harbour fortifications, and Mr Todhunter remembered that he had read somewhere that the dreadful disease of typhoid was endemic to Valparaiso – he must be very careful what he ate.

He thought again about the traitor Savory: all those ships, the ships that linked the world to Valparaiso. Savory could have come in on any one of them, or might be due in shortly, or, again, if he got wind of Mr Todhunter on his trail, he might leave in any of them too. Savory might perhaps eat indiscriminately and contract the typhoid, thus putting himself beyond human reach, beyond reach of the Gladstone bag and all. A wasted journey . . .

To General Codecino's instructions, the carriage stopped by magnificent gates giving on to a parade ground and beyond which was a noble pile that looked to Mr Todhunter like a town hall but was in fact the local military headquarters. General Codecino spoke briefly to a sentry, a guard was turned out in his honour, and the carriage rolled through to the parade ground. It stopped again by some steps. Halfhyde got down with the General and Canon Rampling, bidding the Detective Inspector remain.

'The traitor Savory, sir – '

'I've not forgotten, Mr Todhunter.'

'I'm relieved to hear it.' Todhunter's voice was a shade frigid: three times more during the journey, women had been a feature of the night scene and though Halfhyde had blossomed afresh after each encounter, seeming to draw strength, vigour and good temper from sin, Todhunter had inwardly deplored the flaunting of the conventions and had felt that such dissipation must weaken the response to duty's call. 'Will you be good enough to take me to police headquarters as soon as you've finished, Mr Halfhyde?'

Halfhyde smiled. 'You may be sure I shall.' He turned away with his mixed bag of companions, Captain Watkiss' written apology in his pocket, and climbed the flight of stone steps to be met at the top by another armed sentry. The way was cleared for them by General Codecino and his gilded uniform, and they were escorted by a sergeant, no less, into the building and along a passage lined with portraits of dead Chileans once eminent in military and presidential circles. They were ushered into an ante-room opening off this passage, and the sergeant addressed himself to General Codecino, who nodded and gestured dismissively.

'Waiting,' he announced to Halfhyde as the sergeant departed. 'Short sit down.'

The days' rides had been long; Halfhyde said, 'I'll stand. I'm suffering from chapel bottom.' He patted his rump; Codecino seemed to understand, for he smiled and winked. While Codecino and Rampling sat, Halfhyde went to one of three large windows and stared out across the two-and-a-half-mile wide bay where Rear-Admiral Daintree's Detached Cruiser Squadron lay at anchor close off Fort San Antonio: the first-class cruiser *Halcyon* wearing the Rear-Admiral's flag, with *Cardiff* and *Hector*, also first-class cruisers, in company. They were isolated in their deep-water anchorage from all the other vessels in the bay and there was a Chilean cruiser on station as guardship, presumably to prevent the squadron leaving. The lower- and quarter-booms were rigged in all the British ships, but all the boats were hoisted and griped-in to the davits: evidently there was no communication permitted with the shore. Figures were seen moving about the decks and the *Cardiff* was painting ship, with men slung over the side in boatswain's chairs. The Royal Navy permitted no idle hands, and arrest was no excuse for a make-and-mend, or holiday. Halfhyde turned from his view of the bay as the ante-room door opened and an officer appeared, saluted General Codecino and spoke in Spanish to him, then turned to Halfhyde. In good English he said, 'His Excellency the Military Governor will see General Codecino first, then you.'

Halfhyde nodded. 'Thank you.'

The officer clicked his heels like a German and left the ante-room with Codecino and the ADC. Halfhyde and Rampling sat mostly in silence; after some fifteen minutes the Chilean officer came back and announced that the Military Governor was ready for them. 'Follow me, please,' he said. Halfhyde and Rampling proceeded in his wake along the corridor, past more eminent Chileans peering down from the walls, and through a door at the end. They walked into a splendid apartment, long, high-ceilinged and luxuriously furnished, and were announced in ringing tones that seemed to fit the room's opulence.

'Lieutenant Halfhyde of the British Royal Navy, Your Excellency, and the Reverend Canon Rampling of the Church of England and also of the British Royal Navy, Chaplain to the squadron of Rear-Admiral Daintree.' The introduction had been made in English and was followed by an exposition of His Excellency himself. 'His Excellency General Arturo Oyanedel, Military Governor of Valparaiso.' The officer bowed, clicked his heels again, and ushered them forward towards His Excellency who was standing with Codecino beneath an immense marble chimneypiece that seemed to reach to the ceiling itself. It dwarfed General Oyanedel, who was in any case not tall, and General Codecino, who was. Halting in front of the two Generals, Halfhyde gave a formal bow, then waited for Oyanedel to extend a friendly hand. This the Military Governor did not do. Instead he said coldly,

'I am told you bring messages from your Captain, who initially entered Puerto Montt without permission.'

Halfhyde said, 'It is true I bring messages, General. As to permission or not, I cannot say.'

'I have told you. Now the message.'

Halfhyde hesitated for a moment, then reached into his pocket. Watkiss' envelope was addressed 'To Whom It May Concern', and General Oyanedel would fill that bill as well as anyone. He handed over the envelope; the Military Governor passed it to his ADC to open. The sheet of writing paper was then handed to him and, bringing a pair of gold pince-nez from a pocket, he read. Having read, he stared Halfhyde in the eye. 'An apology for the bad manners of Rear-Admiral Daintree. Good. This is satisfactory progress, Lieutenant Halfhyde.'

'Admiral Daintree will be released, General?'

Oyanedel spread his hands. 'This is not for me to say, but for my President. The apology will be sent to Santiago and instructions will then be given. This will take many days.'

'I see. And in the meantime?'

'In the meantime you and your associates will have the restricted freedom of Valparaiso – the restriction being that you will not be permitted access to the naval or military area other than the apartments which will be allotted to you in this headquarters, nor will you be permitted to embark upon the water to make contact with the British squadron. This is clear?'

Halfhyde returned the General's stare: the man was like an ape, he thought, gross and dangerous, much more dangerous than the amiable Codecino. He said, 'It is clear, General, but I have one request to make.'

'Make it.'

'Admiral Daintree is, I understand, a tired man of failing health – '

'He is an old fool, Lieutenant Halfhyde, and my country is not in a mood to show sympathy.'

'That is understandable, General, but a little clemency in allowing his chaplain, perhaps, to visit him would be much appreciated by my government, with whom so far Chile has maintained most friendly relations.' Halfhyde paused. 'You will, of course, appreciate that a chaplain, as a man of God, has a special relationship with his commander. He is not a man of war. By his ministrations, waters can be smoothed.' He turned to Rampling. 'Is this not so, Padre?'

'Indeed it is,' Rampling answered heartily. 'Indeed it is! Admiral Daintree is a God-fearing man, General, one who never misses communion except when the exigencies of the service demand. No doubt you yourself are attentive to your religion, General – '

'Yes.'

'Then you will understand that to deprive any man of communion with God can be looked upon as a sin.' The cassocked priest clasped his hands together as though in prayer. 'On the other hand, the recording angel – '

'Do not instruct me in my religious duties, you who are not of the holy Roman faith!'

'But I am of Admiral Daintree's faith, General, and wish only to bring the presence of God closer to a frail old man . . . a man whom you would not, I think, wish to die whilst in your hands.'

There was a scornful laugh. 'He is nowhere near death!'

'That is a statement only God can make with accuracy. As for me, I have observed Admiral Daintree closely over many months, and I stand by what I have said – everything I have said. I am known to General Codecino, as no doubt he will have told you. I am known to other persons in Chile, priests of your own church. The Most Reverend Cesar Diaz for example . . .'

*   *   *

'Who, precisely,' Halfhyde asked when they had left the Military Governor's presence, 'is the Most Reverend Cesar Diaz?'

Rampling said, 'A good friend – the Archbishop of Santiago. Very influential, and likely soon to join the College of Cardinals.'

'He seemed to work a miracle today at all events!'

'I fear I took his name to some extent in vain, my dear Halfhyde. Excommunication was a very empty threat and is reserved for His Holiness, but General Oyanedel was taking no chances. Nevertheless, we must work fast now.' Rampling pulled out a gold hunter watch from his pocket. They were back in the ante-room awaiting an escort for the parson to the guarded apartment in the military headquarters occupied by Daintree. 'I shall hope not to be long with the Admiral. Is there any particular message you wish passed from Captain Watkiss, other than word of the written apology?'

'No message,' Halfhyde said, then frowned. 'If you can probe . . . I had the feeling something's been left unsaid, that there's more behind Daintree's arrest than a mere insult.'

'I, too,' Rampling said. 'Never fear, I shall do my best – though it may prove difficult,' he added.

'Why so?'

'Daintree's not a communicative man.'

'Other than at communion!'

Rampling blew out his cheeks in a sigh. 'A prevarication, I fear.' He tapped his travelling communion set. 'I have never administered the sacraments to my Admiral – and when he reads the lesson at divine service he lacks conviction to put it mildly. He prefers reading out the Ten Commandments, because they can be issued as orders.' Rampling went off at a tangent. 'What about Todhunter?'

'I shall take him to police headquarters while you're with the Admiral.'

*　　*　　*

Waiting in the carriage, Todhunter looked relieved to see Halfhyde. 'You've been a long time, Mr Halfhyde, and my imagination ran away with me, which it shouldn't have done. I put it down to being in a foreign land, however, where funny things do tend to happen. Was there any mention of the traitor Savory?'

'No. And for my part, I didn't raise the matter.'

'Quite right, Mr Halfhyde,' Todhunter said approvingly. 'It's not to do with the military and we police like to handle things our own way. Are you ready to proceed now?'

Halfhyde nodded. 'Yes.' He conveyed to the coachman that he wished to be taken to police headquarters and the horses were set in motion. 'You'll manage all right with the Chilean police, I take it?'

'Oh, yes, indeed, Mr Halfhyde, we're all brothers in the world's police forces, all brothers.' The carriage jogged out of the guarded gateway and through the streets of the port, streets filled with seafaring men of many nations – British, French, German, North American. There were Negroes and Chinese, mulattos, every group that made up the great race of men who fought a living from the sea and the world's trade routes. Men buying drink and tobacco, men buying women – the brothels were highlighted by the queues outside them; Mr Todhunter pursed his lips. Policemen were naturally broad-minded, there was no facet of human lust, of human frailty that they had not seen, but Mr Todhunter turned his face the other way. Sternly he alighted at police headquaters, saying he would prefer to interview the Chileans on his own. Halfhyde, who had apprised the Detective Inspector of the facts regarding their restricted freedom and the arrangements made for their accommodation, told Todhunter to rendezvous back at the military establishment when he had concluded his business.

'And you, Mr Halfhyde?'

'I shall walk around the town, Mr Todhunter. Valparaiso is a new place to me and therefore interesting.'

Todhunter gave a dubious nod that spoke volumes about the dangers inherent in seaports and brothels, and went into the police building to bring brotherly tidings from distant London. Halfhyde meandered, conspicuous in the blue and gold and white of his lieutenant's uniform, seeking what he might find in the way of diversion and in the way of his duty: all was grist to the mill of a British naval officer protecting his country's interests. Much could be picked up in bar conversation that would not shine through in official communication and contact. German seamen in particular could be made boastful with a little judicious priming, and it was always useful to listen to boasts that customarily contained a grain or two of truth. On this occasion, however, Halfhyde was out of luck. The only Germans he came across in the Valparaiso bars were useless: if they were not blind drunk, they had no English, and Halfhyde had no German. Footsore, he returned during the afternoon, having taken an appalling lunch in an eating house, and found Todhunter awaiting him at the foot of the steps of the military headquarters, a saddened and discouraged Todhunter by the look of him.

Halfhyde lifted an eyebrow. 'Not brothers, Mr Todhunter? Do I detect a lack of co-operation?'

'You have it, Mr. Halfhyde. A case of stone-walling, I fancy. The traitor Savory has good friends. I am convinced the Valparaiso police know his whereabouts. I have a detective's nose for the truth, you understand.'

ELEVEN

One person, at all events, was happy: Canon Rampling knocked at the door of the room allotted to Halfhyde and was admitted. 'Eureka!' he said, and held out a Bible. 'I'm so glad you're back at last. I've had a long wait for you since seeing the Admiral.'

Halfhyde regarded the Bible. 'I see you have a parable to tell me. Is the Bible relevant?'

'Very. It's all there – read it and see for yourself.' Rampling opened the Bible in the middle of Ezekiel. 'I administered communion, not without difficulty since the Admiral was unwilling and there was a soldier in the room with a rifle, but with God's help I triumphed. Daintree was pleased to see me, and I managed to convey, quietly, that to take communion would be in his best interest. Not that it isn't always in everyone's, of course,' he added hastily.

'Yes.' Halfhyde looked at Ezekiel. Across the top of the page where Chapter Four began was written in pencilled capitals: RING LETTERS TO FORM MESSAGE.

'I passed him a pencil,' Rampling said. 'He understood at once, and formed his message under cover of my ministrations. He is a small man, and I am large, and I managed to obscure him totally. I read the whole communion service, all of it, even the parts I should have omitted – the alternatives, you know. Since leaving the Admiral, I've made a transcript.' He handed over a sheet of paper torn from a notebook. The message was simple. It read: *Get me out they are removing me to Santiago soon so*

*as to inhibit my squadron while I stand trial and von Merkatz
sails for Germany with Savory.*

Halfhyde blew out his cheeks in astonishment. 'It seems we
have some answers! It's not unexpected – but there are still
many questions in the air. Why, for instance, does Germany
want Savory?'

Rampling spread his hands. 'Why indeed? And why did
Savory come to Chile rather than head direct for Germany in
the first place?'

'Perhaps because he didn't want to go there.'

'But – '

'He may not be going of his own free will, Padre. We have
much yet to learn.' Halfhyde looked up from the message. 'You
didn't get any clue as to when Daintree's being removed – other
than, as he writes, soon?'

'No, I didn't, but there's a sound of urgency in his message.'

'Yes. How was he in himself?'

Rampling frowned and said, 'Oddly subdued – frightened,
almost. He's not normally a frightened man, rather the opposite.
I suppose it's natural for him to be apprehensive about being
put on trial, but personally I doubt if he has much to worry
about. The Chileans won't risk upsetting Britain to the extent of
actually punishing him, surely? It'll simply be staged as a
show.'

'Perhaps, but to him the least result will be the end of his
career at sea. He could scarcely be given any future command
appropriate to his rank.'

'And if he escapes, with our connivance – even if that's possible, won't the effect still be the same?'

'I don't know, frankly. This is a matter for Petrie-Smith's
advice, if only it were available! But I know one thing for certain,
since it's not.'

'And that is?'

Halfhyde smashed a fist into his palm. 'It's my duty to get
Daintree out. There's no question about that.' He paced up and
down the room, deep in thought, taking long strides like a
panther, his face worried. 'But how? Padre, I'd like you to

describe Daintree's room – in detail, positions of windows, the view from them, furniture, relative whereabouts in the building, what form his guard takes – you know what I mean. Quickly!'

Rampling did so, forming a mental image for Halfhyde. The guard, Rampling said, consisted of a single armed soldier outside the door of the room; he had no idea how often the guard was changed. Halfhyde reckoned it would be either two-hourly or four-hourly, probably the former. The room was at the back of the building, high up, and there was a view over most of the anchorage, but this view did not include the British warships or the Chilean guardship: useless information perhaps, but part of the whole.

'Does it help?' Rampling asked, moving his boxer-like shoulders as though ready to attack the Admiral's sentry in person.

'I shall think of a stratagem,' Halfhyde answered moodily, conscious that he might not have much time. He was conscious, too, that he was shouldering a burden of state: Admiral Daintree had been stupidly indiscreet if the Chilean charge was a true one, and anyone who assisted in his absconding from the country might well incur official displeasure – might even become the scapegoat, an easier and more expendable scapegoat than a rear-admiral, for the all-powerful Foreign Office. Nevertheless, Halfhyde would not stand by and see an old man treated with contempt by foreigners and held under threat. Acting currently for his own commanding officer, he knew that Watkiss' reactions would have been precisely similar and expressed in no uncertain terms. Thoughts of Captain Watkiss moved Halfhyde to further reflection and he said, half to himself, 'At this moment, von Merkatz is by way of being hemmed into Reloncavi Bay, I fancy! To sail, he'll need to pass the old *Meridian*.'

'True.' Rampling looked up. 'What do you suppose Watkiss will do if he tries to pass?'

*   *   *

Down south, off Puerto Montt, Captain Watkiss, as any good commander should, had been busy projecting into the future and making decisions as to what his course of action must be in various eventualities. Although he had no knowledge of the German plans as indicated via the Bible to Canon Rampling, an outward movement on the part of the German squadron was in fact the principal eventuality to be provided for in advance, and Watkiss had sent for the navigating officer, Mr Lamphorn, plus the gunner, the boatswain, the engineer, and Mr Midshipman Perrin, and had put the position baldly.

'My ships can be said to be impeding any movement or departure of the Huns by their very presence – ' Watkiss broke off and glared at Lamphorn. 'Yes, Mr Lamphorn, what is it, pray?'

'If I may put a point, sir.' Lieutenant Lamphorn coughed in some embarrassment: he was a shy man and all present seemed to be hanging upon his words and the Captain was already impatient. 'There is water enough for the German ships to pass – '

'Oh, for God's sake, Mr Lamphorn, if you can't find something useful to say, I'd be so much obliged if you'd kindly hold your tongue. I am well enough aware of the depth of water. My reference was to my guns. Shall I use them or shall I not – that is the question. Shall I bring von Merkatz to action if he attempts to pass, or shall I let him go?'

Lamphorn, as the next senior officer aboard in Halfhyde's absence, conscientiously tried again. 'I think Mr Petrie-Smith should be consulted on that point, sir.'

Watkiss, who had remained standing, bounced up and down on the balls of his feet. 'Do you, Mr Lamphorn?'

'Yes, sir.'

'Then you are a fool, and an unobservant fool which is an ill thing in my navigator. It has passed your notice that I have carefully *refrained* from including Petrie-Smith in this conference. That I did with full intent, and God help any of you who allows Petrie-Smith to find out my intentions in regard to the future handling of my ships and my guns. Is that quite clear?'

There was a chorus of hasty assent. Watkiss, his jaw thrust out pugnaciously and his monocle screwed into his eye socket, proceeded. 'Mr Mottram, as you're aware, my guns are at this moment unmanned.'

'Yes, sir.'

'That situation is to continue until I say otherwise, or unless Admiral von Merkatz should attempt to proceed to sea. The moment he is seen to be weighing his anchors, I shall man my guns – but without actually sounding for action. Is that clear, Mr Mottram?'

'Aye, sir,' the gunner said. 'You wish the guns to be manned nocturnally, sir?'

'*Clandestinely*, Mr Mottram. Yes, I rely upon you to pass the word to the captains of the guns, who will personally inform their crews that all guns and torpedo-tubes will be manned the instant I give the signal. The signal will be two blasts upon the steam syren. You, Mr Engineer Duffett, will see to it that the syren is working efficiently, which is not always the damn case, and also you'll see to it that steam pressure is not allowed to drop – we remain at instant readiness for sea and for full speed when required.'

'Aye, aye, sir.'

Watkiss turned to the boatswain. 'Mr Pinch, you and Mr Duffett will see to it that when I give my signal the damage control parties are mustered to stand by and that all watertight doors and hatches are shut as soon as my ship's company is at stations – just as though I had fully sounded for action and beat to quarters.'

'Aye, aye, sir.' Benjamin Pinch looked troubled. 'Does this mean you intend to open upon the German squadron, sir?'

'I don't know yet, Mr Pinch, I've not decided,' Watkiss said calmly, releasing his monocle. There was a tinkle as it struck a brass button on his jacket. 'A good captain never strait-jackets his mind, Mr Pinch, but makes his decision finally as events dictate.'

'I see, sir.'

'I may open fire, I may not. In the first instance, I have a good scheme in the use of my steam syren.' There was a smirk now upon Watkiss' face. 'Mr Perrin, pray be so good as to tell me what I am indicating when I make two long blasts on my steam syren?'

'Well, sir, it depends, sir, does it not?' Perrin shuffled uncomfortably.

'Does it, Mr Perrin?' Watkiss asked with studied politeness. 'Upon what, may I ask?'

'If you are under way, but stopped, sir, in fog, falling snow – '

'Oh, for God's sake.'

'If you are not stopped, sir, and if you are visible, it indicates you are directing your course to port.'

'You've finished, Mr Perrin? No, don't answer for heaven's sake or I shall throw my telescope at you. For your information, Mr Perrin, I am none of the things you have mentioned, nor am I a sailing vessel on the port tack. Do you know what I am?'

It was a dangerous question, but Perrin was not a youth to be impertinent to his Captain. 'Yes, sir. A battleship, sir. At anchor, sir.' There was a pause during which Perrin grew red and again shifted his feet. 'A ship at anchor does not make sound signals, sir.'

'Exactly, Mr Perrin, well done. It does not! And when it does, it will confuse Admiral von Merkatz, possibly to the extent that he will sheer away and implant his damn squadron firmly in the mud. Mr Lamphorn?'

'Sir?'

'A close study of your chart, if you please, and I am to be informed of the precise depth all round me as far as the shore,' Watkiss ordered in total disregard of his earlier assertion of knowledge. 'Now, Mr Perrin, the matter of rats.'

'Rats, sir?'

'I have observed a number of them below whilst making rounds, congregating largely in the vicinity of the store-rooms. We are in a filthy dago country, Mr Perrin, and filthy dago countries have filthy dago diseases. All rats are to be killed, and you will see that they are killed with the assistance of Mr Luckings who will provide the keys of the store-rooms.'

* * *

'A man, an old man,' Halfhyde said ruminatively, 'locked in a room with an armed sentry outside his door, the room in question being inside a military headquarters where the smallest untoward occurrence would bring a swarm of military Chilean bees about the ears of – of Hercules, even.'

'And Admiral Daintree is no Hercules,' Rampling said, hunching his cassocked shoulders. 'We should get no physical support from within.'

'As I thought.' Halfhyde frowned and ran a hand over his long jaw. 'Has the Church expended all its ammunition, Padre?'

'In what sense?'

Halfhyde said, 'A frontal assault on Daintree's quarters would have no hope of success. We must find other means. Such, for instance, as the Most Reverend the Archbishop of Santiago.'

'I think not. He's a loyal Chilean.'

'He's worked once in our favour.'

'By proxy only. The favour may not be long extended, as I told you.'

'True.' Once again, Halfhyde ran a hand over his jaw, thoughtfully. 'What's Daintree like physically?'

'Small, as I've already remarked,' Rampling said. 'Short and thin – bird-like, one might say. Not much substance in his body, but his personality makes up for it. In some ways he's not unlike Watkiss – I don't mean physically, but in his outlook.'

Halfhyde grinned. 'Doesn't like dagoes?'

'Precisely! And somewhat self-important.'

'He's just being an admiral,' Halfhyde murmured. 'It's by no means unusual. Captain Watkiss is merely a little premature. I wonder how Daintree would react to our Mr Todhunter, Padre?'

Rampling shook his head. 'Badly, I fear. Mr Todhunter is not sea material.'

'No. But if he were to come as a rescuer?'

'Well . . . all is grist to some mills, Halfhyde, is it not? What are you suggesting now?'

Halfhyde said, 'We shall go and talk to the Detective Inspector, and rummage in his Gladstone bag, which carries a wealth of official papers. Come, Padre.' He strode purposefully from his room, followed by the parson; along the passage they knocked at Todhunter's door but there was no answer.

'What now?' Rampling asked

'We shall sleuth the sleuth. Mr Todhunter is predictable, and I predict we shall find him somewhere down by the harbour, seeking Savory.'

'Why the harbour?' Rampling gathered up the skirts of his cassock as they made their way to the entrance and the steps to the parade ground. 'If Savory's in Chile . . . if he came in via Valparaiso, surely he'll not linger in the town?'

'That depends on his ultimate destination and where his friends are, Padre. And Todhunter won't leave Valparaiso on a wild goose chase, nor without informing me – and in the meantime, harbours are the best places in the world for obtaining information and clues.'

*   *   *

Halfhyde was proved both right and wrong: right that Mr Todhunter had proceeded towards the harbour area with its vices and squalor and its heady tang of distant seas and its potential for sheltering wicked men, wrong that he had embarked on a manhunt. Mr Todhunter, naturally enough, knew that wherever in the world you find vice and squalor, the tang of seas and shelter for wicked men, you also find the Salvation Army; and he was encountered quite by chance outside the Valparaiso citadel bidding goodbye to a portly, jovial man in a dark blue tunic with a maroon collar bearing the insignia of a major in religion. It was part of the duty of a good Salvationist to call upon citadels in far distant corners of the world, and the pursuit of the traitor Savory had been temporarily laid aside in the pursuit of that other, nobler duty.

'Why, Mr Halfhyde,' Todhunter said, lifting his bowler hat politely. 'I scarcely expected to see you here I must say. May I have the pleasure of introducing Major Barnsley? Lieutenant Halfhyde, Royal Navy, of whom I have spoken, Major, and the Reverend Canon Rampling.'

'Welcome, gentlemen, welcome!' There was a big, beaming smile and hands were shaken, pumped up and down, indeed, by the Major. 'May I ask you to come in and partake of the cup that cheers but does not inebriate? It would be my pleasure.'

'Ours, too,' Halfhyde said, and meant it. He had not known of any connection between Todhunter and the Salvation Army; now, he wondered why he – or Todhunter which was more to the point – had not thought before of seeking their assistance in the gathering of clues. But perhaps Todhunter had. . . . They all followed the Major into the citadel, a barely furnished place but earnest in its endeavour to draw into its portals wicked seafaring men and save their souls in spite of their base desires when ashore. A number of seafaring men were to be seen inside, their calling proclaimed by salt-stained blue jackets, seaboots, and a smell of tar. Many of them were undoubtedly wicked – probably, Halfhyde thought, just waiting their chances to prise open the tea till and spend the proceeds in the brothels down the road. Some were rigid with drink already taken – the Sally was well known as a good place for sleeping it off in moderate comfort. But the Major had a happy word and his beaming smile for all.

'Good fellows really,' he said to Halfhyde, ushering his guests to a horsehair settee, 'as I'm sure you well appreciate, Lieutenant. The sea's a hard taskmaster and they can't be blamed for taking a nip or two, do you not agree?'

'I do indeed.' There were enough nips present in the citadel that afternoon to float the Channel Squadron. 'And for your part, Major Barnsley, you hope to wean them?'

'Ah, that's so, yes.' The Major rubbed his hands together briskly. 'The experience of being in here will help those lads, you just mark my words, the atmosphere penetrates, you know.' It did: it was like a distillery. 'They appreciate the kindly welcome, well we try to make it kindly, instead of being kicked into the gutter by some passing – ' Halfhyde was sure the Major had meant to say "policeman" but had remembered Todhunter's calling just in time. Somewhat lamely he ended, 'boatswain.'

'Quite, I do understand.'

'Why, I thought you would, and now let's all have tea.'

The tea, with cakes, was brought by a homely woman – Mrs Major Barnsley herself, as chubby and smiling as her husband. Halfhyde found himself warming to them both. The tea was good and was welcome. As the Major chatted professionally with Canon Rampling, and after Mrs Barnsley had departed to see to the kettle, Halfhyde asked Todhunter in a low voice if he had come to the citadel to seek information, and Mr Todhunter sucked in a horrified breath. 'Oh, dear me, no, Mr Halfhyde, I should think not! The Army does not operate as a police agency, that would never do. Think of all the betrayed trusts. It's not done to ask those sort of questions, not, that is, from one Salvationist to another.'

Halfhyde nodded. 'I take your point. But if a non-Salvation-ist – '

'No, Mr Halfhyde,' Todhunter said firmly. 'I must ask you to remember that you're in a sense my guest here, and there-fore – '

'Quite, quite. I apologize, Mr Todhunter. And in any case Savory's not my main concern at this moment. I assume the Army's prepared to use its offices, as it were, on behalf of persons in trouble?'

'Why, yes, of course. Who have you in mind, Mr Halfhyde?'

'Admiral Daintree,' Halfhyde whispered in the policeman's ear. 'I have a stratagem. It has just this moment come to me. Tell me this: is there not an extradition agreement between Great Britain and Chile?'

'Yes, there is, but not – '

'Its terms, and quickly, before Mrs Barnsley comes back.'

'Oh, dear.' Todhunter sighed, but conceded. 'The treaty covers outrages by anarchists, which Admiral Daintree is not . . . fugitives may be apprehended in treaty countries and after they have been fifteen days in apprehension may be handed over to the requesting authorities, in this case I assume Great Britain, for crimes of murder, manslaughter, coining, forgery, embezzle-ment . . .'

'Yes – '

'Larceny, if you wish a complete list, false pretences, fraud by a bailee, burglary, arson, threats, rape, perjury, kidnapping, bribery and bankruptcy offences. The – '

'I see you know it all – '

'None of which unfortunately apply to the traitor Savory any more than to Admiral Daintree, since political offences are not extraditable. Mrs Barnsley is now coming back.'

'So I see. Yes, thank you, ma'am, another cup would be delightful.'

*　　*　　*

From the horsehair settee they moved to Major Barnsley's office. Before doing so Halfhyde had elicited from Todhunter that the Major was to be trusted entirely : in point of fact, the happy, innocent face proclaimed that for itself and Halfhyde had no qualms about speaking freely. Barnsley, of course, had heard that the Rear-Admiral commanding the squadron in the bay was being held at military headquarters and on the mention of Daintree's name he sucked in his cheeks.

'Dear, dear, so injudicious in a high-placed naval officer, but I'm dreadfully sorry it's come to such a pass, Lieutenant, I am really.'

'An old man – '

'Yes, indeed. Poor old gentleman! I'm sorry to have to say it, but the natives do make even me, well, *tetchy* from time to time.'

'Yes. And far from well.'

'Really? Oh, dear me.'

'So many years of service in . . . unwholesome areas, as Canon Rampling will confirm.'

'Yes,' Rampling said.

'And I see,' Halfhyde went on, nodding towards an ungainly black instrument set into the wall of the office, its wires and pole having already been noted outside in the street, 'that you are connected to the telephone service.'

'Yes, yes, indeed, a boon and a blessing at times, at other times rather a nuisance – '

'Can it reach Santiago?'

'Oh yes, that is if you know how to use the instrument, which is immensely complicated, and the exchange operators are very slow and hard to hear.'

'I dare say I can manage.'

'Manage? You wish to use the instrument, Lieutenant Half-hyde?'

'If you'll be so kind as to allow it, Major Barnsley.' Halfhyde paused, coughed, cleared his throat with a portentous sound and whilst so doing fixed his stare on Mr Todhunter. It was a warning look, a look that told the Detective Inspector he would do well to keep his mouth very firmly shut. Halfhyde then spoke to the Salvation Army Commander. 'Major, my good friend Todhunter has, for reasons of state security, given you not my name but my alias. What I am about to tell you must on no account be spoken of to any person whatsoever – the secret is for your ears alone. Do you understand me?'

Barnsley, his face alarmed, nodded. 'Who are you, then, Lieutenant Halfhyde?'

'Not Lieutenant Halfhyde. I am not a naval officer. I am from Whitehall, Major Barnsley, representing the British Government. My name is Petrie-Smith, and I have the rank of senior clerk in Her Majesty's Foreign Office. And I require to speak on the telephone immediately to Her Majesty's Minister in Santiago.'

There was a silence, a heavy one. Canon Rampling carefully studied the feet peeping out from below his cassock. Mr Todhunter, possibly so as to make out he hadn't heard a word, opened his Gladstone bag and extracted some Metropolitan Police literature, which he shuffled through with an official air. But no one contradicted Halfhyde. Barnsley's face was a study in itself: bafflement, excitement, dislike of involving his religious command, pride in being trusted and in being about to partake in Her Majesty's affairs of state . . . the telephone was made promptly available to Mr Petrie-Smith, who thereafter was addressed punc-tiliously as 'sir'. Handles were whirled, bells rang, receivers clicked, and much time passed. Chilean voices interminably repeated, '*Oiga, oiga? Diga me*,' as the wonderful electric call was passed through its stages to Santiago. At long last, after fob-bing-off attempts by the military attaché and a first secretary, the British Minister himself responded : it was, Halfhyde knew, a very long shot that he would know Petrie-Smith's voice, let alone recognize it through the buzzes and crackles and fizzing interruptions of the Chilean telephone service.

'My name is Petrie-Smith. You'll know my mission, I think, Minister.'

The voice was faint, distorted. 'Petrie-Smith, yes. My dear fellow, isn't this indiscreet?'

'Perhaps, but it's also most urgent. I repeat, most urgent. This is in reference to a certain personage held in Valparaiso. I have instructions for you and these instructions must remain strictly within the limits of Chile – do you understand fully, Minister? There is to be no telegraph communication with Whitehall – this is vital for the safety of the personage, for his very life.' Half-hyde had secured an attentive ear; wrapped in the powerful glory of a person ranking only just below the Permanent Under-Secretary of State, he issued his orders, rammed them home firmly in an authoritative voice, listened to expostulations about the time customarily taken over extradition proceedings, dealt with this tartly, then replaced the receiver upon its hook and turned to Major Barnsley.

'Thank you, Major. Rest assured that the warrant for which you heard me ask is intended only to secure Admiral Daintree's release. He will face no charges upon his safe return to England.'

'A *false* warrant, sir?'

'A stratagem in a good cause. You have been of much assist-ance, Major Barnsley, and your good lady brews a magnificent cup of tea. A very good day to both of you.'

Halfhyde virtually swept out into the street, with Rampling and Todhunter in his wake. Todhunter was shaking with anxiety and anger. 'What did all that mean, Mr Halfhyde?' he deman-ded. 'I've been made party to a blooming lie, and I – '

'In a good cause, I say again. You will have heard my con-versation, but let me summarize : as fast as the railway can bring it, a warrant for Admiral Daintree's arrest in the name of Her

Majesty will arrive from Santiago, signed and stamped by Her Majesty's Minister himself, with a request that Daintree be handed over to British justice to be dealt with for bankruptcy offences – '

' But really – '

' Which you yourself have confirmed are extraditable offences – '

' Extradition can take blooming months – '

' So said the Minister, my dear Todhunter, but in this case I think the matter will be speedily dealt with. Admiral Daintree must be an embarrassment to the Chilean authorities, and this will appear as an intervention by the Lord to save their faces. You, Mr Todhunter, will confront General Oyanedel with your warrant, you will serve it upon Admiral Daintree, and you will arrest him.'

Todhunter blew out his breath through set teeth. 'And then what, for heaven's sake, Mr Halfhyde?'

' Then, Mr Todhunter, arrangements having been made by us in the meantime, Admiral Daintree vanishes from the scene.'

' But why vanish, Mr Halfhyde? Cannot we take Admiral Daintree out to his ship, all open and obvious without *vanishing*?'

' No, Mr Todhunter, that would never do. Our stratagem will not hold water for long, I fear. We shall tell General Oyanedel that Admiral Daintree will be taken south by road or train to Puerto Montt to be embarked aboard one of Captain Watkiss' vessels. General Oyanedel will then direct his efforts, should word reach him of our chicanery, towards re-arresting Daintree either en route or in Puerto Montt. What will actually happen is this : we shall seek the assistance of a merchant shipmaster in need of a crew, and a crimp-house where drunken men are customarily shanghai-ed to sea.'

' But the Minister, sir ! Surely he'll – '

' Check?' Halfhyde laughed. 'Not with Whitehall, I fancy ! With your Salvation Army citadel here in Valparaiso, without a doubt – and will be informed by a major of unimpeachable integrity that Mr Petrie-Smith's identity and bona fides were most amply vouched for by a canon of the Church of England

and also by your good self – a Detective Inspector of the Metropolitan Police, no less, an officer already known to the Minister as being here in Chile and to whom the warrant is to be addressed – ' Halfhyde broke off as the policeman clutched excitedly at his arm and pointed down the sleazy street. 'What is it, Mr Todhunter?'

'Sir, it's the traitor Savory! As God's my judge I do believe it's Savory!'

Todhunter took to his heels, belting after what he imagined to be his quarry, a hand feeling automatically for his Metropolitan Police whistle. Halfhyde, who had quite failed to identify anyone who looked remotely like Savory, ran behind. Behind again came Canon Rampling, his cassock billowing in a black cloud like a street-bound thunderstorm and his bull-like face shining with the sweat of exertion as though he were chasing a cow in season.

TWELVE

Todhunter stopped and swore : ' Bother take it !'

' Gone ?'

' I wouldn't be sure now that it *was* him, Mr Halfhyde, not altogether.'

' As for me, I saw no one – '

' No, Mr Halfhyde, I fear it was a misidentification after all, a flight of fancy such as can happen to anybody.'

' Quite, quite.'

Canon Rampling pounded up. ' Where did the man go ?'

' He vanished,' Todhunter said, angry with himself for professional ineptitude. ' Just simply blooming well vanished, but I don't believe it was him anyway.' He looked around : they had stopped immediately outside a brothel and there was a vacancy for a client : a woman stared lewdly from a window, and made an inviting gesture, and another of a different nature at the cassocked figure of an obvious heretic in church clothing. ' Shall we move on, Mr Halfhyde ?' Todhunter asked.

' As you wish. Are you certain the man didn't go in there ?'

' Quite certain, thank you.' Mr Todhunter shooed hysterically at a crowd of small boys who had gathered and were making shrill Spanish comments, and giggling. When the attentions followed him down the street, he looked desperate and felt in his pocket for small change, looking frugally at an English penny when he had withdrawn it : Mr Todhunter, whose remuneration as a Detective Inspector was not large, disliked parting with money, but needs must when the devil drove. He was, however, prevented in the nick of time.

Halfhyde put a hand on his arm. 'I wouldn't if I were you, Mr Todhunter. They'll never leave you alone afterwards. Unless you want to buy their sisters, of course.'

The penny went back into Todhunter's pocket fast and he pursed his lips. Halfhyde raised his voice in a quarterdeck bellow, and the small boys scampered to a safe distance. 'Let us take time by the forelock, Mr Todhunter, and let not the grass grow beneath our feet! This is where we split our forces.'

'Oh, yes, sir?'

'I suggest you go back to Major Barnsley and pass the night beneath the citadel roof. The citadel is where the Minister's despatch will be sent. Whilst awaiting its arrival, you'd do well to enlist the Major's aid in finding a suitable shipmaster for our purpose – one, that is, who lacks members of his crew.'

'Surely, Mr Halfhyde, ships arrive here with full crews?'

'Yes, but some fall sick and others jump ship to seek their fortunes in the gold mines and other places. And many ship-masters must be good Salvationists, and will call upon the citadel to take tea – is that not so?'

'Yes, I dare say it is, but – '

'Then go to it, Mr Todhunter,' Halfhyde said, placing a friendly arm about the policeman's shoulder. 'At the same time keep your ears acock-bill for word of Savory . . . but of course without compromising your conscience as a Salvationist.'

'Of course, Mr Halfhyde. And you, if I may make so bold?'

'You may. I shall be investigating the other side of the coin so to speak – the crimp-houses, and the boarding-house masters who run them. It would be unsafe to try to shuffle Admiral Daintree out in a boat ourselves, but the port authorities are always in the pockets of the crimps, and will never question a senseless load of drunks being ferried to the sailing ships in the anchorage – the trade is a legitimate and licensed one, as it happens, although the men who form the stock-in-trade are sup-posed to be both sober and willing rather than drunk and incapable of protest. When you find your shipmaster, Mr

Todhunter, be very certain he is bound home around Cape Horn, and not across the Pacific and the Southern Ocean for Australia!' Halfhyde caught the parson's eye. 'And now there is you, Padre. Whom do you wish to accompany?'

'Neither, thank you,' was the tart reply. 'I would feel out-of-place overnight in both establishments, I fancy. I shall return to military headquarters to be available should my Admiral have a need of me.'

*   *   *

In the gloom of the various store-rooms below the waterline, amid a variegated stench of paint and oil and turpentine, potatoes growing mouldy, paraffin, weevily biscuits and salt pork, stagnant drinking water and worm-ridden sides of beef, Mr Perrin and Assistant Paymaster Luckings moved warily behind the eerie glow of candle lanterns. Rats they could hear and smell and sometimes feel; occasionally they could be seen as pairs of eyes shining brightly in the lanterns before moving away at great speed and with shrill squeaks of anger and frustration. The filthy diseases mentioned by Captain Watkiss were much on their minds; true, the rats could be presumed not to have gone ashore to consort with other rats, dago rats, but one never knew; some diseases were airborne. With the leaders of the extermination party moved also their entourage: Master-at-Arms Titmuss in his frock coat with three brass buttons on either cuff, and his sword; the gunner's mate with a cutlass; and a number of able-seamen with rifles and bayonets. Each time a rat was sighted, the excitement was tremendous: sword and cutlass flashed and the rifles were discharged in a below-decks pandemonium of smoke, flame, noise and smell. In the store-rooms there were casualties: some tins of bully beef pierced, a sack of rice colandered and, worst tragedy of all, in the spirit room a barricoe of rum was broached by a bullet; whether this was intentional or not, the Master-at-Arms shouted wrathfully about stupid clumsy buggers who shouldn't ever have bloody joined and needed a something nanny to hold their fornicating hands. 'With respect, young sir,' he added to

Mr Midshipman Perrin as the rum gushed and was stemmed by a thumb.

'That's all right, Master.'

'Yessir, thankee, sir. The rum, now. The spillage when I removes me thumb. There's a routine laid down, sir, as is incumbent upon me to remind you of.'

This was nearly true. At the daily spirit issue of three-water grog to leading hands and below and neat rum to the virtuous petty officers who would not dream of bottling it except out of sight of officers, there was always some excess left over from the watering-down, which was seldom measured exactly. It was customary for the executive officer attending the issue to give the formal order: 'Throw it in the scuppers.' 'The scuppers', strictly the drainholes on deck, was a term fairly liberally interpreted, but duty had been done, the order given. Now reminded, Mr Perrin did his duty.

'Throw it in the scuppers, Master.'

'Aye, aye, sir.' The Master-at-Arms swiftly produced his own personal scupper, bottle shaped, and gathered in that of the gunner's mate in addition. These he filled, then turned the barricoe hole-up so no more rum flowed out. 'It being the case, young sir, that the scuppers ain't exactly here but can be poured into later on, see. All right, sir?'

Mr Perrin was too young to dispute the facts. 'All right, Master, carry on,' he said. Assistant Paymaster Luckings looked on in mute astonishment: much was wrong with the Navy if this sort of thing passed for discipline, but he was merely a bird of passage, so why worry? Probably, if he remonstrated, no one would take any notice of him in any case. Meanwhile, the Master-at-Arms was not yet at the end of his ingenuity.

'It being the case also, young sir,' he said obsequiously, pulling down his frock coat, 'that you are the senior executive orficer here present, might I make a suggestion?'

'Go ahead, Master.'

'Yessir, very well then, sir.' The Master-at-Arms' voice was virtuous and held no hint of 'be it on your own head'. He went on, 'It's open to you, young sir, if you so wish, to make your own splice the mainbrace order. Just those of us what's here, like. Better'n see it go to waste by 'vaporating in the atmosphere, sir.'

'Can't the rum be transferred to another barricoe, Master?'

The answer was prompt. 'Oh, no, sir, no! That's agin Queen's Regulations and Admiralty Instructions, sir. That buggers up, if you'll pardon me, the whole spirit issue, that does, sir. The books an' records, like.' The Master-at-Arms sniffed. 'Hanging offence, sir, in a manner o' speaking.'

'Oh, I see.'

'Yessir. And the air's got at it, now, see. You'll give the order, then, sir? It's bin a hard afternoon, sir. Not a bloody corpse and too much ammo expended, as the gunner's mate'll testify.' The Master-at-Arms paused. 'Well, sir?'

With reluctance, Perrin nodded. There was, he felt, a catch somewhere. Holes could be plugged, air or no air, but . . . 'Very well, Master,' Perrin said.

'Yessir. Give the order, sir, if you please. Just to set the record straight, like, sir.'

'Splice the mainbrace,' Perrin said. And they did. Rum slopped about. They fell to, all of them, even Petrie-Smith who was in an aggressively anti-Watkiss mood. Time passed. On deck the day grew dark. The rats scuttled about in safety outside the hatch of the spirit-room, which the Master-at-Arms had sagely clamped down from inside. They reached the singing stage and passed through it to the sentimental, nostalgic one when thoughts of home and mother and the missus took over. They had passed into the thoughtful and silent stage when the peace of the spirit-room was shattered by two almighty blasts on the steam syren, which Engineer Duffett, in obedience to the Captain's wishes, had supplied with an immense pressure of steam.

Mr Perrin, fear striking into his heart, leapt to his feet and then sagged against a bulkhead. 'Action Stations!' he said in a thick voice, and the gunner's mate seized an empty rum barricoe and thudded it against the hatch as if beating to quarters with a whole tattoo of the drums of the Royal Marine Light Infantry.

*   *   *

'Mr Mottram! Balls and bang me arse, where's that blasted gunner?' Watkiss leaned from his compass platform, hurling blasphemy into the night.

The response came from immediately before the bridge. 'Here, sir.'

'Jesus Christ inside a starboard light!' Watkiss roared furiously. 'What's happened to my blasted ship's company? They're all rotten! Rotten, every man-jack of 'em, d'you hear me, Mr Mottram?'

'Yes, sir, but – '

'I'll have every bugger's balls for breakfast, just see if I don't. God give me strength to endure. Mr Lamphorn!'

'Yes, sir?'

'You took almost *five minutes* to bring my ship to quarters, Mr Lamphorn, and the fact will be noted in the deck log. All captains of guns are to be placed in the report, too, and I'm damned if I don't punish every blasted so-called petty officer by warrant.' Watkiss seethed to the port side of the compass platform and back again to confront the Officer of the Watch. 'Not only slow to respond, either! The watch was too damn blind to see von Merkatz moving, or was wilfully helping the bloody Hun! The alarm was given too damn late – '

'Sir, the steam syren stuck at first – '

'*What*!'

'It failed to respond to the lanyard, sir.'

'Then God help Mr Duffett! I'll feed him into his own boilers, or drop him into the bay with bars of pig-iron secured to his blasted feet. The ship is sick – sick – sick.' Each repetition of the word brought Watkiss' telescope sharply into Lamphorn's stomach. 'As for you, Mr Lamphorn, you are a damn leper.'

'Yes, sir.' Lamphorn backed away, and Watkiss chased, striking out with his telescope until, with relief, Lamphorn saw something he could usefully report. 'Sir, the German squadron – it's anchoring, sir!'

'Is it indeed!' Captain Watkiss swung round and glared out

ahead: the *Meridian* had swung at her anchor, and was facing von Merkatz to seaward. The rattle and roar of outgoing cable was clearly to be heard: for a certainty the Germans were letting go their anchors, and Watkiss knew very well why. In a fury, he said so: 'Mr Lamphorn, do you see what your blasted ineptitude, your blasted slowness, and your blasted stupidity in not testing the damn syren in advance has led to? Do you, you fool? If you don't, I'll tell you: von Merkatz has turned the tables upon me! Instead of me blocking the Hun in, the bugger's now blocking *me* in!' He shook his telescope. 'You let him creep past me in the dark like some damn poacher! By God, you're not fit even to be a game-keeper, are you!'

'I'm sorry, sir – '

'Oh, hold your tongue. Send for Petrie-Smith or whatever he calls himself, I may decide to blow von Merkatz out of the water. And where's Mr Perrin, may I ask, and why is he absent from his action station?'

* * *

Far to the north in Valparaiso, Halfhyde had been passing an interesting night with no sleep at all. To begin with he had accompanied Todhunter back to the Salvation Army, where Major Barnsley was persuaded to supply him with plain clothes in place of his lieutenant's uniform: an officer resplendent in gold braid might, in seafaring quarters, appear all too reminiscent of the press gang of old and might inhibit tongues. With a flat cloth cap, a muffler, serge trousers and a very old and dirty jacket of broadcloth, Halfhyde felt more suitably clad; and was able, without exciting any comment, to enter a bar on the waterfront, then another and another. In these bars, knowing the night might be a long one and that he would need his wits about him, he practised moderation and diluted his whisky liberally with water. He rubbed shoulders with seamen of many nations, German, American and British predominating, men who became progressively more drunk as the night wore on. Not all the clients were seafarers: there were native Chileans, men who worked in the docks, men from the country districts who had business in town. There were also foreign nationals who were not seamen, Americans and Europeans, many of them from up country, whose business in mines and ranches brought them to Valparaiso and who were disporting themselves in seeing how the other half lived, drank and fornicated. In the main these persons stayed only three parts drunk, having a reasonable regard for their immediate future; others did not, and it was these, the dead drunks, who formed the nuts and bolts of the boarding-house masters' trade in human beings. When they passed out, they would be hauled off to be dumped on the floors of boarding-houses to vomit, urinate and be robbed; negotiations would then be conducted with shipmasters lacking crews, and in the morning a mixed bag of cowhands, mineworkers, clerks and a handful of genuine seamen would wake up to find themselves aboard a homeward-bounder with a cruel passage of Cape Horn in prospect and the first mate's leather seaboot poised to kick them aloft to the masts and yards when the boatswain's hose had sluiced away the night's vomit. . . .

A hand descended on Halfhyde's shoulder.

He turned from the bar. A big man stood by him, a man as big as Canon Rampling, with a heavy face badly marked by acne in youth, a youth long past. The nose had been partially eaten away by venereal disease, the eyes were small, sharp and shrewd, the expression was friendly, the generosity open, but greed was in the face too, which gave the lie to the generosity. 'A drink for the señor,' the man called to the bartender. 'And for me.' He laid down coins. 'On your ownsome, eh?' he said to Halfhyde.

'That's right.' Halfhyde gave a realistic hiccup, and lolled against the bar. 'You British?'

'Australian. You from a ship out in the bay?'

Halfhyde shook his head. 'No. I'm no sailor.' The whisky came and he knocked it back.

'Another?'

'Thanks.'

The order was repeated. The man asked, 'What's your work, limey?'

'Mining engineer. I've come in from Tarapaca.'

'Gold, eh.'

'That's right, gold.' Halfhyde gave a laugh that ended in a belch. 'It's a living, you might say.'

'Too right, limey, too right.' The man looked at Halfhyde's glass; it was empty again. 'Another?'

'Have this one on me.' Halfhyde pulled out some Chilean money, acquired from Major Barnsley in exchange for his sterling. 'What's it to be?'

'Scotch.'

Halfhyde gave the order, taking another whisky himself. His capacity for whisky was in fact large; but he allowed exaggerated results to show. After a while he and the Australian were joined by another man, a squat South American Indian, probably from Peru or Brazil or the Argentine, a man who grunted a few words of English and showed much capacity for free drink. The Australian provided liberally, having a vested interest. The evening wore on, there was song, there were women, one of whom danced upon the bar counter almost naked. Halfhyde allowed his head to sink into his arms which he had laid upon the bar; the squat Indian, who in a short time consumed three full glasses of neat firewater, slumped to the floor in a heap. Halfhyde found another whisky pushed against his hand, and he reached out groggily and drank it. Enough was enough; he joined the Indian on the floor-boards. There was a perfunctory clicking of the tongue from the Australian, who bent and seized the collars of the two drunks. No one took any notice as the bodies were dragged to the door. The singing and dancing continued and the two men were dragged outside and deposited on the ground, which was wet: torrential rain had started, making it a filthy night. Halfhyde was soon drenched. The Australian, who on emergence had emitted a shrill whistle, waited and picked at his teeth with a pin, guarding something like twenty pounds sterling plus extras as yet to be assessed, a fair night's work. Within a few minutes a cart had rumbled up behind a sad-looking donkey with sores covering its back; Halfhyde and his companion were loaded into the cart beneath a canvas hood and the tailboard was secured. The

Australian got up to join the driver and the cart rumbled away into the sleazier nether regions of the great seaport. It travelled for some thirty minutes, slowly, and when it stopped the two men were dragged out and carried into a two-storied building with a crumbling front and thrown down upon the bare floor of a windowless room. Before the door was locked upon them, the Australian had rifled Halfhyde's pockets and had removed all his cash, some of which was in large-denomination notes.

*　　　*　　　*

'Sir, it was the rat hunt, sir.' Mr Perrin shook like a leaf but managed to bring the words out without slurring. 'A bullet entered a barricoe, sir, and rum flooded out. That is why I smell, sir.'

Watkiss shook his telescope in the midshipman's face. 'A likely story!'

'But it's true, sir!'

'Master-at-Arms?'

'Yessir. As the young gentleman says, sir, it's true as I stand here, sir.'

'You're drunk, man!'

'Beggin' your pardon, sir, that was accidental. The stream of rum, sir, entered my mouth, which was at that time open in surprise, sir. Some of it became swallowed, sir, some of it landed upon my frock coat, sir.'

'And that, I suppose, is why *you* smell?'

'Yessir, that's correct, sir.' The Master-at-Arms coughed into his hand. 'We was late mustering to quarters, sir, because the damage control parties locked us into the spirit room in error, sir.'

Captain Watkiss, who didn't believe a word of this, swung away in a tantrum and bounced back and forth, up and down the compass platform in the darkness, glaring ahead at the Germans, who had now lit their anchor lights as bold as brass. God, how von Merkatz must be laughing up his damn sleeve! What the Master-at-Arms had said about being locked in by the damage control parties was perhaps true; the damage control parties, and woe betide Mr Pinch and Mr Duffett, had undeniably wrought other havoc that night: a hatch into the double bottoms had been left open and Petrie-Smith had fallen through. He had climbed out again, but too late to offer advice the one time it might have been sought, and the stench he had brought with him, a stench of long dead rats and cockroaches, bilge-water, foul gases and excreta that had missed the proper channels into the sea, had obliterated any evidence of rum. True, Petrie-Smith was staggering about like a drunk, but then so would anyone who had fallen into the dreadful atmosphere of the double bottoms, and Petrie-Smith had roundly denied any impropriety. Captain Watkiss knew very well why: a person ranking as a senior clerk in Her Majesty's Foreign Office, than whom there were few more illustrious in the land, could scarcely admit a drunken orgy in a warship's spirit room in company with common ratings. That they had all been blotto, Captain Watkiss knew very well, but they were sober now if only under the spur of total fear and there was absolutely no real evidence so long as they all stuck to their stories. Captain Watkiss, recognizing when his head had struck a brick wall, decided upon dignified acceptance of the inevitable. He halted in front of the miscreants and brandished his telescope.

'Get out of my sight!' he roared. 'Stay out! Mr Perrin?'

'Yessir?'

'You're a disgrace to my gunroom and my ship. You'll take the able-seamen detailed for the rat party, and you'll scrub out the double bottoms.'

'Aye, aye, sir.' Perrin saluted.

'After that you'll spend all daylight hours when not on watch going aloft to the foretop and down again, smartly. This will cease only when I say so.' Watkiss blew out his cheeks. 'God damn it, Mr Perrin, if this had been twenty years ago I'd have had you flogged round the fleet!'

*   *   *

Within half an hour of their being locked in the windowless room, a visitor was admitted to view Halfhyde and the Indian, the latter being still unconscious and breathing like a dray horse running uphill. The two bodies were turned over and were prodded with a stick, and over their heads a price for their shipment was agreed: Halfhyde, feigning drunkenness still but listening hard, gathered that the ship was the sailing vessel *Glen Lyon*, the master one Captain Jericho, and the destination Falmouth for orders. Fifteen pounds sterling was agreed for Halfhyde, seven pounds ten for the Indian, and Captain Jericho's boat was waiting to take them out to the departure anchorage in the bay. This information duly taken in, Halfhyde opened an eye. Captain Jericho, clad in tall hat and frock coat, was white-bearded, with a jovial enough face behind the whiskers, and looked a decent man: crews who had deserted were hard to replace by any means save this, and a shipmaster was always being hurried along the ocean routes by his owners. Delay cost money, a great deal of money . . .

Halfhyde got suddenly to his feet. Captain Jericho and the Australian stared. Halfhyde said, 'Good morning, gentlemen. I imagine it is morning by now?'

'It is,' Jericho said in a deep-sea voice. He seemed puzzled, and turned to the Australian. 'This man doesn't appear drunk to me, Felton. What's going on?' Felton said nothing, but looked dangerous, and Jericho turned once more to Halfhyde. 'Are you willing to sail with me?' he asked.

'I am not, Captain, and since I am very sober indeed, you'll not get me to make my drunken cross on the ship's articles of agreement.'

'Then – '

'One moment, Captain. When do you sail from here?'

'In two hours' time, Mister.'

'I see. I shall return to that, if I may, later. Now, Mr Felton, you are about to do business with *me* – '

'I'm buggered if I am.' Felton's voice was flat and final.

'Oh, but you are! You have stolen my money, and I had taken the precaution of writing down the numbers of the notes before you removed them from my person. Your trade in human beings is one thing, theft is another. If I lay a charge with the police authorities, you stand in danger of losing your licence.'

Felton's face filled with blood, the small eyes became smaller, and with a sudden rush he was upon Halfhyde, whom he sent crashing to the floor. Halfhyde squirmed from beneath him and regained his feet. Felton got up and came for him with his fists flailing. Halfhyde shouted at Captain Jericho not to intervene; and a large bunched fist took him a glancing blow on the head. He staggered a little, but landed a return blow right in Felton's face. Blood squirted from torn flesh, and Felton closed in, grasping Halfhyde and holding him close to his body and gradually, with his superior weight, forcing him back against the wall. Letting go with one hand, he seized Halfhyde's jaw with the other and started smashing his head into the wall. Halfhyde felt immense pain and his vision was filled with flashing coloured lights and he did the one thing he could do : freeing a hand he seized the Australian firmly by the throat and squeezed the adam's apple hard. Felton's grip loosened, Halfhyde struck again and a moment later Felton was on his back, unconscious, his jaw possibly broken and a number of teeth protruding through his lips.

'Well done, my man !' Jericho said.

'Thank you, Captain.' Halfhyde rubbed skinned knuckles. 'Now, if you'll be so good, a search of the premises will reveal the stolen money, and I'd be obliged for your testimony to the police if needed. And we shall talk – you and I, and Mr Felton too. You can be of much service to the Crown, Captain Jericho.'

*   *   *

Halfhyde walked in the early morning through the streets of Valparaiso, humming a tune to himself, a tune of Nelson's navy and stirring deeds of long ago. The night's work had been very satisfactory, and now even the rain had cleared and the day was bright. He made his way to the Salvation Army, where Mr Todhunter was breakfasting on porridge followed by good English bacon and eggs. 'My favourite breakfast, Mr Halfhyde, I do declare. You'll join me ?'

'With pleasure, my dear fellow, after a wash and a shave with a borrowed razor if there is such a thing, and the resumption of my uniform.' Halfhyde, directed by Todhunter, found the ablutions and his own clothing and quickly returned to the breakfast table. There being other residents present, it was not possible to exchange confidences and Halfhyde ate fast so as to catch up. Todhunter talked meanwhile of Salvation Army matters, singing the praises of Major and Mrs Barnsley in their running of a home from home. The best hotel, Todhunter averred, in Valparaiso, no, in all Chile. He drank tea, daintily, with his little finger lifted, washing down toast and marmalade.

'You've finished, Mr Todhunter?'

'Yes, thank you, Mr Halfhyde.'

'Then outside with you, and we shall walk, and talk.' They got up and went out into the street, where stalls and small dirty shops were opening up and the brothels were about to enter their brief hour of siesta : few men fornicated immediately after breakfast. Halfhyde noted rising excitement in the Detective Inspector, an excitement that in fact had been there all through breakfast – Todhunter had important news to tell, obviously, and sleuthlike had steeled himself not to call attention to himself and it by hurrying over the meal. Halfhyde said, 'Out with it, Mr Todhunter.'

'Yours first, sir.'

'Very well.' Halfhyde recounted his night's experience. 'Captain Jericho is backing us – he's loyal to the Crown and is a lieutenant of the Royal Naval Reserve, no less! The man Felton has been well brow-beaten into giving temporary lodging to Admiral Daintree once he is released to your custody – and this, I repeat, will be subject to no delay, I am certain – and then Daintree will be ferried incognito, as a common seaman who has been shanghaied, to the *Glen Lyon*. Captain Jericho will delay his sailing until Daintree is ready to be embarked, and then he will leave the port bound towards the Horn.' Halfhyde paused. 'How's that, Mr Todhunter?'

'Excellent, Mr Halfhyde. And just as well, since I have to report failure on my part to secure the services of a shipmaster. But it doesn't matter now, does it? And now, sir, for *my* news.'

There was a pause and then the words almost fell over themselves. 'The traitor Savory, Mr Halfhyde! I have information leading me to suppose, to suppose beyond doubt in fact, that he is presently in Santiago!'

THIRTEEN

The facts as given by the Detective Inspector were simple: during the previous afternoon a steamship out of Liverpool had arrived in Valparaiso and had proceeded, once entry formalities had been completed, to the mole in front of the Customs House. There she had landed four passengers: a Commander Jeavons, retired from the Royal Navy, with his wife; a Miss Slindon, formerly a governess; and a Mr Rufus Ackroyd, a London merchant with interests in Chilean copper and silver ores, who was met by an attentive person from the German consulate.

'How did you find all this out?' Halfhyde asked.

Todhunter said primly, 'As a police officer, you may be sure I have my methods. There is such a thing as . . . well, liaison.'

'So brotherly love reasserted itself?'

'In a manner of speaking, Mr Halfhyde, you might say it did. An officer from the Valparaiso police called at the citadel to make certain enquiries. I was in Major Barnsley's office when he arrived. Major Barnsley accompanied the police officer when the latter went to examine the effects of a fellow Salvationist, a seaman who had unfortunately, it appears, been murdered the previous night – killed, you understand, in a dockland brawl.' Todhunter coughed and seemed more than a little embarrassed. 'The police officer, who happened to mention that he had recently boarded the s s *Taragona*, just in from Liverpool, had left a file of documents on Major Barnsley's desk.'

'And you looked at them, Mr Todhunter?'

'Yes, I did. I felt it was my duty. The police officer having said the German consul had boarded the *Taragona*, had made me, as it were, prick up my ears, Mr Halfhyde.'

'Go on. You begin to interest me.'

'I fancied I might. Well, the top paper in the file contained a list of the passengers aboard the *Taragona*, also a crew list. The name of one passenger, Mr Rufus Ackroyd, had been ringed in pencil, and there was a notation. In Spanish, of course, a tongue with which I am not familiar, but still. It was self-evident, really. *Embajada Alemán*, Santiago. "Allemandes" is Germans in French, so I deduced – '

'I see. Is there any reason why Rufus Ackroyd shouldn't have some connection with the German Embassy?'

'Not really, Mr Halfhyde, no. But it seemed to me there was a certain contiguity of events, an emerging pattern if you follow me. Liverpool, to which city we know the traitor Savory proceeded after his escape . . . the sailing date of the *Taragona*, given on the police officer's documentation, fits also . . . the involvement of the German consul here in Valparaiso, and of the German Embassy in Santiago. My suspicions became aroused.'

'And what did you do, Mr Todhunter?'

'I went aboard the *Taragona*, Mr Halfhyde, using my Metropolitan Police pass to enter the docks – foreigners are very simple people, and are easily impressed by documents and an authoritative manner on the part of the person producing them. I confided in the ship's master, and then I spoke in private to the man Ackroyd's steward. It appeared Ackroyd had lax morals and so had another passenger, Miss Slindon.'

'Cabin crawling?'

'Pardon? Oh – I follow you, Mr Halfhyde, yes. Cabin crawling, very descriptive. A sexual relationship developed.' Todhunter paused. 'Or I should say, was already in existence. That is, according to the steward, who assured me he was not mistaken. Ships' stewards, he said, after a lifetime attending upon passengers, whose morals frequently loosen at sea when the constraints of the land are cast off – I am reporting what was said, you understand, I have no personal experience – '

'Quite, yes.'

'Well, the man used a vulgar expression to convey that Ackroyd and Miss Slindon had been cohabiting before embarkation – '

'If you're about to suggest,' Halfhyde broke in, 'that Ackroyd and Savory are one and the same – '

'Yes, that is what – '

'But presumably Savory had been in Dartmoor until shortly before the *Taragona* left Liverpool?'

Todhunter nodded. 'Certainly. I had not forgotten that, you may be sure. I have more to tell you. The steward was a person who listened at cabin doors. Much of what he heard meant little enough to him, certainly, but when I probed and questioned, it became quite clear in my mind. Among other things, Miss Slindon had been in Chile before . . . and the steward, when shown a photograph of the traitor Savory, stated that he could well be the person known as Ackroyd in spite of certain physical changes no doubt adopted for the specific purpose of disguise.' Todhunter coughed. 'This is not the time to go into great detail, Mr Halfhyde, sir, but you may take my word for it that Ackroyd is the traitor Savory and Miss Slindon, which will be found not to be her real name, was his accomplice, his mistress until he went to gaol, and the woman who made the arrangements prior to his escape for his passage to Chile. We do know that he was visited as often as regulations permited, whilst in Dartmoor Prison, by a female person.' Todhunter brought out a handkerchief and blew his nose vigorously. 'I am confident the traitor Savory and possibly the woman Slindon will be found in Santiago.'

Halfhyde nodded somewhat doubtfully. 'Perhaps, perhaps. A needle in a haystack, however. Santiago's a biggish place.'

'As an officer of the Criminal Investigation Department, I have found many needles in many haystacks, sir.'

'I'm sure you have, but time presses – '

'My duty – '

'*My* duty, Mr Todhunter, is first to Admiral Daintree, and since I believe firmly that extradition proceedings will not be long drawn, I shall require you to extract him from the Chileans as soon as your warrant is to hand. After that, Savory.'

'I protest most strongly. Most strongly!'

Halfhyde put a hand on Todhunter's shoulder. 'Don't take it to heart. There's a better way than scouring Santiago for a man well protected by the German Embassy, I promise you. Remember what Daintree said to the good Canon Rampling: von Merkatz is to sail for Germany – *with Savory*!'

*   *   *

As they walked back to the Salvation Army to await the warrant from the British Minister, Halfhyde reflected upon Savory. Speed was now vital. As soon as Daintree was safely aboard the *Glen Lyon*, he and Todhunter must head south to cut Savory off before he was put aboard the German flagship off Puerto Montt. More than likely Savory would be despatched by train to Osorno; if so, any pursuing journey by road would take much too long. They, too, must take the train, and in advance, and apprehend Savory in Osorno. If, as seemed likely, he was being delivered to von Merkatz under protest, he would be accompanied by an escort. There would be a fight on Chilean soil and diplomacy would go for a burton. Releasing Daintree by a strategem was one thing, and was indeed an affair in which the Chilean authorities were themselves far from blameless in having made such an arrest; but to intercept and overcome – if indeed they could – a Chilean escort, was another. Again, the Chileans had no right to hand a British national over to von Merkatz . . . while the British themselves, in the circumstances of political offences not being extraditable, had no rights either. It was going to be devilish tricky. . . .

Shortly after Halfhyde and Todhunter had returned to the citadel, a special messenger arrived off the train from Santiago with an envelope addressed to Detective Inspector Todhunter, Metropolitan Police. In it was the warrant, duly and impressively signed in the name of Her Britannic Majesty, and also a letter, sealed into another envelope, from the British Minister to

His Excellency General Oyanedel, Military Governor of Valparaiso.

'I don't like it, Mr Halfhyde,' Todhunter said.

'Courage, my dear fellow! You'll be proud to tell your grand-children of your part in this, one day.'

'Grandchildren!' Todhunter said bitterly. 'Why, I'm not even married!'

*   *   *

Before going to the military headquarters Halfhyde once again used Barnsley's telephone and called the British consul; arrangements were made for a carriage to be in attendance outside the headquarters building for the conveyance of Admiral Daintree. In it would be a parcel containing clothes appropriate to a person about to be shanghai-ed. This settled, Halfhyde went with Todhunter to Oyanedel's headquarters but did not go at once to the General. Instead he sought out Canon Rampling, finding him in his room checking his communion set.

'Ah, Halfhyde, I was becoming anxious.'

'Without need, Padre, since all is well. Are you busy?'

Rampling indicated his stock-in-trade. 'I'm about to administer communion to Daintree. Not that he's asked for it, but it's a means of keeping in touch.'

'With more than God! I'm glad. There's something you can do, if you will, and it must be done quickly.' In as few words as possible Halfhyde explained his plans for the future, adding, 'Daintree has to know the charges we trumped up, or he'll give the game away when he's sent for by Oyanedel.'

Rampling nodded without enthusiasm. 'I see your point, of course, but how does one tell an admiral he's being accused of bankruptcy offences? He's as rich as Croesus as it happens.'

'Hasn't he a sense of humour?'

'Not the sort that would be relevant.'

'Then you must do your best, Padre, and pray as you've never prayed before.' Halfhyde pulled out his watch, and glanced at Todhunter, who was looking pale and nervous. 'I'll give you ten minutes from now, Padre, then I'll ask for an interview with Oyanedel. Soon after that, I imagine, Daintree is likely to be sent for.'

'You don't think this ploy will fail, Halfhyde?'

Halfhyde shook his head. 'I do not. Her Majesty's Minister . . . the Chileans won't cut off too many of their noses to spite their faces, Padre! British trade's vital.'

'And the Germans?'

'They're still in the process of trying to get a foot in. With any luck, we'll put a spanner in the works.'

'Not via Daintree, I assume?'

'No. Via Savory.'

Rampling looked blank. 'How?'

'I don't know yet.' Once again, Halfhyde looked at his watch. Rampling took the hint, snapped shut the lid of his mobile communion set, and left the room buttoning up his cassock. Halfhyde and Todhunter waited, then, when the ten minutes had passed, Halfhyde led the way to the ante-room to which they had been taken on their original arrival from Puerto Montt. There he jerked at a bell-pull. Within a couple of minutes an A D C entered and gave a stiff bow.

Halfhyde said, 'We would like an interview with General Oyanedel, if you please.'

The A D C smiled a shade bleakly. 'A coincidence, gentlemen. His Excellency wishes also to see you. Please come.'

*   *   *

Captain Watkiss swung round from his roll-top desk where, assisted by his clerk, he was dealing with Admiralty documents regarding stores and requisitions for coal. 'What is it? Oh, it's you, Mr Lamphorn. I'm busy.'

'Yes, sir. It's the man Tidy, sir.'

'Tidy?' Watkiss looked blank.

'The churchwarden from Yorkshire, sir, Canon Rampling's man.'

'God! What about him, pray?'

'He wishes to ask you for news of the rector, sir.'

'Rector!' Watkiss pushed himself back at arm's length from his desk. 'Is that what he said, *rector*?'

'Yes, sir.'

There was a hissing sound. 'Tell him there isn't any such person and there isn't any news.' Another angry sound emerged. 'Tell him something else: tell him ratings do not make direct approaches to any officer, let alone the Captain, but put their requests through their divisional petty officers. Tell him that, Mr Lamphorn, and go away.'

Lamphorn stood his ground. 'He says he's personal servant to the re – to the chaplain, sir, not a rating as such – '

'Then tell him he's wrong.' Watkiss waved his arms as Lamphorn attempted to speak again. 'Go away or your name will be put in the deck log for disobedience of my orders.'

Lamphorn gave it up. There was no point, really, in telling the Captain that Tidy had in fact further wishes – that he wished to be put ashore, and journey by rail to Valparaiso to join his rector – for Watkiss would have been unlikely to agree in any case. But Tidy was a Yorkshireman, one who did not give up easily. When told by Lamphorn that his quest was fruitless, Tidy went with aggrieved but determined manner to his hammock stowage, and packed his belongings in a kitbag. Then he climbed, breathing hard under the kitbag's weight, to the quarterdeck, where he had what he later described as a piece of 'reet good luck': a cutter had been called away and was dropping aft to the accommodation ladder from the lower boom.

Tidy, somewhat bow-legged, approached Mr Perrin. 'Eh, lad.'

Perrin looked surprised. 'What?'

'Wheer's boat going?'

'Inshore – Puerto Montt for beef. Why?'

'Reckon I'm going in it, young feller-me-lad,' Tidy said firmly.

'Have you been given permission?' Mr Perrin asked, looking baffled.

'Aye, the Lord's. Reckon thee'll stop me, eh?' Tidy's Yorkshire face loomed before the midshipman, self-contained and sure of itself. 'I'm not one o' you pressed men, I'm rector's warden, free t'come, free t'go an' all – t'Admiralty says so.' Tidy moved towards the ladder in the wake of two ratings bearing coils of rope and heavy blocks. 'I'll be coming back again, don't fret.'

*   *   *

With General Oyanedel was the familiar, happy face of General Codecino. Oyanedel was looking relieved; his own high command had in fact already confirmed that Admiral Daintree, as a result of an intervention by the British Minister, was to be released to Todhunter's custody – and released, as Halfhyde had been hoping, immediately; the prognosis had evidently been correct – Daintree had become an embarrassment and now that the loophole was offered the Chileans couldn't wait to be rid of him, especially as he would be going home in disgrace and arrest.

'The laws of extradition,' Oyanedel said smoothly, 'must of course be obeyed, and in view of your government's representations as conveyed by His Excellency the British Minister in Santiago, they are indeed being greatly expedited. Your Admiral will not now be proceeded against in regard to his insult to our flag – at least, not in our country. I trust your British authorities will bear in mind what he has done.'

'Oh, yes indeed, sir,' Todhunter said, relief spreading in sweat upon his brow. 'It's been most reprehensible. He'll be dealt with, never fear!'

'Good. He will be free to go in a few minutes so far as we are concerned.' Oyanedel spoke to his ADC, who left the chamber. 'How is he to reach England, Lieutenant Halfhyde? His ships will also be free to leave when the formalities have been completed. Will he travel in arrest in his own squadron?'

'I think that would be untactful considering his high position, General,' Halfhyde said. In point of fact, a new dimension had arisen: with the cruiser squadron free to leave, it would in theory be possible to take Daintree straight off to his flagship. On the other hand, 'formalities' on sailing from Chilean ports could take time and Halfhyde felt in his bones that his stratagem could not

165

hold out for much longer; already, perhaps, the telegraph lines would be busy from the Chilean authorities in Santiago to Whitehall, seeking further elucidation. Whitehall and its valuable senior clerks might understand, reading between the lines, and might co-operate, but probably would not: totally barefaced lies were seldom the currency of governments, at least when they were ultimately checkable, and the politicians would play for safety. Besides, it could be dangerous to change horses, as it were, at this stage. The original plan must be adhered to and the sooner Daintree could be put into the hands of the crimp and Captain Jericho, the better. . . . Halfhyde went on, tongue in cheek, 'He'll be taken to Puerto Montt, General, for embarkation aboard one of the sloops that acted as escorts for the *Meridian.*'

'By the train?'

'By the train.' This was dangerous, since Halfhyde, Rampling and Todhunter, minus Daintree, would be aboard the train themselves shortly and could be handily placed for arrest when the truth emerged; but Halfhyde saw no alternative. Codecino might offer his carriage, but in the carriage the British Admiral's absence could scarcely be concealed from the General. . . .

Oyanedel seemed about to speak again when a racket was heard from outside the room: a thin voice raised in very loud complaint, accompanied by the soothing tones of Canon Rampling. Just as Oyanedel's ADC appeared in the doorway ahead of Daintree and Rampling, there was the sound of a crash and a chalice rolled past the ADC's feet. Rampling burst in, looking furious, gathered up the chalice and replaced it in his communion box, which he snapped shut with an aggressive movement. Then Admiral Daintree appeared, shaking with anger. White hair stuck out like a fringe around a face pale and set. The mouth was like a rat-trap. Halfhyde stepped forward, catching Rampling's forbearing look in passing. He addressed the Admiral.

'Sir – '

'So you're the man,' Daintree snapped.

'Sir, if I – '

'I'll have you court martialled, young man. I'll have the bloody Padre court martialled. I'll have the Ambassador court martialled. I am far from bankrupt and I have never committed an offence in my life. I refuse to leave Valparaiso. General Oyanedel, I expect you to preserve me against the evil machinations of these persons.'

FOURTEEN

There was a tense silence; Rampling whispered in Halfhyde's ear: 'He simply wouldn't listen, I'm afraid. He only took in the charge, not the explanation. He believes he's upset someone at the Admiralty and this is their idea of revenge. Something like that, at all events.'

Admiral Daintree meanwhile had advanced upon Oyanedel, who was now standing behind his desk, a massive knee-hole affair that would hold the enraged Briton at some distance unless he should outflank it. Oyanedel said flatly, 'I am most sorry. I cannot stand in the way of an extradition. You must now leave Chile.'

'I shall not.'

'The orders state – '

'You have no authority to hand me over to vandals.'

Oyanedel stared, started to say something, then burst out into laughter. Through the rat-trap mouth Daintree said, 'You are a rude man.'

'No, Admiral, it was you who was rude – you insulted our flag and through it our country and our President.'

'I am prepared to do it again. You are a hard man as well as rude – '

'No. This is not by my wish – '

'I am an old man and my character is under attack.'

Oyanedel shrugged. 'All must obey the law, of their own and other countries. High officers must be incorruptible.'

Much colour came to Daintree's pale cheeks. He lifted a

shaking hand and pointed at the Chilean. 'Ho! Incorruptible indeed! Like all dagoes you've been lining your pockets – your hand constantly in the till of state I don't doubt for one moment!' There was, at the corner of General Oyanedel's desk, a small replica of the national flag of Chile mounted upon a model of the House of Congress in Santiago, which acted as a paperweight. Admiral Daintree's jaw moved in sudden activity, his mouth gathering spit. Seeing this, Halfhyde lost no more time.

'Mr Todhunter, serve your warrant, if you please.'

'I, Mr Halfhyde?'

'You are the police officer, Mr Todhunter.'

'Yes, but an Admiral – '

'Get on with it!' Halfhyde hissed. Daintree's mouth filled. In the nick of time Todhunter interposed himself and laid a hand on Daintree's shoulder. Involuntarily, Daintree swallowed; the moment of prime danger passed.

'Sir, I – '

'Who are you?'

'Detective Inspector Todhunter, sir, of the Metropolitan Police.'

'Really?' Daintree's thin shoulders sagged. The rat-trap mouth trembled.

'Yes, sir, I'm afraid so.' Sweating slightly, Todhunter opened his Gladstone bag and brought out the warrant, coughed, shot his cuffs, and began in a solemn voice: 'Clement William de la Poer Daintree, Rear-Admiral in Her Majesty's Fleet. I arrest you in the name of the law. You are not obliged to say anything but if you do so what you say will be taken down in writing and may be offered in evidence.' The solemn voice of the law's retribution fumbled a little. 'Oh, dear, Mr Halfhyde, the Admiral seems unwell . . .'

*   *   *

Todhunter, placing his Gladstone bag carefully on the floor of the official-looking brougham provided by the British consul, leaned across and whispered to Halfhyde, 'I believe his angry

169

response to have been the best possible for our purpose.' He glanced across at Daintree, revived fairly speedily by the administration of smelling-salts provided by General Oyanedel's ADC. 'He was so angry that it could not appear otherwise than entirely genuine.'

'Quite so.' Daintree was still not entirely *compos mentis* and Halfhyde could only hope the shock had not had some ill effect upon his mind: certainly, according to Rampling, his arrest and detention by the Chileans had done him no good, and God alone could say what might be the result of Todhunter's supposed arrest of him. However, explanations would be better left until they reached the premises of the Australian crimp, for which they were now bound as fast as the horse could take them. Daintree sat small and forlorn in a corner, attended by his chaplain. His eyes stared blankly from the window at the passing scene; it was just as well he would be a passenger to the Falklands, Halfhyde thought. He was in no state to command a cruiser squadron, but, even in his present condition, there was something about him, some sort of emanation of an innate obstinacy akin to that of Watkiss, that said he would try to do so. In the meantime there was work to be done: Daintree's gold-encrusted monkey-jacket was removed, and a merchant seaman's pilot-cloth watchcoat was substituted; the oak-leaved cap went into Todhunter's Gladstone bag, Daintree's protests being ignored. They reached the semi-derelict house and the carriage stopped. Rampling took Daintree in his arms and brought him out of the carriage like a baby, an unpopular act that went far towards restoring the Admiral's health.

'Leave me alone.'

'You are ill, sir.' Rampling held on as the Admiral's feet touched ground.

'Utter nonsense, complete drivel. Why am I being brought to such a place?'

Rampling looked at Halfhyde. Halfhyde said, 'Come inside, sir, and you shall be told all.'

Taking a pace forward, Daintree sniffed. 'Looks like a brothel.'

'I assure you it is not, sir.'

'Pity.' There was a brief cackle of dry laughter: Daintree was improving. The carriage was despatched back to the consulate, the driver under dire threat as to what would happen to wagging tongues, and the party moved inside, along the narrow passage that formed the hallway, Todhunter bringing up the rear with his Gladstone bag and its important contents. From the end of the passage came the Australian, his expression sour.

'This 'im?'

'Yes,' Halfhyde answered, and his face hardened. 'He's to be properly treated with the respect due to an old gentleman, and you'll remember to keep a still tongue in your head – or else. I need not, I think, remind you that Her Majesty's Government has a long arm wherever in the world you may be.'

The Australian sucked his teeth. ''Ow about the cash, eh?'

'It will be paid to you by Captain Jericho as soon as my friend is embarked aboard the boat for the *Glen Lyon*. Not before. You are being well paid and you will make sure you earn the money first.'

'It's generous enough,' the man said ungraciously.

Daintree said, 'I demand an explanation. I think everyone has gone mad. Who is this man?'

Halfhyde gestured to the boarding-house master to make himself scarce. 'Explanations are coming, sir,' he said to Daintree. He led the way into the room where he had been held during the previous night. A chair had been placed ready for the Admiral, and Daintree sat with some relief. 'Now, sir,' Halfhyde said, and told his story. Daintree listened without comment and Halfhyde wondered if indeed he had heard a word, or, if he had heard, whether he had understood. An important point might be worth repetition. 'You are not being arrested, sir. It was a stratagem to free you from the Chileans.'

'I gathered that, Mr Halfhyde. A stupid one if you ask me. They'll be after me the moment they smell it out. But I must confess I'm most relieved not to continue in that policeman's clutches.' Daintree blew out his cheeks. 'Well, you'd better get me aboard my flagship at once, had you not?'

'No, sir, it would be better not. I have planned something

safer.' Halfhyde told the Admiral of the arrangements, and Daintree chuckled, seeming oddly pleased.

'Bless my soul, Halfhyde, I never thought I'd land up in a crimp's hands! And a sailing ship . . . a pleasure. I served as a midshipman in the old sailing navy, you know.' He paused. 'My squadron – will my acting Flag Captain be told the facts?'

'He will, sir, by means of a boat from the *Glen Lyon* – I've asked Captain Jericho to pass messages after nightfall, and this he would have found a way of doing whatever the difficulties, but now his task is eased, since the Chilean guardship will be withdrawn. Jericho will pass orders, if you approve them, for your squadron to leave for the Falklands, rendezvousing with the *Glen Lyon* off Chiloé Island outside Puerto Montt for you to be transferred back to your flagship.'

'Yes. Well done, Halfhyde.' Daintree frowned somewhat disagreeably. 'Captain Watkiss, now. He's to become my Flag Captain. How's he to join?'

'That has yet to be gone into, sir, but I suggest that if all goes well and if the time element can be made to fit he also can rendezvous off Chiloé Island with his sloops, after handing over the *Meridian*, and – '

'Yes, yes. Watkiss . . . I didn't *ask* for him, you know. I'm aware of him by repute, not an easy man. It's usual for an admiral to be given a choice, but there we are. Don't know what the service is coming to! However, that's by the way for now. What do you gentlemen wish me to do?'

'Lie low till dark, sir. After dark, Captain Jericho will come for you and another man, a man who is genuinely to be shanghai-ed, and – '

'Poor fellow. I don't approve of shanghai-ing. Which is not to say I'm ungrateful.' Daintree paused. 'I suppose you know about that man Savory?'

'Yes, sir. Your chaplain – '

'Ah yes, the Bible, a clever scheme of Rampling's. Well, to expand on that – Savory's expected to reach Valparaiso – '

'He's landed already, sir.'

'Has he indeed? Well, the Germans are after him – I learned

this during my detention. That's why they entered Puerto Montt instead of Valparaiso. You see, von Merkatz would have expected the *Meridian* to enter Valparaiso, and what with all the jiggery-pokery, *and* the fact he would have known my squadron was in the bay . . . I dare say you can follow his reasoning, Halfhyde. Much easier to take the man aboard from Puerto Montt.'

'Or was, until *Meridian*'s arrival, sir.'

'Yes, indeed. Mind you, the Chileans will be out to prevent von Merkatz embarking him.'

'As, indeed, so shall I be, and Mr Todhunter, who is to arrest him.'

'Then I wish you both luck, my dear fellow. Savory means no good to Her Majesty, you know. I've overheard things . . . there is jiggery-pokery on many sides . . . Oyanedel's a double-dealer, so is that fat fellow Codecino.' Daintree put his head in his hands. 'My brain's in a whirl, you know. So much of it is Greek to a simple sailor, but the gist is that Savory's playing off one side against the other. The original idea was for Savory and von Merkatz to rendezvous out here – Savory's own idea, that. As if by chance . . . and of course that gave Savory the opportunity of making arrangements with the Chileans – '

'To double-cross the German, sir?'

'Yes. I believe so. When my mind clears I may be of more help. Meanwhile, I think you'd better find him, Halfhyde.'

'Easier said than done, sir,' Halfhyde murmured, 'it's not the least of our problems and concerns Mr Todhunter particularly – does it not, Mr Todhunter?'

'Indeed it does, sir, and it is a large problem. Savory's offences against Britain, are, as we know, not extraditable, and Captain Watkiss will not permit him to be arrested on Chilean soil. If such an arrest is made, Captain Watkiss will be sure to refuse to take him aboard whatever I say.' Todhunter almost wrung his hands. 'I'll get it right in the neck from my Chief Super. . . .'

*   *   *

Daintree was left in the safe hands of the crimp, hands that with the promise of money and the threat of information being laid to the authorities about his thieving would, Halfhyde was confident, remain safe. In the meantime the British party made its way to the railway station, having been informed by the consul that, by a stroke of luck, today was the day that the train ran to Osorno in Llanquihue province, some seventy-five miles north of Puerto Montt. The station was a primitive place but busy, with Chileans from town and country lining the dusty tracks and awaiting trains to Santiago, La Ligua, and points east and south. Some of them appeared to be camping out for a long wait: there were signs of cooking utensils and bedding and there were yelling Indian babies stowed in things like quivers on their mothers' backs. Owing to a delay there was to be a wait of some two hours for the train, and having paid for tickets the three conspirators left the station in order to remain inconspicuous in the town, and laid as low as possible upon their return to the station's bustle. Halfhyde, with Daintree's observations to support his theorizing, was confident enough that Savory would sooner or later be transported south to Puerto Montt via the services of the German Embassy in Santiago. Todhunter nagged away about the advisability of attacking the Embassy direct; Halfhyde was short with such suggestions, as he had been earlier. Neither he nor Todhunter could storm into sovereign German territory demanding Savory, and the only result would be to positively alert the Germans to the fact that the British were on the scent.

'They will know this, sir, from Admiral von Merkatz.'

'They will know only that Savory is being looked for. Not that we have definite information. This must be left to me, Mr Todhunter.'

Todhunter sulked; he continued sulking after they had boarded the railway train. The train was not especially full, but the culinary arrangements were non-existent: the Chilean passengers had brought their own picnic-baskets, the contents of which they cruelly demolished from time to time around a hungry Todhunter. The journey was to take two full days, which meant that two nights of terrible discomfort loomed ahead. The seats were immensely hard and the train developed a horrible swing as it chuffed along. The smoke from the engine was terrible, thick and black and choking when it swept back through the windows, beneath one of which sat Mr Todhunter. He argued with a fat Chilean seated opposite, but to no avail; the Chilean liked the window wide open, and he had more than equal rights in his own country. Life was torture, empty of food or drink apart from an occasional swig from Mr Halfhyde's whisky flask that was shared between all three; and he would be bedless at night.

Mr Todhunter suffered.

Thank God, the train stopped at various stations en route, causing delay it was true but also allowing some food to be purchased from native women with donkeys and panniers who awaited the train's arrival. Mr Todhunter bought fresh bread and some fruit, including some dates that did not look particularly fresh, but beggars, as Mr Todhunter's old mother used to say, couldn't be choosers. It may have been the fruit, it may have been the dates; whatever it was, it had an effect upon the Detective Inspector's stomach by next day and he was forced to sit in dreadful pain and misery until the first morning stop, for the train had no lavatory. When the train came to rest, Mr Todhunter got to his feet rapidly and alighted, and found what was meant to be a lavatory in a small shed beside the track. Emerging from this place, Mr Todhunter all but bumped into a person waiting to take his place, one of a long line. Mr Todhunter politely moved aside.

'*Danke schön*,' the man said. The door, only half a door it was, closed upon him. Mr Todhunter's heart pounded: German! Well, well – coincidence, or not? Savory had certainly not been expected to come south so soon. But the British party, remaining inconspicuously out of the way as the Osorno train had steamed slowly into Valparaiso, could very easily have missed the embarkation of a party from the German Embassy – in any case, such a party would no doubt have got aboard in Santiago, would it not? Mr Todhunter made his way back aboard the train thoughtfully, looked out through a window and noted that the German was entering the next coach but one towards the rear. Todhunter then resumed his seat, saying nothing as yet to Halfhyde. First he wished to be sure of his facts, and the train was not an easy place in which to hold a conference anyway; while certainly not packed, there were no completely empty compartments.

The train started off south again, rumbling, jerking, swinging. Todhunter tapped his fingers on the woodwork ledge below the window and every time pungent smoke smote his face and clothing thought balefully about the blooming Chilean opposite him. When the next stop came, Mr Todhunter once again descended, his purpose on this occasion being to change coaches. He leapt aboard the coach containing the German and walked fast along the central corridor. At the end, as in his own coach, there was a compartment to which a closed door gave access. This, he fancied, was a special compartment, superior even to the First Class, for important persons or parties wishing total privacy. Tentatively, under cover of turning round, Mr Todhunter felt the handle.

Locked! Suspicions mounted. In the open compartments there was no sign of the German. Ergo, if he hadn't descended to the lavatory, and there had been no sign of him there, he was beyond the locked door.

Mr Todhunter dithered. He didn't normally dither – never in London. But there was something very off-putting about a foreign country, one false move and you could start a revolution. He dithered too long: with a double jerk the train started off again and Mr Todhunter went flat on his face. In falling he struck an aged countrywoman with a basket of eggs. They broke on the floor, and the revolution started. By the time it had been more or less settled in favour of the countrywoman, who extracted almost all of Mr Todhunter's money by way of compensation, the train had well and truly started and Mr Todhunter was cut off from all assistance. He mopped his brow, bent, and retrieved his bowler hat from beneath a seat. There was some egg on it. Whilst rubbing the egg away, he backed against the locked door of the intriguing compartment behind him, and he caught the sound of a loud laugh, an unmistakably female laugh.

If only he could contact Mr Halfhyde! He hadn't even got

his Gladstone bag with him, with the essential revolver.

Mr Todhunter came away from the door and teetered towards a seat, being thrown about violently as he moved; the track was treacherous, a real disgrace. . . . Mr Todhunter sat gloomily next to a man who smelled of sheep dung; the train rattled on and on. At last it stopped again and Mr Todhunter scuttled for the door to rejoin Halfhyde and the parson and after he had got down to the dirt of the wayside stop the locked door opened, and General Codecino came out to relieve himself beside the track.

*   *   *

There was nothing of Yorkshire about Puerto Montt, but it had taken more than that to stop churchwarden Tidy: once ashore, he managed to make contact with a cart going north, which for a fee would drop him at Osorno, where in due course he arrived with his kitbag and asked the way, by sign language and a deal of shouting in his Yorkshire dialect, to the railway station. Here he dumped his kitbag by the ticket office and, like Todhunter farther north, sought the lavatory and for a similar reason: there was disturbance in his stomach. In his case the cause was different: the appearance of a rash upon his leg had propelled him to the *Meridian*'s sick-bay a couple of days before, and following good naval medical practice the functionary known aboard ship as the po boatswain had prescribed Black Draught, a most noxious liquid fed by Queen's Regulations to all boy ratings under the age of eighteen each Sunday forenoon before church, and to all sick persons. This liquid panacea cured all manner of diseases. In Osorno it had the effect of keeping Tidy occupied for some while, and when he emerged he saw a man, a native in what he believed was a sombrero, handling his kitbag.

'Eh there, lad!' Tidy called, and hastened to the kitbag's protection. 'Doan't thee muck about wi' that, it's mine!'

The sombrero or whatever it was, was lifted and something was said in Spanish, unintelligibly; however, it sounded polite.

Tidy said reluctantly, 'Aye, well, all's well as ends well, just as long as thee knows like.'

There was a wide smile. 'Eenglees, yes?'

'Yorkshire.'

'Not Eenglees, señor?'

'Aye, English, lad.'

'Señor Savoree?'

'No, lad, not me. Henry Tidy's t'name.'

'Not Señor Savoree?'

'No. I just said that, like. Doan't you believe me?' Tidy grew impatient. Yorkshiremen were men of few words and didn't like to have to repeat what they did utter. And natives were natives, thieving so-and-so's mucking about with other people's property! Tidy swiped a hand towards the native, who ducked and looked vicious, as though he wished to kill the Englishman. Thinking better of that, he turned away, but not before Tidy had seen a short, thin dagger half up his sleeve, its blade not quite concealed by the arm and wrist. Small but probably lethal: in these parts they poisoned their knife blades, as Tidy knew. He whistled in concern as the native made off; then he shrugged and went to enquire about tickets and trains. He was right out of luck: he was told there was no train for Valparaiso for the next four days, no less. Tidy was exasperated; he argued, but it was no use, they wouldn't listen. Fed up, Tidy wondered what he was to do now. The rector was a long way off and he couldn't reach him; likely enough by the time the train was ready to go up to Valparaiso, the rector would be on his way back again. Tidy wandered through the ramshackle station building, shaking his head. Looking down the road he saw the knife-bearing local lad and he saw something else too: a man in uniform, naval uniform, turning away from the Chilean and entering a shed, like an engine shed it was . . . Tidy fancied the uniform was German. Not British anyway. A curious sort of headdress, with trailing ribbons, and the jumper was different. It was only then that something stirred in the former churchwarden's mind that should have stirred before: something overheard – no, he told himself a lie, *said* to him aboard the battleship. By the Captain's steward: the name of Savory, the one all the fuss had been about in the newspapers a year or two, maybe three, back. The one the Germans were after, or something.

Savory. *Sa-vor-ee* . . . come to think of it, there was no mistaking it, allowing for English being rendered in a dago tongue. Sir Russell Savory, the traitor!

Once more, Tidy whistled.

He was a conscientious man, wouldn't ever have been rector's warden else. That Watkiss, he was as obstinate as a pig, but duty was duty all said and done. Besides, what the heck was he going to do for four days in Osorno? Tidy humped his kitbag on to his shoulder and left the station. He looked at the shed in passing; the door was closed and he could see no more Germans. Better not pry, perhaps, with that Chilean and his knife likely to be around still. Tidy went back to where the cart from Puerto Montt had set him down and after a while an omnibus came along behind eight horses.

*　　*　　*

Early next morning a knock came at the Captain's door: Mr Perrin stood visible, his cap beneath his left arm.

'Yes, Mr Perrin, what is it, I am busy.'

'A boat coming off, sir – '

'From the German?'

'No, sir, from Puerto Montt, sir. The man Tidy is aboard.'

'Is he, by God! Then he'll have some explaining to do, Mr Perrin, will he not?' Watkiss' face grew angry; the monocle flew to the end of its toggle. 'My compliments to the Officer of the Watch and Tidy's to be put in the report charged with going ashore without permission.'

'Sir, Tidy – '

'Don't argue with me, Mr Perrin, just do as I say.'

'Aye, aye, sir.' Perrin disappeared, back to the quarterdeck. The Captain moved out to his sternwalk and sniffed the air: there was rain about. He watched the approach of a filthy boat from Puerto Montt. Two dirty oarsmen who looked as though

179

they needed the attentions of a boatswain's boot up their back-sides, and the wretched Tidy. Watkiss scowled. Rustics did not fit aboard one of Her Majesty's battleships and someone at the Admiralty deserved to be kicked out for allowing the man to attach himself to Rampling. It was scandalous, nothing short of that. The boat vanished from Watkiss' view as it approached the battleship's side farther for'ard, and sounds came down as of the wretched craft bumping the bottom platform of Watkiss' ladder. His face suffused; he bounced inside and seized the voicepipe from his cabin to the quartermaster's lobby inside the after screen. He blew vigorously and was answered.

'Quarterdeck.'

'This is the Captain. Send that bumboat to the lower boom immediately. I'll not have ratings using the quarterdeck ladders.'

'Aye, aye, sir.'

Breathing hard, Watkiss retired back to the sternwalk. He heard voices . . . believe it or not, the man Tidy was arguing! Watkiss' fingers clenched round his telescope and he bared his teeth. The next thing he heard was the sound of clumping foot-steps upon the deckhead, then upon the ladder descending from the quarterdeck hatch; a few moments later the curtain across the doorway of his day cabin was hurled back and Tidy entered, face red and hair awry. Behind him were Mr Perrin and the Officer of the Watch with a boatswain's mate, but Tidy managed to penetrate all the same.

'Eh, Captain,' he said angrily, 'just call these boogers off!' He seemed immediately ashamed of unchurchwarden-like lan-guage uttered in the heat of the chase but did not apologize. 'I've summat to tell thee, like, and t'won't wait.'

*　　*　　*

Mr Todhunter, after re-embarking in his original coach, apol-ogized to Halfhyde, who had been most anxious when he had disappeared but had been unable to make an extended search aboard a corridorless train. The apologies made, the Detective Inspector, glancing out at the track, spotted General Codecino returning from his mission. He reported in a whisper to Halfhyde. 'There's no mistaking him, Mr Halfhyde. Look.' Halfhyde looked, but Codecino had re-entered his coach. Todhunter, not caring now about Chilean company, gave *sotto voce* elaborations upon recent events and the chain of circumstances that had led him to find the locked compartment. 'I'm certain the traitor Savory is there, Mr Halfhyde, and I am now suspicious of the good faith of General Codecino.'

'As was Admiral Daintree, you'll recall.'

'I have half a mind to execute my warrant, Mr Halfhyde, and arrest Savory.'

Halfhyde said warningly, 'If I were you, Mr Todhunter, I'd listen to the other half of your mind. We are strongly outnumbered and an arrest would not in any case be legal.'

'No.' Todhunter was bitter. 'Sometimes I wonder why I was sent at all, Mr Halfhyde, if I can't execute my warrant.'

'You can't execute it on Chilean soil, but you can execute it aboard a British ship – '

'That's what Captain Watkiss said.'

'And he was right, of course.' Halfhyde grinned. 'But never forget, I too have been sent, and I see a strong link between you and me, Mr Todhunter.'

'I don't follow, I'm afraid, sir.'

'I am to assist you in making your arrest. What I do is perhaps of less import to international law than what you, as a representative of the police authority, do. If that confuses you, don't dwell upon it. The ways of the Admiralty are strange and are known only to naval officers.'

'They're certainly incomprehensible to police officers, Mr Halfhyde,' Todhunter grumbled. Halfhyde comforted him : a stratagem, he said, would present itself, and meanwhile they must just await the Osorno arrival. It was unlikely they would meet trouble from Codecino with regard to the impudent extraction of Admiral Daintree, he said; both Codecino and the Savory escort party would have left Valparaiso before there had been time for any of the truth to emerge. The train rattled on its way; the shades of evening descended once again and Mr Todhunter tried

for the second night to sleep, bolt upright on the hard seat. It was
an uphill task: Canon Rampling did fall asleep and his snores
were loud ones. His mouth sagged open unbecomingly and a trail
of saliva ran like the slime from a snail's mucous gland down his
cassock. It was an abominable journey.

*   *   *

Captain Watkiss had been much enraged by Tidy's extraordinary
invasion of his cabin and had peremptorily ordered hands to be
laid upon the rector's warden. 'I'm damned if I'll not clap you in
irons!' he stormed.

'Eh, but you can't do that, can you?'

'I am the Captain and I can do anything I wish, and that's
fact, I said it – '

'Tisn't fact at all,' Tidy broke in with flat disparagement of
what he knew to be nonsense. 'I'm not a pressed man, I'm not
enlisted – '

'You – you – '

'Tisn't no use you blethering, Captain, you just ask t'Admiralty. Like I said, I've summat to tell thee, and when tha's
got rid of thy men, I'll say it an' not before, see?'

Watkiss rose and fell on the balls of his feet and shook his
telescope speechlessly. When the Officer of the Watch was not
ordered to leave, Tidy, taking a leaf from his own earlier reflec-
tions upon Watkiss, said calmly, 'I've known pigs a damn sight
less obstinate than thee. Look at thyself! Tha lewks like bun on
toothpick wi' that stummick and skinny legs. If you'll not send
thi lads away, I'll say't after all, and to hell like: *Savory.*'

Watkiss checked himself in mid thrust of his telescope. 'Did
you say Savory?'

'Aye, that's reet. Savory.'

'What, may I ask, do you know of Savory?'

'Ah.' Tidy closed an eye conspiratorially: he had got the
measure of the old geezer at last and he knew it. 'Wouldn't tha
like to know!'

Watkiss breathed out hard, turned away and for a few moments paced his cabin, his thoughts tumbling over each other in a riot of utter confusion. Rampling – a damn rector's warden – Admiral von Merkatz close behind him still in his anchorage – and Savory! He had, of course, to know what was going on . . . he turned again and faced the group in the day cabin. 'Very well,' he said to the Officer of the Watch, 'you may leave this man to me.'

'Aye, aye, sir.' The party left.

'Now,' Watkiss said ungraciously.

Tidy made his report: in unadorned Yorkshire, a scruffy native lad had taken him for Savory. 'On t'railway station at Osorno, that were, like.' Tidy added thoughtfully, 'T'lad had a dagger.'

'Blasted dagoes. Did he attack you, Tidy?'

'No. I gave him a piece o' my mind, like, and he ran off.'

'Where to?'

Tidy shook his head. 'I doan't know, Captain.'

'I see. What construction do you place upon this, Tidy? What's your view of what the dago was up to?'

Tidy lifted a hand and scratched his head. 'Hard to say, like. I reckon t'lad were waiting for this Savory.'

'To *kill* him – with the dagger?'

'I doan't know,' Tidy said again, then frowned and added, 'No, I'd not say that. I doan't know, but . . . summat told me he were just waiting, likely, to take him somewhere else.'

'A messenger, a guide, would you say?' Watkiss asked keenly.

'Aye, reckon I would . . . yes. Summat like that. An' there were t'German, too.' This was Tidy's *pièce de résistance*, and the reaction was satisfactory.

'*German*? What German?' Watkiss leapt from his chair, eyes staring. 'By God, why didn't you report that before?' Tidy didn't answer, merely shrugged; but he gave Watkiss the details. Wheels now revolved rapidly in Captain Watkiss' mind, revolved and slotted into place with other wheels, engaging to produce a forward-moving machine.

'Well, Tidy, you've been of great assistance – may have been, that is to say. I'm grateful.'

183

'It's all reet.'

'Nothing will now be said about your having gone ashore without permission.'

'Doan't give a hoot if it is,' Tidy said, and turned away.

There was an oath from Watkiss and a sharp voice followed the rector's warden out of the day cabin, adjuring him to mend his manners if he wished to live. For a moment Watkiss relieved the pressure within by raising both fists and shaking them violently in the air. Then he calmed down. The man was a boor, was of the common people – and all Yorkshiremen were impossible; but the fact had to be faced that he was beyond Watkiss' power to punish unless he became an actual danger to the ship. That acknowledged, there was much to be done – much indeed! There was no reason at all to doubt Tidy's veracity and so it was obvious that dirty work was afoot and Watkiss felt certain that von Merkatz, imagining himself inviolable behind his gleaming guns, was the instigator of it.

He must and would be stopped. Captain Watkiss' chest swelled out. This began to look like the climax; if he, Watkiss, could circumvent the machinations of the Hun, much honour would accrue to him. Watkiss paraded his quarters, thinking hard. Entering his sleeping cabin in order to pass through to his bathroom, Watkiss halted in front of a long looking-glass. He failed to find any resemblance to a bun on a toothpick; but he saw much gold, much rank, plus a good deal of astuteness in the face. The picture pleased him. He bounced into his bathroom, bounced out again after an interval, and sent for Lieutenant Lamphorn, acting second-in-command until the wretched Halfhyde should see fit to return aboard and report. By the time Lamphorn knocked upon the doorpost of the curtained day cabin, Watkiss was back to full resilience.

'Ah, Mr Lamphorn. Matters are moving fast. I am in possession of vital information.'

'Yes, sir?'

'Yes. Tidy – he went ashore as you know.'

'Yes, sir.'

'A subterfuge. I could have had him stopped, of course. I

preferred his disobedience to pass . . . I had a feeling he might prove a, what is it, a catalyst. That is, Mr Lamphorn, he might *provoke a reaction*, do you see?'

Lamphorn did not. 'Yes, sir.'

'Which is what he has done.' Briefly Watkiss passed the facts. 'Because of my ruse in appearing to permit disobedience and slackness, von Merkatz will not know that I know, you understand.' Watkiss paused. 'Oh, what is it now, Mr Lamphorn?'

'Sir, I'm afraid I don't quite see what you – '

'Oh, hold your tongue and don't argue with me, Mr Lamphorn, I have far too much to think about. Pay attention, if you please. I intend putting a landing party ashore as fast as possible, which means now. Do you understand *that*?'

'Yes, sir.'

'Thank God, Mr Lamphorn, thank God. Twenty-four seamen, gunnery rates. They will go to Osorno, to the railway station, where I expect the man Savory to appear – from the train, no doubt, out of Valparaiso. Are you following me?'

'Yes, sir.' Lamphorn paused, then asked, 'Are they to march, sir, in full – '

'March, fiddlesticks, you idiot, it's too damn far to march! Seventy odd miles. No, there should be a horse omnibus, I fancy. The man Tidy caught one at all events, when returning here.' The incongruity of a naval advance by public transport did not appear to strike Captain Watkiss. 'If not I shall commandeer horses or mules. Tidy, I understand, hired northward passage in a cart. They'll not go in uniform, Mr Lamphorn, they will muster in plain clothes.'

'There's not much available, sir.'

'It's not to be a parade of fashion, Mr Lamphorn, anything so long as it's not obviously uniform will do. Rifles and side-arms to be taken but concealed about the person and it's up to each man to conceal his rifle properly and not argue the toss. Sailors are not without ingenuity. Von Merkatz is to have the wool drawn over his eyes. Now what is it?'

'The position under international law, sir. You yourself made the point that Savory – '

'Needs must when the devil drives, Mr Lamphorn,' Watkiss said loftily, 'so hold your tongue and be gone about your duties. You're very nearly as bad as Mr Beauchamp, my last First Lieutenant. One more thing.'

'Sir?'

'I shall go myself in command, and I shall take that over-weight youth Perrin. The expedition calls for experience and I am no stranger to landing parties, nor am I afraid of shot and shell. Woe betide you, Mr Lamphorn, if you should hazard my ship in my absence.'

Muttering to himself, Lieutenant Lamphorn turned away, only to be called back once again. 'Mr Lamphorn, another thing. Assistant Paymaster Luckings. He's not to be told about this. To avoid his getting wind of it, he's to be sent down to the spirit-room until my party's left the ship.'

'Aye, aye, sir.'

'Kindly inform the Paymaster privately that Luckings is to measure out the contents of all the barricoes – or something like that. With luck, the fellow will become blind drunk again and cease to bother me for a while. Off you go.'

Lamphorn left the cuddy and proceeded to the quarterdeck. Sending for Mr Mottram, he passed the orders. There was incredulous merriment when these orders reached the lower deck: anything for a lark was the reaction, plus the added spice of danger in a foreign land. Working fast, twenty-four men with the non-substantive rate of seaman gunner, plus the gunner's mate and two leading-seamen, prepared to land. They mustered by the starboard lower boom in a motley collection of rigs: blue jerseys, vests, long woollen scarves and never mind the warmth, funny hats found in a store-room, relics of a party held aboard for the warrant officers during the battleship's last commission in the Portsmouth command, a variety of non-uniform trousers provided from the officer's wardrobes: ratings were not permitted to bring plain clothes aboard. One wore a dinner jacket belonging to the Paymaster, another the Engineer's civilian overcoat; the gunner's mate wore Mr Pinch's nightshirt tucked into uniform trousers. As to the rifles, these were concealed with equal ingenuity: several of the seamen appeared stiff-legged, capable only with difficulty of moving at all. One or two had their rifles hidden beneath cocoons of Admiralty canvas, like fishing rods. The gunner's mate's cutlass was wrapped in an oilskin, while one of the leading-seamen had his rifle thrust into a golf bag borrowed from Halfhyde's cabin, its butt covered with a pair of flannel underpants. The negotiation of the lower boom and the descent from it into the boats via a swaying rope ladder dangling at its end was made with great difficulty in many cases; and when the two boats were ready the leading one came alongside the starboard quarterdeck ladder for the embarkation of Captain Watkiss. Before reporting the muster present and correct to Mr Perrin, who was wearing a Norfolk jacket and a deerstalker hat, Mr Mottram had issued the detailed orders in ringing tones.

'No weapons to be shown, right? An' where possible, and when in company o' foreign persons, no talkin' unless any o' you knows Spanish. From the jetty to the place where the transport leaves from, you'll slouch not march. God alone knows 'ow long the journey will take. It won't be comfortable. God knows 'ow every man's to be found even clinging-on room aboard the horse bus, but if God don't provide, the Captain will. Any questions?'

One was asked: rumour had spoken already, and a leading-seaman wished to know how the party, whilst boatborne for the shore, was to remain unseen from the German squadron. Mr Mottram's reply was terse. 'You can refer that to God an' all.' But the services of God were not required: Captain Watkiss had covered the eventuality as best he could, and had at the same time covered other eventualities. A signal had been made by all-round lamp to the port authority with the winking light standing fully visible from all points of the compass at the masthead. This signal asked permission to land recreation parties: the ship must be kept healthy, and British seamen had a need of exercise. This permission given, Captain Watkiss had no fear of being turned back from the jetty upon arrival inshore. Embarking, Captain Watkiss shook his walking-stick triumphantly towards the *Friedrich der Grosse* and its flaunting ensign of black, white and red, of insolent eagle and trumpery iron cross. Von

Merkatz would be very nicely fooled; Captain Watkiss congratulated himself hugely. Halfhyde was not the only person in the Empire who was capable of stratagems.

*   *   *

There was in fact an omnibus, but it ran only weekly, and today was not its day for returning north : Captain Watkiss, baulked, raised hell and sent men scouring for mules. Enough were found and commandeered; the British consul, Watkiss said, was to be presented with the bill, which Her Majesty would settle. Captain Watkiss, dressed in a curious black alpaca coat like a grocer, worn atop his overlong white shorts and topped in its turn by a panama hat, his gold-oak-leaved uniform cap now concealed in a Gladstone bag not unlike Mr Todhunter's, mounted. They all mounted and straggled into some sort of file; no cavalryman, the gunner's mate wisely, as he thought, kept his mouth shut and hoped for the best. This was, in fact, not wise.

'Gunner's mate !'

'Sir ?'

'Don't you know anything at all about handling mules ?'

'No, sir – '

'Don't argue with me, Gunner's mate.' Watkiss lifted his voice and shouted incomprehensible instructions and the mounted ragbag got under way for Osorno. And victory.

*   *   *

A matter of a few hours after Watkiss' departure, and as night began to come down over Puerto Montt, two Chilean boats left the shore with three men embarked as passengers in the leading one. Men of much gilded splendour, only a shade less than that of General Codecino, they sat comfortably in the sternsheets beneath a dirty white canopy, fingering revolvers in holsters at their belts and not indulging in much conversation. A little way for'ard of them, not beneath the canopy and on a less splendid seat, sat another man, a civilian in a crumpled white suit and a panama hat, clutching a leather attaché case. In the second boat sat a number of uniformed musicians. These boats edged out from Puerto Montt and headed for the anchorage, making in due course a wide sweep to come alongside the starboard ladder of the *Meridian*.

FIFTEEN

Mr Todhunter awoke and cast a bleary eye at the dawn. Canon Rampling was making a most terrible noise and the Detective Inspector could, after a while, put up with it no longer. He jabbed his knee into the parson's thigh : that did the trick.

'Bless my soul,' Rampling said. 'The night has gone! Praise God.' He looked out of the window and rubbed his hands together briskly. He was, Halfhyde thought as he surveyed Rampling from opposite, much too hearty for the time of day. Now they were not far from Osorno – that was, if the train was keeping to schedule, which very likely it was not. There had been periods during a largely sleepless night when the engine had slowed almost to walking pace as it met inclines, and periods when it had ground to a halt altogether and an unhealthy sound of rushing steam had been heard. Rampling went on, 'I believe I smell the sea.'

'We've not been far from the sea all the way south, Padre.'

'Ah.'

'A thin country.'

'Quite so.' The parson's gaze surveyed the other passengers. They were mainly fat, like General Codecino. The train pulled on, chugging and chuffing. Soon it would be time for breakfast, which they might be able to find from the saleswomen of country produce at Osorno – or again, they might not. The arrival at Osorno promised to be the time for action rather than for breakfast. Canon Rampling shifted about uncomfortably upon his seat : he had problems apart from breakfast. Under cover of the night a window had been lowered and one of the fat Chileans had relieved himself from it, a proceeding that Rampling had wished to follow but as an Englishman and a cleric dared not. Ruminating upon how Chilean women might manage, he had fallen asleep again and the urge had lain dormant, but now it had come back strongly. Not, please God, much longer . . .

*　　*　　*

The ordeal for the mounted seamen had been a long one but had come to an end when virtually all the mules in unison had metaphorically dug in their toes and refused to budge an inch more. Watkiss had raved but had had to concede. Mules were mules. March the men had to, and there were some fifteen miles yet to go, but luck was with them and a farm cart happened to come along empty and was duly commandeered and overloaded. Now, this morning, Watkiss' eye darted along the railway track at Osorno, seeking what Tidy had referred to as the ' Chilean lad '. There were indeed several who could have fitted that description, along with older persons of both sexes. But there was no one who looked in the least like a German or even like someone lurking with evil intent, the intent to remove Savory to a place unknown until he could safely be put aboard the German flagship. Watkiss scowled beneath the panama hat. Perhaps he should have brought Tidy. Tidy could perhaps have made an identification of the Chilean. Meanwhile the midshipman looked as if he wished to communicate, but, having been instructed that on no account was he to use the word ' sir ', didn't know how to. Watkiss clicked his tongue and said, ' Well, Mr Perrin, what is it ?'

The ' sir ' was uttered beneath Perrin's breath. ' It occurred to me that Tidy might have helped.'

' Oh, nonsense, Mr Perrin, what a stupid thing to say.'

' I'm sorry . . .'

' All damn dagoes look alike, like Chinamen. In any case, it is always a pointless exercise to ponder on what *might* have been done, is it not, Mr Perrin ?'

' Yes, sir.'

' Hold your tongue, you fool.'

'I'm sorry, sir.' Habit was still too strong.

'God give me strength, Mr Perrin, *shut up*.'

The wait for the Valparaiso train, which was late like all dago moving things, continued. The landing party drifted about beside the dusty track, looking consciously un-naval, a hard thing to accomplish in the presence not only of the gunner's mate but also of their Captain. It was not done to shamble before a Captain; and the old bugger looked as if he knew that too, and despite his own orders might at any moment burst a blood vessel. For his part, he could never look anything but of the Royal Navy: his bouncy self-assurance, his arrogant blue-eyed stare that looked through a man without seeing him on the way, proclaimed his calling as clearly as if he wore his commissioning pennant streaming from his right ear. The railway track was currently his quarterdeck, and he strode it, hands behind the back of the grocer's alpaca, panama hat on square and shipshape and lacking only the gold oak leaves, monocle dangling from its customary toggle, the colourful tattoo-ed snake showing itself on his forearm each time the monocle was lifted and thrust into his eye the better to watch for approaching action. Sardonic tars watched the gunner's mate too: the gunner's mate, as was the way of gunner's mates, brought the Whale Island Gunnery School to Osorno platform, as he would to everywhere else from Hong Kong to Bermuda, from Gibraltar to Simon's Town, as if it were the most natural thing in the world. All gas and gaiters were gunner's mates, and as full of bull as a cowpat.

Distantly, a whistle blew. The Valparaiso train . . . the gunner's mate swung round, a beautiful about turn, and marched along beside the track with his nightshirted arms a-swing, left-right-left, to execute a crash halt in front of Mr Midshipman Perrin. No salute; but Mr Perrin politely acknowledged the gunner's mate's rigidity by raising his deerstalker.

*   *   *

Halfhyde now had Todhunter's revolver concealed in his waistband and had passed the word to Rampling and Todhunter to stand by: it was evident from the busy actions of the Chilean

192

passengers that Osorno was now looming up. Wicker baskets were being prepared for disembarkation, stacked handy for the doors. Limbs were being stretched, clothing pulled straight. Rampling could hardly wait : the last few seconds before the joy of relief were always the worst. He scarcely dared stand up. Already Half-hyde, with all three heads close together in secret session, had passed the action orders : they were simplicity itself and all that could be done in the circumstances. The moment the occupants of the locked compartment emerged – and it was still not known how many occupants there were – the British party was to close in and Halfhyde would allow his revolver to be glimpsed, after which it would be thrust into the side of the traitor Savory. Or of General Codecino if the Chilean should prove a handier target. The miscreants would then be ordered to remain quiet and to walk calmly out of the station.

'And then?' Rampling asked.

'We take things as they come, Padre. Transport must be found, of course. I shall find it, you may rely upon it.'

'Suppose they call for help from the crowd?'

'I think they will not. Savory is of value and must not be shot, while something tells me General Codecino is not a brave man. The revolver shall be our guarantee. That, and our resolution. Is that not so, Mr Todhunter?'

'Oh, yes, indeed it is,' Todhunter whispered back, and thought of his Chief Super at the Yard. His Chief Super never accepted excuses, he was a hard man. This had to be brought off against all the odds, the odds that included that there Captain Watkiss and his insistence that the traitor Savory be arrested only aboard a British vessel. Todhunter steeled himself : everything would be there with him – the Crown as represented by Lieutenant Half-hyde of the Royal Navy, the Church of State as represented by Canon Rampling, the law and the civil power as represented by himself. The Queen and Parliament and the Archbishop of Canterbury; and a thunderous revolver.

The train, which had slowed already, slowed still more. Walk-ing pace now . . . Osorno railway station slid into view with a remarkable number of persons waiting by the track. Halfhyde thrust open a door, elbowed the Chileans out of the way, and jumped down. There was a jerk and a clatter of bumpers as the train stopped. Mr Todhunter almost fell out, with Canon Rampling behind him. Halfhyde ran through the dust for the next-but-one coach to the rear and stood by the door with his fingers round the revolver. As he waited and closely watched the crowd issuing from the train, he was accosted by a fat youth in a deerstalker hat and a Norfolk jacket.

'Good morning, sir.'

Halfhyde stared. 'Perrin! What the devil – '

'The Captain's here, sir, with an armed landing party.' Perrin pointed down the line, and Halfhyde turned to look over his shoulder. The gunner's mate had come back into his own: the landing party, sartorially a ragbag, was doubling in file towards Halfhyde, rifles out from hiding and in their hands, and bayonets fixed. A heartening sight; in rear came Captain Watkiss with his walking-stick. He was still in his grocer's alpaca but with the panama hat now jettisoned in favour of his uniform cap, all gold and glitter in the morning sun.

'Mr Halfhyde!' Watkiss called in a loud voice.

'Sir?'

'I have reason to believe the man Savory is aboard this train.'

'So have I, sir.'

'What? Frankly, I didn't expect to see you, Mr Halfhyde, what the devil are you up to now?'

'I am about to arrest Savory, sir.' At that moment Captain Watkiss vanished from sight, submerged in the astounded crowd of Chileans. His voice was heard in very loud indignation, shouting about damn dagoes and smelly peasants, but his short body was invisible. Halfhyde turned back to watch the exit of passengers from the train; approaching the door now was General Codecino, behind him a woman, behind her a man that Halfhyde recognized beyond doubt as Savory; and behind him again, three square-headed men in white suits. Halfhyde brought out his revolver and held it, still out of sight of the crowd, aimed at the emerging stomach of General Codecino. He was about to caution the Chilean to have a care and keep his calm if he wished to live, when a high shout came from the station building behind the track:

'Captain Watkiss! Captain Watkiss! Where's Captain Watkiss?'

'Here,' came another angry shout. 'What the devil are *you* doing here, Mr blasted Petrie-Smith?'

*   *   *

General Codecino, fat and smiling, still genial, had taken full advantage of the interruption. He was astonishingly fast on the move: a hand darted out and laid hold of the barrel of Halfhyde's revolver and twisted it away; at the same time one of the white-suited men, squirming round General Codecino's stomach, kicked Halfhyde in the groin before he could react, while another sent a fist into Canon Rampling's face. The man of God, about to turn man of war, lurched back on to Mr Todhunter and rout, at least temporarily, was complete. The naval party, deprived of positive orders, milled about in the mob of Chileans, impeded, confused and bloody-minded. Thereafter Codecino, one large hand propelling Savory by the collar, charged like a bull and cleared a passage for his followers, who included the woman referred to by Todhunter, the woman who was obviously Miss Slindon from the s s *Taragona*. Halfhyde, recovering himself, fought through the crowd towards the station exit behind the fugitives. This took time; too many persons got in his way. Reaching the exit he found a surprising sight: Codecino and Savory, the woman and the white-suited men, were on the move in the centre of an armed German naval guard, some ten files of seamen who were already moving away at the double past an engine shed towards a large covered vehicle with a team of a dozen horses in the traces. Cursing, Halfhyde fought back through the amazed crowd of Chileans to make contact with his Captain. Reaching him, he was disregarded: Watkiss was making the air tremble.

'You are a vile man, Mr Petrie-Smith, a *reptile*. I shall have you drummed out of the Foreign Office, just see if I don't!'

'I think not, Captain Watkiss, since I have just prevented an international incident, not to mention a war – '

'Stuff and nonsense, a war my backside!' Watkiss became aware of Halfhyde. 'Ah, Mr Halfhyde. You shall mount a counter-attack and seize – '

'He shall not, Captain. He shall most positively not, nor shall you. I forbid it,' Petrie-Smith stormed. 'As Her Majesty's representative at this moment, I shall order your own men to restrain you by arrest if you make any attempt to engage in a pitched battle with the Germans.' Petrie-Smith, his bald head bobbing about like that of a hairless china doll, pointed vindictively through the station exit. 'It's too late anyway, my dear sir – out there is a German naval guard, as Mr Halfhyde will testify, well armed, provided by Admiral von Merkatz – '

'How the devil – '

'I have spoken to the Lieutenant in Command. They have been some days in Osorno, having been landed in Puerto Montt before our own arrival – '

'Waiting for Savory?'

'Yes.'

'Whom you were sent to Chile to help apprehend, Mr Petrie-Smith! Now where is he – hey?' Watkiss was dancing in fury. 'You are yourself a damn traitor – a damn lunatic who has acted against the Queen's interests – '

'Oh, nonsense. I have prevented a very nasty incident, as I said – '

'You are a lily-livered *coward*, sir – '

'And it was *not* my business to apprehend Savory, but to preserve diplomacy. It was Todhunter's job to arrest Savory, who, while important certainly, is of less import than the avoidance of war – as must be obvious to the meanest intellect – and the requirements of civilized diplomacy. To land armed men in an act of insanity is – '

'Don't damn well be impertinent!' Watkiss waved his arms. 'Why, von Merkatz has landed men, and you don't call that insanity, do you, you bloody traitorous *villain*!'

Petrie-Smith shrugged. 'It matters little what I call them,

Captain Watkiss. They are Germans, and beyond my authority. If they wish to be insane, that is their affair. We, at least, have now acted correctly.'

Captain Watkiss remembered something and was not slow to point it out. 'Your authority, Mr Petrie-Smith, Mr Luckings perhaps I should say, is currently confined to my ship's files and stores indents. You are a damn little tick, Mr Petrie-Smith, and a damn paymaster tick at that. How did you get here in the first place?'

'An automobile – '

'Horseless carriage! Where did you find it?'

'Our consul in Puerto Montt – '

'I thought you were supposed to remain incognito?'

'The intelligent person, Captain, knows when to expose – to reveal himself. The diplomatic mind does not put itself into stays like a woman – '

'Oh, hold your tongue, Mr Petrie-Smith – Mr Luckings.' Watkiss extended a hand and pointed. 'Put yourself back into your horseless carriage and return instantly aboard my ship and inform my Officer of the Watch that you are in arrest.' His voice rose above the heads of the tittering crowd of Chileans: even the return of the train to Valparaiso would be delayed until the pantomime was over. 'Go now, at once, or I shall order my gunner's mate to provide an armed escort of seamen to remove you.'

*　　*　　*

Captain Watkiss held himself incommunicado after formally taking note of Halfhyde's full report of events in Valparaiso; he would thereafter speak to no one. Mr Lamphorn, when he returned to deal with him, for which he could scarcely wait, would be placed in arrest himself and his name entered in the log for allowing Petrie-Smith to go ashore. In the meantime, it was a pity about the horseless carriage, which would have had room for himself and might have been speedier than the public stage-coach, but he would not have trusted himself to sit alongside the bounder Petrie-Smith, at least not without throttling him. Watkiss bounced up and down angrily, raising Chilean dust about his person, outside the station. The German guard had marched away victorious, with Savory and the fat Codecino . . . oh, it was too bad! Savory in his clutches as if by a miracle, and then the stinking Foreign Office had to go and intervene, the set of cowardly pimps! After a while Watkiss simmered down a little and decided to resume relations, since get back to his ship he must.

'Mr Halfhyde.'

Halfhyde put his head out of the door of a primitive waiting room. 'Sir?'

'Come here at once, don't peer at me like a monkey from a cage.'

'Aye, aye, sir.' Halfhyde emerged and approached his Captain.

'Mr Halfhyde, you will fall the men in properly and have them marched to where mules or carts may be found. You will send a runner ahead to demand relays of transport of whatever kind for Her Majesty's Fleet. You will succeed in arranging for its provision, what's more,' Watkiss added vindictively. 'That's fact, I said it!'

'Aye, aye, sir.'

The orders were passed via Mr Perrin to the gunner's mate and the curious party fell in for the march, rifles now in the open and at the slope as they marched away towards a hostelry from where the public horse-drawn omnibus left. Two seamen whistled *Rule Britannia* until shouted at to stop. In the rear went Half-hyde, Rampling, Todhunter and Captain Watkiss, the latter already planning his counter-stroke: Savory would not be allowed to sail for Germany and that was that and to hell with Petrie-Smith. Upon the high seas, if it should come to that, Petrie-Smith could yelp and complain and quack as much as he liked: Captain Watkiss upon the high seas was back to Godhead. And the high seas were open, untrammelled by the methods of pimps and nancy boys. A time would come. Yes, *his* time would come, and soon! Captain Watkiss strode out, keeping time now to the step as shouted by the gunner's mate. He was not done, by God! Just give him the open sea and a rolling deck, his guns and torpedo-tubes and faster engines than von Merkatz – a problem, the latter, certainly – and the Hun would live to rue his filthy duplicity. Captain Watkiss turned to glance at the policeman : a miserable little man, and his blue serge suit looked shinier than ever, but he too had faced disappointment that morning. Watkiss called to him.

'Todhunter!'

'Yes, sir?'

'Come here. At the double.'

'Yes, sir.' Todhunter doubled up, his trailing moustache stuck to his chin with sweat.

'Bad luck, Todhunter.'

'Yes, indeed, sir.'

'I am satisfied that you did your best, and shall thus report to whom it may concern.'

'Oh, thank you, sir! My Chief Super, sir.'

'A higher authority than he, I fancy, but he shall be informed also. You have nothing to fear, but I damn well know who has!' Fresh anger swept into Watkiss' face. 'But never mind. At least I understand that Admiral Daintree is on his way. Right will triumph, Todhunter, in the end. Be of good cheer.'

'I shall be, sir.'

'Try to keep step. You may be of the civil power, but there is no need to walk like a whore with clap. Send Canon Rampling to me.'

'Yes, sir.' Todhunter doffed his bowler and approached the parson, who came up alongside Watkiss.

'You wished to speak to me, sir?' Rampling asked.

'Yes. You will utter prayers, Padre. Find a relevant portion of the Bible.'

'Prayer book, sir.'

'Oh, very well then, prayer book, it's all the same to me. Prayers will be said, and said in the proper manner. The man Savory is to be delivered up to me . . . and fiddlesticks to Petrie-Smith!'

*　　*　　*

Weary, hungry, mostly down-in-the-mouth, having found no sign of the Germans or of Savory en route, the landing party arrived back in Puerto Montt next day on mule-back and was marched to the jetty in the port. Boats were commandeered, or at any rate hired and paid for on the Admiralty's account, since Watkiss had no intention of waiting around for a signal to be made by semaphore for a ship's boat. As they waited, the gunner's mate was seen to be staring towards the distant masts of the *Meridian*, a hand shading his eyes against the bright sun, his brow furrowed. He then approached Perrin, who approached Halfhyde.

'Sir, the *Meridian*, sir!'

'Yes, Mr Perrin?'

'Sir, the Chilean flag's flying superior to the White Ensign, sir!'

'*What*!'

Mr Perrin coughed. 'Sir, I was wondering who is going to tell the Captain.'

SIXTEEN

At the head of the accommodation ladder as Captain Watkiss rejoined his command, Lieutenant Lamphorn stood at the salute with the Officer of the Watch and a midshipman together with a piping party. When Watkiss, Halfhyde, Rampling and Tod-hunter had disembarked to the bottom platform, the shoreside boats were sent for'ard to the lower boom to discharge the ratings of the landing party and Mr Perrin.

Captain Watkiss climbed nimbly to his quarterdeck, where he shook a fist at the Chilean flag.

'Now, Mr Lamphorn.'

'Sir?'

'Why is that — that *thing* flaunting itself from my masthead?'

'The Chilean authorities boarded, sir, shortly after you had left for the shore with the landing party. It seems they were under orders from Santiago, sir.'

'Orders, Mr Lamphorn? In my absence? Orders to board my ship?'

'Yes, sir. To take possession . . . to take delivery, sir, in accord-ance with the bill of sale from the Admiralty.'

'Yes, I see.' Captain Watkiss' voice was like ice. 'And *have* they taken possession?'

'Well, yes, sir, they have.'

'And you allowed it, Mr Lamphorn?'

'I had no alternative, sir. The Chilean officers were acting for their government — they are an advance party, with the main steaming party due to join by sea shortly from Valparaiso, and they were concerned that you were not handing over as arranged in Valparaiso – '

'Damn impertinence.'

'Yes, sir. They brought musicians – '

'*Musicians?*'

'Bandsmen, sir, to provide stirring music for the ceremony.' Lamphorn coughed. 'You will appreciate that we are in Chilean waters, sir . . . and that the documents of entitlement were fully in order.'

'Were they?'

Lamphorn swallowed. 'Yes, sir. I checked carefully.'

'Oh, good. These officers . . . did they board in a warlike fashion, with guns aimed at you, Mr Lamphorn?' Watkiss' tone was almost solicitous.

'Er . . . no, sir. The affair was handled with dignity, sir. Peacefully.'

'A peaceful take-over of my ship?'

'Yes, sir.'

Watkiss, his control going fast, brandished his fists. 'I've never heard the like in all my years of service! You are a scoundrel, Mr Lamphorn!'

'I'm – '

'Hold your tongue and don't argue with me, Mr Lamphorn, you are a lily-livered *bum*. That's fact, I said it, and you will acknowledge it! You shall repeat it loudly and clearly! What are you, Mr Lamphorn?' Watkiss took a pace forward and thrust his face close to Lamphorn's, his eyes murderous. '*What are you?*'

Lamphorn licked his lips. 'A lily-livered bum, sir.'

'Exactly, Mr Lamphorn. Now go to your cabin and remain there until I send for you. You are relieved of all duties and you are in arrest. On return to England you will face court martial!'

'And the charges, sir?' Lamphorn demanded with a show of spirit.

'Yet to be framed. Mr Halfhyde!'

'Sir?'

Watkiss pointed at the Chilean flag. 'Get that bloody excrescence down immediately.' He turned on Lamphorn again. 'Well, what are you waiting for? You have been ordered to your cabin. Kindly go.'

'Sir, there is a further report I should make first.'

'Oh, very well, make it, then go.'

'Yes, sir.' Lamphorn looked as though he were praying for the deck to open beneath his feet. 'The Chileans, sir. They wished to take over your quarters, since you were absent. I – I persuaded them to make do with your spare cabin, sir.'

* * *

Watkiss went below with Halfhyde. His spare cabin resembled a dockside bar or gaming room. Thick with cigar smoke, it contained three figures recumbent round a card table, with loosened uniform collars and glasses in their hands. A fourth figure, a civilian, lay drunk on the deck as if dead. Captain Watkiss, after one look, beat a retreat towards the voicepipe in his day cabin, whence he called the quartermaster's lobby.

'This is the Captain. Fall in the duty part of the watch, the men to muster outside my quarters with rifles.' He banged the brass cover back and turned to face Halfhyde. 'I shall have their balls for breakfast!' he announced.

'A natural reaction indeed, sir,' Halfhyde said soothingly. 'But may I ask what your *actual* intentions are?'

'I shall throw them into the sea, Mr Halfhyde.'

'Of course, sir. But with respect, it might be wiser not to go so far as that.'

'Oh, rubbish, why not for God's sake?'

'Repercussions, sir. Mr Lamphorn was right that we are still in Chilean waters, and we must remain so until we have Savory in our hands.'

'Savory – yes, yes. But ultimately we are to be handed over, we know that. Handed over – *not seized*. What about Savory then?'

'We shall come to that, sir. In the meantime, I suggest that the Chileans in your spare cabin – '

'Where they shall not remain.'

'Quite so. But they may have a use, sir.'

'Use? What use?'

'As hostages, sir.'

'Hostages?' Watkiss' eyes gleamed with sudden interest.

'Yes, sir. Not that we should tell them as much. Let us call their forthcoming removal and detention by the duty part of the watch . . . let us call it a misunderstanding, sir, perhaps a difficulty of language – '

'Ah—ha, yes, by God, you may have a point! You may indeed!'

Halfhyde inclined his head. 'Thank you, sir. They may also prove useful in regard to Savory, who knows?'

'Yes, yes, they may! They may!' Watkiss bounced around the day cabin, a tubby figure in the black alpaca coat. 'Yes, a good thing I decided not to throw them in the sea, the buggers, is it not? I shall make use of them as hostages, Mr Halfhyde, kindly see to that – ' He broke off; sounds in the lobby outside his quarters indicated the muster of the duty part of the watch. 'Mr Halfhyde, tell the hands to have my spare cabin cleared, cleaned and aired and the dagoes provided with hammocks in the midshipmen's chest flat – under guard. They're not to leave the flat without my permission.'

*   *   *

Only minutes later it became apparent that the German squadron, which already had steam, was about to leave port: von Merkatz was on the bridge of his flagship and bugles were sounding. When the report of this reached Captain Watkiss, who was back in uniform again after a lightning change, he sent for Halfhyde and with him bounced up the ladder to his quarterdeck. 'What the hell do we do now?' he demanded.

'The hostages, sir. Captain Montero, who is to command once you've handed over – '

'And not before.'

'I suggest, sir, that he does.'

'What?'

'A mere ruse, sir, to fool von Merkatz. The Chilean naval ensign . . . it's flying still, for which I apologize. A question of time – '

'Yes, yes, Mr Halfhyde!'

'And it's as well, sir, as it happens, for a need of it has now come.'

'I'd be obliged if you'd not talk to me in riddles, Mr Halfhyde.'

'What I mean, sir, is this: von Merkatz, seeing the Chilean naval ensign, will believe you to have genuinely handed over to – '

'To the dagoes?' Watkiss flourished his telescope, joy coming into his face. 'By God, you're right, my dear fellow! Montero in command . . . and then I send a cleverly worded signal to the Hun, as from Captain Montero – yes!' He gave a sound of triumph. 'By God, von Merkatz shall find out I'm not to be trifled with, nor disregarded! Excellent! Send for my yeoman, if you please, Mr Halfhyde.'

'Aye, aye, sir.'

Called from the flag deck by the voicepipe, the yeoman reported without delay and saluted the Captain. 'Yessir?'

'Make to the German flag from Captain Montero commanding the Chilean vessel *Meridian*, and remove that odd expression from your face, yeoman, since I have not taken leave of my senses – '

'Sorry, sir – '

'Make: I am ordered by President whoever it is, damn – '

'Errazuriz, sir,' Halfhyde said.

'Thank you, Mr Halfhyde, I was aware of that. And the Minister for War, oh, all right, take the name from Mr Halfhyde, it's – '

'Domingo Amuñategui, sir.'

'Oh, hold your tongue, where was I?' Watkiss breathed hard down his nose. 'I am ordered to request you remain within the port area until . . . until . . .'

'Until important despatches from His Imperial Majesty the Emperor of Germany are to hand, sir.'

Watkiss nodded distantly. 'Yes. That is what I wish to say, yeoman. Make the signal immediately.' He turned his back on the yeoman, who doubled away, silent upon bare feet. Within three minutes the signal was in transit. As it went another report, an astonishing one, came down from the flag deck: a three-masted square-rigger under reefed topsails, identified by her signal letters as the *Glen Lyon*, was entering by the sailing-ship track from the Gulf de Ancud to the south of Reloncavi Bay; she was flying the signal to indicate that she had a passenger to disembark.

'Who can that be, Mr Halfhyde, for God's sake?'

'I suggest Admiral Daintree, sir.'

'Daintree? Was he not to be landed at the Falklands? Has he gone mad, do you suppose?'

'No doubt we shall find out, sir.'

Watkiss glared speechlessly. He and Halfhyde, with Mr Todhunter now, watched the sailing ship enter.

'A fine sight, Mr Halfhyde.'

'Yes, indeed, Mr Todhunter.' Halfhyde scowled across the water: Daintree was behaving foolishly, was putting his head dangerously close to the lion's den if anything should go wrong. The *Glen Lyon* drifted onward, her crew visible as they lay out along the yards, swaying on the footropes as they took the remaining canvas off her. She came up to the anchorage and let go, then lay still and silent on the blue water, the sun striking fire from brass fittings on her deck.

'Call away my galley, if you please,' Watkiss said to the Officer of the Watch. 'Embark Admiral Daintree – stand by to pipe the side.'

'Aye, aye, sir.'

The galley was called away, and quickly left the quarter-boom. Halfhyde, who had now observed the small, thin figure of Daintree standing on the *Glen Lyon*'s poopdeck, kept an eye lifting towards the German ships still in their anchorage: so far, they did not appear to have shortened in. The mischievous signal seemed to be doing its work very nicely indeed . . . they all waited, none of them speaking now. Quite soon the Captain's galley was seen to be returning with Daintree in the sternsheets. Captain Watkiss hastened to the head of the starboard accommodation ladder and was standing at the salute as the Admiral ascended to the shrilling of the boatswain's calls.

'Welcome aboard, sir, though I confess I had thought you safe away for the Falklands. I trust you are recovered from your dreadful experiences.'

'Thank you, Captain, I am fully recovered. Once off Chiloé Island, I changed my mind and decided to enter. It is not in my nature to run and leave my subordinates – even those, such as your ships, not under my command – I would not run and leave them to face possible hazard. Ah, Halfhyde.'

'I'm delighted to see you well, sir.'

'Thank you, thank you.' Daintree's eye swivelled back to Watkiss. 'Why are you wearing the Chilean flag, Captain Watkiss?' The voice was cold; after all, his arrest had been due to his attitude towards the Chilean flag, as Watkiss now remembered.

'A stratagem of Mr Halfhyde's, sir.' Watkiss explained fully.

'Ah, I see. A good stratagem.'

'One with which I concurred, sir. My intention is to hold the German squadron until – until – '

'Until Mr Halfhyde has another stratagem?'

Watkiss' mouth opened: a rear-admiral was a rear-admiral, but the tone had been sarcastic. Watkiss found speech. 'Until your squadron arrives off Chiloé Island, sir, to contain them and to enforce the hand-over of the man Savory.'

Daintree nodded. 'My squadron was to weigh out of Valparaiso shortly after I left aboard the *Glen Lyon*, and indeed they have closed already. They were within signalling distance before I entered, and I have ordered them to follow in on the steamship track.'

'Excellent, sir,' Watkiss said, beaming.

Daintree looked him up and down. 'I'm not over keen to provoke war between my sovereign and her grandson Willy. On the other hand we have our Chilean trading interests to consider, and the Chileans don't want Savory to leave the country. If we should aid them by ensuring that he remains, the Foreign Office would be well pleased, I fancy.'

Watkiss grew impatient. 'You seem not to understand, sir. I am to take Savory to England.'

Daintree nodded. 'Yes, yes. A conflict of interests. I understand you have a man named Petrie-Smith aboard. I think you should send for him, Captain. Then – '

'One moment, sir,' Watkiss interrupted: the voicepipe had whistled in the quartermaster's lobby. It was answered by a boatswain's mate. 'Well?'

'Flag deck, sir,' the seaman reported. 'The German squadron is weighing, sir.'

'Is it, by God!' Watkiss glared; the glare said that Halfhyde's stratagem had been a poor one after all, seen through with ease. Watkiss dithered for a moment, then anger brought him to a final decision: von Merkatz, blast him, was not going to get away with this, damned if he was. All Watkiss' frustrations came to boiling point and he waved his telescope at his Officer of the Watch. 'Sound for action!' he cried out, and stamped a foot. 'Where's Mr Mottram? My guns are to be swung to bear upon the German flag.' As Halfhyde, looking out to starboard, ran for the guardrail with his own telescope lifted, Watkiss called, 'What is it now, Mr Halfhyde?'

'A boat has left the flag, sir. I believe I saw General Codecino before he ducked down below the canopy.'

'Balls – '

'Captain.' Daintree laid a hand on Watkiss' arm. 'May I suggest that you might with advantage ask General Codecino to step aboard you? I believe a little pressure, properly applied . . . Codecino is a fat man of, I would say, little real courage – '

'I, too, sir, dislike fat men,' Watkiss said unctuously.

Daintree was observed to cast an eye towards Watkiss' stomach; Halfhyde prevented verbal collision by asking if he should have a boat called away. Watkiss scowled, but nodded. 'Yes, Mr Halfhyde, send a boat's crew to ask General Codecino to repair aboard my ship – and make damn sure he obeys, what's more!' He swung round upon the Officer of the Watch. 'Pass to the flag deck, the yeoman's to make a signal to Admiral von Merkatz, worded thus : I am about to exercise action. I suggest you stand clear of my line of fire.'

'Aye, aye, sir.'

Captain Watkiss rubbed his hands together gleefully, his telescope beneath his arm. 'By God, he'll find it difficult! My guns will follow the bugger to kingdom come if necessary!'

*　　*　　*

Watkiss danced upon his compass platform : Mr Mottram's gunlayers had done splendid work. A shell, aimed high, had taken the flagship's foretopmast and had brought it down to the deck atop a gun-turret, which now lay beneath a tangle of rigging and broken woodwork and burned flags.

'Yeoman, make my apologies to the Hun.' Watkiss leaned over the guardrail and shouted to the gunner. 'Mr Mottram, lay upon his port-side davits and destroy his boats.'

'Aye, aye, sir.'

A moment later *Meridian*'s guns spoke again : not such fine aim this time. There was a tremendous spout of water, followed seconds later by a great booming sound and a mountainous upsurge of the sea close alongside the flagship's port plating. Captain Watkiss' stomach suddenly turned to water : the booming sound had been very nasty. It had all been far too close in fact to be explained away by poor gunnery and he, Watkiss, could stand in much danger of being harried by the accursed Foreign Office when he returned in due course to British territory. Once again he sent his immediate apologies by signal. There was great activity aboard the *Friedrich der Grosse*, seamen running hither and thither, a large party of them dragging out the collision mat to drape it over the side. The flagship's anchor went down again with a roar of outgoing cable. So did those of the other German ships. Furious signals came : the British idiot had holed the flagship below the protective deck, a report would be made to Berlin, reparations would be demanded, the dolt's dismissal from the service sought.

Watkiss shook his telescope towards the German Admiral. 'Secure from action stations,' he ordered. 'I've stopped the bugger in his tracks! I am to be informed immediately if there is any attempt to transfer Savory to another ship of the squadron. Now where's Mr Halfhyde?'

SEVENTEEN

General Codecino, brought aboard the *Meridian* by the tactful use of *force majeure*, was oily and polite although clearly scared, not least by the appalling smoke of battle. When he attempted to use his execrable English to ask questions of Watkiss, who had descended from the compass platform, he was peremptorily silenced: Captain Watkiss, all-seeing, had espied another development and had lifted his telescope towards the *Friedrich der Grosse*. A moment later he gave an exclamation of satisfaction.

'Mr Halfhyde, man the side and stand by to pipe. Von Merkatz appears to be coming aboard in person.'

'With Savory?' Daintree asked.

'Not with Savory, sir. With his Flag Lieutenant.' Watkiss swung round upon Halfhyde. 'Mr Halfhyde, be so good as to have General Codecino stowed out of sight. He is to be taken below under guard.'

'Aye, aye, sir.' Protesting, the fat Chilean was removed from the quarterdeck, and his boat was ordered to secure to the lower boom on the port side of the battleship.

Daintree said warningly, 'We must exercise discretion now, Watkiss.'

'Indeed we must, sir, and I shall. I sense a climb-down on the part of the German Emperor's lick-spittle! Von Merkatz might have been expected to ask me to board him, but he is coming to me instead!' Watkiss bounced on the balls of his feet, importantly. 'By God, the bugger recognizes the power of the British fleet!'

Daintree frowned. 'I spoke of discretion, Watkiss. I hope I need not stress it.'

'Never fear, sir.'

'You strike me as an indiscreet officer – '

'I shall ask you not to interfere with my command, sir. I'm not your Flag Captain yet, and until I hand over my ship, this remains my command and not yours.' Captain Watkiss rudely bounced away aft along his quarterdeck, brandishing his telescope at no one in particular.

*   *   *

The atmosphere in the cuddy was on a knife-edge: Watkiss sat at his roll-top desk, drumming his fingers on the polished wood. Vice-Admiral von Merkatz sat stiffly in a chintz-covered armchair and opposite him was the small figure of Rear-Admiral Daintree with his eyes closed as if in deep slumber. Halfhyde stood by the door as though ready at the Captain's word to arrest the German and his Flag Lieutenant, also standing. Petrie-Smith, obviously on tenterhooks, stood by the Captain's side. In the pantry the Captain's servant, not yet ordered to bring gin, hovered with ears flapping to catch mention of affairs of state for eventual retailing along the lower deck.

'My Emperor,' von Merkatz announced, not for the first time, 'will react most strongly against such shooting from foreign ships.'

'*British* ships, I'm not a damn Chinese,' said Watkiss.

The German made a gesture of irritation, and glanced with forbearance at Petrie-Smith who had been introduced to him as representing the British Government. 'Damage,' he said heavily, 'has been done and will be paid for – '

'The British Treasury,' Watkiss snapped, 'is not bankrupt – '

'We must not commit the Treasury,' Petrie-Smith interrupted in a sharp tone.

'Hold your tongue, Mr Petrie-Smith, and balls to the Treasury. The damage is clearly not serious enough to prevent von Merkatz sailing. If in effect Savory has to be paid for, then I shall not quibble and neither will the Treasury unless it's insane. On the other hand, of course, the public purse must be where possible protected.'

'Exactly!'

'And will be. Now, sir.' Watkiss swung to bear upon von Merkatz. 'The man Savory, whom I have reason to believe is aboard your flagship – '

'I do not deny this, Captain. He is there, and he will remain there until I reach Germany.'

'I see. You're entitled to believe what you please, of course.' Watkiss' tone was mild. 'Savory appears to be of an interest beyond his importance – '

'To you, I think, as well as to me, Captain!'

'Yes, indeed. And you know very well why: he is an escaped convict and must be returned to Dartmoor Prison. You seem willing enough to aid the escape of a convict, Admiral, and I would be most interested to know why.'

Von Merkatz shrugged. 'Because he has been of assistance to us in the past . . . or tried to be at all events.'

'Ah, yes. And your Emperor does not forget his friends.'

'Quite so.'

'Yes. But this time the friend's a pretty useless one, is he not? A failed spy, Admiral – and one that's somewhat out of date by now!'

'There is nevertheless gratitude.'

'To the extent that your Emperor is willing to upset Her Majesty and her law – I think not, Admiral, I think not. There is another reason, and one I wish to learn about, one that I fancy is connected with the reason for your own presence in Chilean waters.' Captain Watkiss reached out with his telescope and tapped Admiral Daintree on a knee-cap. 'Will you kindly come awake, sir, if you please – '

'I *am* awake, Watkiss,' Daintree said irritably, opening his eyes.

'Then perhaps you'll tell Admiral von Merkatz what you learned in Valparaiso, sir, as reported in outline to me by Mr Halfhyde.'

'Very well.' Daintree stared at the German. 'The reason given for my arrest by General Oyanedel was that I had treated the Chilean flag with disrespect, as you will have heard, no doubt.'

'Yes, I have heard this.'

'Well, that was no more than a stupid excuse to hold me. It was necessary that I should be out of effective action until Savory had entered Valparaiso and been despatched safely if unofficially to the German Embassy in Santiago. Do you understand?'

Von Merkatz nodded. 'Yes, I understand your words, but I fail to appreciate what is behind them.'

'Really? I'm most surprised,' Daintree said mildly, then chuckled. 'I overheard talk . . . words between Oyanedel and Codecino. Savory was wanted in Germany, to work upon the German naval construction programme as he had worked upon the British. He was, and still is no doubt, a brilliant man in his field, and with his deep basic knowledge of British ship construction would have proved a tower of strength in the re-equipping of the German fleet. But he was wanted in Chile too – wasn't he, von Merkatz? He once had strong connections with the Committee of Privy Council for Trade in Britain, and his knowledge of trade and trading agreements is both detailed and world-wide. As for you, you were in Chilean waters to show the German flag and to pay compliments specifically to cement a trading agreement for Germany – and together with your Emperor's ambassador, Baron von Gutschmid, to talk about the establishment of coaling bases for German vessels. You sought Savory's intercessionary help for that also – and he, of course, was well aware of his value to you and at the same time his value to the Chilean Government. He was very nicely placed . . . but intended in fact to place himself ultimately under the official protection of Chile. But there happened to be another agreement, secretly, between Oyanedel and Codecino and yourself.' Bird-like eyes peered brightly at the German. 'What have you to say to that, Admiral von Merkatz?'

'That it is ridiculous falsehood.'

'Ah, but I think not, and can prove so. Not only the evidence of my own ears . . . as you may or may not have noticed, General Codecino boarded the *Meridian* a short while ago, and already he has made certain statements, and will shortly be persuaded to make more,' Daintree said, tongue in cheek. 'In all this there is great danger for yourself and your Emperor.'

The German, his face bleak, shrugged. 'It is of no concern to you, Admiral Daintree, in any event.'

'But possibly to President Errazuriz, if he should be informed that two of his generals conspired with you to ensure that his own wishes were defied – to ensure that Savory was taken into German protection rather than Chilean?'

Von Merkatz spread his hands wide and laughed. 'President Errazuriz must take that matter up with the generals concerned, Admiral. It is – as you would say – no skin off my nose now!'

'I believe it may become so. I believe President Errazuriz will prevent the sailing of your squadron from Reloncavi Bay until Savory has been handed over – and you will then incur much displeasure from your Emperor, who will be revealed as a man who uses cat's paws to conclude underhand agreements contrary to normal decent procedures between great nations.' Daintree glanced up at Petrie-Smith. 'The world's reaction will be harsh against the German Emperor, would you not agree, Mr Petrie-Smith?'

The diplomat nodded vehemently. 'It will indeed. The Emperor will be revealed as a plotter, an intriguer rather than as a soldier, one whose word is to be trusted by no government of consequence.'

'Exactly! Well, Admiral von Merkatz?'

'I treat your notions with contempt, Admiral.' The German's face was livid, his mouth a thin, hard line. 'You talk child's nonsense, the kind of nonsense that is to be expected of a senior officer who makes stupid gestures against foreign flags – ' He broke off as a knock came at the Captain's door-post and a midshipman pulled the curtain aside to stand revealed with his cap beneath his arm.

'Yes, what is it, Mr Perrin?' Watkiss asked.

'Admiral Daintree's squadron is entering from Calbuco, sir, and the flagship has signalled that the ships intend lying off at the entrance to the bay, sir.'

'Thank you, Mr Perrin, kindly ensure that in future your white

trousers are clean before presenting yourself at my cabin door.'
Watkiss turned to Rear-Admiral Daintree. 'Well, sir?'

Daintree chuckled once more. 'I suggest to Admiral von
Merkatz that his simplest choice is to turn Savory over to you,
Captain, after which President Errazuriz will find it a happier
thing to accept a *fait accompli* and take it out on Generals
Oyanedel and Codecino afterwards. Do you not think so, Mr
Petrie-Smith?'

'Indeed I concur, indeed I do most heartily.' The sweat of
relief poured down the Senior Clerk's face: at long last, some
sort of diplomacy was being observed, though the firing of
Watkiss' guns was going to take some explaining – and for that,
the wretched Watkiss would have to take full responsibility. 'An
excellent ending, Admiral.'

Daintree nodded. 'And you, too, would agree, Admiral von
Merkatz?'

'You have a most colossal nerve, my dear sir, if you think for
one moment – '

'And I have ships as well as nerve,' Daintree interrupted
happily. 'Believe me, I shall not hesitate to hold them at the
entrance to the bay until you find yourself in agreement with my
proposals. You shall not go past – except to dig your ships into
the bottom of the port approaches!'

*   *   *

Ill-temperedly, von Merkatz faced defeat: in dudgeon, he drafted
a signal to his Flag Captain, ordering him to send Savory across
to the British ship. As Savory stepped aboard, Mr Todhunter, on
firm ground now, executed his warrant and the prisoner was
taken below under strong escort to remain in the cells until he was
transferred to Daintree's flagship for onward passage to the Falklands and thence to England. With Savory secure aboard, von
Merkatz was allowed to proceed back to his own ship; and
General Codecino's boat was called alongside from the lower
boom.

Codecino was in a good mood now, beaming happily upon

his sudden release untormented by the British. From his confinement under guard he had heard nothing of the recently-accomplished transfer of Savory from German hands. As for him, he had pulled off a profitable enough deal; von Merkatz had been generous, and his, Codecino's, part in knavery should not come out to crease his President's face in angry frowns . . . also, he had wonderfully outwitted the stupid, pig-headed British sailors and their bombastic Captain. As the stupid British lifted their hands in salute, General Codecino returned the polite gesture and beamed more than ever. 'Goodbye, Captain,' he said. 'I 'ope you 'ave enjoy ze ztay in Puerto Montt?'

'Very much indeed, thank you.'

'Ees zere anyzings you weesh?'

'No.'

'Zen I go.' General Codecino turned and descended the ladder. His boat cast off and was pulled round in an unseamanlike circle for the shore. As it dropped past the battleship's stern General Codecino was seen to be laughing heartily, holding his ample sides and making an obscene gesture towards the British ship. Watkiss turned his back and strode with Halfhyde to the port side of his quarterdeck.

'Greasy bugger, Mr Halfhyde. How I wish I could have *told* him I'd won!' Watkiss breathed in and out hard for a few moments 'However, we must not lose sight of the fact that von Merkatz is also beaten – and that's what we came for, is it not?'

'It is indeed, sir.'

'He'll not cross me again, my dear fellow. I think I dealt with him pretty firmly.'

'Yes, indeed, sir.'

'And without needing to use those dago hostages.'

'Quite, sir. But speaking of them – '

'Yes, Mr Halfhyde,' Watkiss said distantly, 'you have no need to remind me, I am only too damn well aware that I must now hand my ship over to filth, bugs, lice, and doubtful moral practices – that's the one fly in the ointment, is it not?'

Halfhyde rubbed his nose thoughtfully. 'There are other difficulties to be overcome, sir – '

'What difficulties?'

'Well, sir, my deception in Valparaiso – my personification of a diplomat – and the firing of your guns. Mr Petrie-Smith will have much – '

'Oh, balls to Petrie-Smith, Mr Halfhyde, he's of no consequence now. I've won and that's all there is to be said. I'll settle Petrie-Smith's hash within five minutes of my report reaching the Admiralty.'

*　　　*　　　*

Daintree lost no time in taking his cruisers outside the narrows, and beyond the limit of Chilean territorial waters, having first embarked Mr Todhunter with the prisoner Savory, Canon Rampling, churchwarden Tidy, and Petrie-Smith. In his wake went Captain Jericho with the *Glen Lyon*. Daintree had informed Captain Watkiss that he would close again towards the territorial limit to embark the *Meridian*'s company aboard his ships from the *Biddle* and the *Delia* after the hand-over to the Chilean Navy had been officially made. In due time the Chilean steaming party arrived from the north to take over, bringing with them tidings from Valparaiso and Santiago: the British Foreign Office, it seemed, had reacted smoothly enough to representations from the Chilean Government about the removal of Rear-Admiral Daintree. Indeed he was required in London, and, though the Foreign Office had been reticent as to bankruptcy proceedings, gratitude had been expressed for Daintree's swift release. There was no mention of Savory on the part of the Chileans, and neither Watkiss nor Halfhyde were surprised at that, though it was but a pious hope that Generals Oyanedel and Codecino would by now have suffered the displeasure of President Errazuriz. . . .

With the *Meridian* officially handed over and the White Ensign lowered for the last time, her erstwhile Captain saluted the quarterdeck, his no longer, and with his officers and seamen left her ladder for Her Majesty's sloops *Biddle* and *Delia* and the outward passage for Daintree's waiting squadron. Received aboard *Delia* with ceremony, for word of him had gone before,

Watkiss was coldly formal. There was no room to swing a cat . . . the anchor creaked home on its rusty cable– rust was a disgrace and would have to be chipped away – and the orders were given for taking the sloop to sea. As she moved, Captain Watkiss began slowly to return to normal pompousness. He swelled his chest out : true, a sloop was a sloop and totally unfitted for a post captain to leave a dago port in, but he had plenty to be pleased about. Plenty! Savory had been flushed out, thanks to his own astuteness in sending armed men ashore to Osorno at precisely the right moment; von Merkatz had been most neatly outwitted – most neatly; the Hun had been kept at arm's length from the Chilean trade, guano and all, that belonged by right to Great Britain and the Empire. The Chileans – indeed all the blasted inhabitants of South America – would know by now who remained the mistress of the seas! As Captain Watkiss stared importantly ahead towards the great open sea, a band assembled aboard the *Meridian*, slouching and shambling into position in the starboard side of the waist. There were curious instruments : two trumpets, a huge thing of brass already baying tentatively, some flutes, even a concertina, a violin, and a double bass. Most of the instrumentalists were genuine dagoes but two were South American Indians and one was black and had a bare chest while the others were in some sort of comic opera apology for uniform. Watkiss closed his eyes for a moment and thought of the band of the Royal Marine Light Infantry. Then, as the sloop moved up towards the old battleship, the music took tune and shape and unbelievably *Rule Britannia* emerged.

Watkiss' chest swelled more. It was quite a moment, to hear that tune in foreign waters, a moment that made a man proud of his country, of his calling as a seadog, as a subject of Her Majesty the Queen. Really, the dagoes were behaving with unexpected decency, behaving perfectly properly. Of course, they knew their place in the scheme of things, fully realized the might and right of the Royal Navy . . . they could not in truth be blamed for not being British, it was the luck of the draw, the chance allocation by God in his wisdom that sent the best souls to England. From the *Meridian*'s already filthy quarterdeck a dago dropped a bucket of potato-peelings over the side, then turned to kick out at a dog that was peacefully lifting its leg against the stanchion of the guardrail atop the Captain's hatch. In the waist, one of the dagoes picked his nose and missed a note, but Captain Watkiss saw none of this. In flat refusal to lift his hand in salute to the dago flag, and never mind the compliment of *Rule Britannia*, he had turned his back.